DEVIL'S FANCY

TRACKDOWN II

MICHAEL A. BLACK

WOLFPACK
PUBLISHING
— EST 2013 —

WOLFPACK PUBLISHING
— EST 2013 —

Devil's Fancy

Paperback Edition
Copyright © 2020 Michael A. Black

Wolfpack Publishing
5130 S. Fort Apache Road, 215-380
Las Vegas, NV 89148

wolfpackpublishing.com

Paperback ISBN 978-1-64734-138-1
eBook ISBN 978-1-64734-137-4

DEVIL'S FANCY

To all who have served

Tell me where is fancy bred,
Or in the heart or in the head

The Merchant of Venice
William Shakespeare

CHAPTER 1

PHOENIX, ARIZONA

The blue Altima pulled into the driveway of the light-green stucco house, and Wolf watched as Lorna Adams got out and looked up and down the block twice before removing the brown paper grocery bag from the back seat. The vehicle's rear bumper was almost hovering over the sidewalk because Luth's pickup, wheel-less and propped up on four cement blocks, took up most of the driveway leading up to the house. She went into the house. She wasn't a bad-looking woman and certainly deserved better than the lot she'd drawn.

Much better.

Wolf had sought her out, asking for information on her boyfriend, and at first, she'd been less than cooperative. Then she'd called him from the grocery store and asked for a meet. The discoloration under her left eye told Wolf all he needed to know.

Tim Luth was a hundred-percent grade-A scumbag, and he deserved to be in jail.

It had taken one too many beatings to finally bring her around to realizing that too.

You don't want to piss off the chicks, Wolf thought. Especially not if you skip your court date.

He adjusted his binoculars and focused on the side window on the front porch. It was an old-style house made of stucco and cedar board with an extended front section. It had seen better days. The house deserved better, too. Luth needed to spend more time on home improvement and less sampling his own product.

The long, bamboo-strip shade in the front window rolled down, then up, then down again.

That was the signal they'd agreed upon about ten minutes prior at the grocery store. The pigeon was in the coop, but this guy couldn't exactly be described as a pigeon. He was closer to a rooster, but hopefully, he'd be the kind who was all crowing and little in the way of pecking and scratching.

Lowering his binoculars, Wolf checked his phone for the incoming text.

The better part of a minute went by before the phone chirped.

Front door unlocked.

K, he texted back. *Gun?*

No. I think.

As soon as he read her response, Wolf wondered what that meant as he dropped the phone on the seat.

I think.

Not the best reassurance when you were bringing a Taser to what might quite possibly turn into a gunfight.

Shades of Mexico.

He readjusted the straps on the vest Mac had given him, shifted the Escalade into gear, and drove down the block at a rapid speed.

It wasn't exactly how he wanted to play it, but with Mac still being out and nobody to help him, flying solo was his only option.

Flying solo and unarmed and going to arrest a meth head for an outstanding warrant—not a good combination. Meth heads could be tricky, and grabbing somebody inside his own house was just asking for trouble. He was certified on the Taser, but it would have been nice to have the comfort and reassurance of a gun.

But ex-cons couldn't get concealed carry permits in the state of Arizona.

He wondered if that was true in other states as well and imagined it was. Once you'd served time, you were always placed in that restricted category—a second-class citizen in every sense of the word. He couldn't vote, not that he wanted to anyway. He couldn't even reenlist in the Army, or ever again wear his campaign ribbons again, or look at his stripes, or claim any of the veterans' benefits he'd earned during six years as an Army Ranger.

But that was what happened when you got saddled with a DD and four years in Leavenworth.

Wolf cast a quick glance toward the target house as he went by, then slammed on the brakes, jerked the Escalade to a halt, and pulled into the driveway adjacent to the green house. There was a white Ford pickup in that driveway. Wolf knew he was blocking it in and most likely pissing off the guy who lived there, but he couldn't take the chance of pulling up directly in front of Lorna's house. Not with a gun possibly being involved. She'd said he had a nine-millimeter he usually kept under the mattress in the bedroom, but if he happened to be looking out the window and had decided to tuck the gun in his pants, Wolf would make a dandy target pulling up in front. He had her safety to think about, too. She had already taken a big chance by dropping a dime on this abusive jerk, and at the grocery store, she'd said he was awake and a little paranoid from doing meth all night.

That would make Luth unpredictable and this apprehension problematic.

Wolf pulled the chain around his neck to free the gold badge that said BAIL ENFORCEMENT AGENT on the front. It was pinned to a leather base and dangled in the middle of his chest. It looked official, and hopefully, Luth wouldn't pick up on the fact that Wolf wasn't real law enforcement, had no weapon, no radio, and no back up on the way. But he did have the black vest on that Mac had given him. It also looked official and was guaranteed to be bullet-resistant.

He hoped he wouldn't have to check out the veracity of that guarantee as he shifted the Escalade into park, pulled out the keys, and gripped the door handle.

One hundred percent guaranteed, he thought. Or your money back.

He wondered if Mac would get that refund if it wasn't. It also left a lot of Wolf's body unprotected.

The oppressive heat rolled over him like a wave as he jumped out of the Escalade, reminding him of his three tours in Iraq. That body armor had been a lot heavier, and he'd been well-armed back then.

Wolf slammed the door, hit the remote to lock it, and did a quick dash for the front door of the target house. He saw a flash of movement inside the adjacent structure, the house with the driveway he'd usurped.

He flattened against the wall, gripped the doorknob, and twisted.

It was indeed unlocked.

Maybe my luck will hold out, he thought as he slipped the Taser out of its holster.

"Hey, buddy," a loud voice called from his left. "What the hell you doing? Get your truck outta my driveway."

A middle-aged Hispanic man wearing a wife-beater and holding a can of beer was standing in front of the white pickup in the adjacent driveway.

"I'll be just a minute," Wolf said, holding up his Bail Bond Enforcement Agent badge from under his vest. "Official business."

"What?" the man said, his mouth twisting downward in a scowl. "You a cop?"

"No, he ain't," another voice said as the door in front of Wolf whipped open. Tim Luth stood there, matted hair hanging down to his shoulders, leveling a Glock semi-automatic pistol at Wolf's chest. "He's just some piece-of-shit bounty hunter."

Luth's face twisted into a maniacal grin, and Wolf saw the other man's finger tighten. The look in his eyes was wild and unfocused. Wolf instinctively twisted to the side as a burst of flame and smoke erupted from the muzzle of the Glock, but it felt like a heavyweight boxer had just delivered a whistling body blow to his right side. He saw the shell casing flipping upward in slow motion as the slide snapped back into place. The Taser discharged into the dirty carpeting beside Luth's left foot. Wolf's body was still twisting as he slammed his left palm into the back of Luth's right hand, knocking the Glock away. Letting the Taser slip out of his right hand, Wolf grabbed the weapon and surged forward. The gun felt hot, and the metal slide ripped his palm as it fired again, this time at the ceiling or wall. Another shell casing erupted, and Wolf's hands were seared by the gaseous expulsion.

Both of them tumbled to the floor, things inexplicably shifting back to real-time as their bodies collided. Luth's breaths flicked out particulates of spittle as they struggled to obtain total control of the weapon. Wolf twisted the barrel to the right, the weakest part of Luth's grip, and managed to dislodge the Glock from the other man's hands. Luth gleamed with a patina of sweat and had a pungent and sour body odor.

The Glock tumbled on the floor a few feet away, and Luth reached for it.

Wolf grabbed his wrist but could barely hold on due to the slickness from the perspiration. Looping his hand and forearm under Luth's right arm, Wolf yanked the other man away from the errant weapon and used his body weight to roll him over.

Luth somehow managed to slip away and slammed his left fist into Wolf's jaw.

It was only an arm punch, so it stung more than hurt. Wolf smashed a hard left hook into Luth's exposed right side. He grunted and scrambled to his feet, apparently still trying to go for the gun, but Wolf managed to grab a hank of hair and pulled him back, then got his legs under him and sprang upward, still controlling his adversary's head. Luth spun away, leaving Wolf with a handful of uprooted hair.

Luth staggered forward, fists clenched, his face a portrait of rage.

"I'm gonna kill you, motherfucker." His voice was a low growl.

"You don't want to do that," Wolf said, delivering a kick to Luth's left knee.

That stopped his advance, and Wolf set the other man up with a grazing left jab before stepping in and slamming home a right to Luth's liver. Knowing that blows like that usually took a couple seconds to register, Wolf pivoted and sent a left hook to the solar plexus.

Luth expelled a foul-smelling burst of air and sank to his knees.

Body punches, thought Wolf. Worked every time.

Kill the body, as Joe Frazier used to say, and the head will die.

Wolf straddled his now-prone opponent and bent Luth's left arm behind his back. Kneeling on the biceps, Wolf locked the bent left arm in place with his thigh. Using both hands, he gripped Luth's right arm and bent it back, and then, after taking out his handcuffs, he ratcheted them over Luth's wrists.

"What's going on?" a woman said.

It was Lorna. She'd told him before that she didn't want Luth to know she'd dimed him, so Wolf played along.

"Bail Enforcement Agent, ma'am," he said. "I have

a warrant for his arres—"

"Your ass, bitch," Luth said. "You did this. You snitched on me, and I'm gonna make you pay."

Wolf exhaled. Was anything going to go right today?

He realized a substantial amount of the wet hair he'd pulled out of Luth's head before was now clinging to his forearm. Wolf wiped the hair off on the other man's t-shirt, which was ripped.

"I'll kill you," Luth said. "You, bitch, and this prick, too."

Wolf gripped more of Luth's shaggy hair and pressed his face into the carpet.

"Shut your mouth, asshole," Wolf said. "You're going to jail, and for the record, she didn't snitch. I've been watching this place for a week."

"Your ass, motherfuc—"

Wolf clipped him on the temple with an open palm. It wasn't meant to injure as much as stun, and it worked.

Wolf lifted him off the floor and began walking him toward the door, pausing to retrieve the Taser. He heard the distant wail of police sirens.

"That gun yours?" he asked Lorna.

She grimaced and shook her head.

"Better give it to the cops when they arrive," he said and pushed Luth out the door.

Hopefully, what Wolf had said would sow the seeds of doubt that Lorna had been instrumental in his capture, but he was going to jail for the foreseeable future. He doubted any of the local bail bondsmen would take a chance and post bond for him after he'd skipped out on Manny.

As they got outside, the Hispanic man with the beer was watching the procession. Lorna stayed at her door.

"You better move your damn car," the man said. "I called the cops on you."

Wolf nodded to the man. After all that had happened, he could hardly blame him: some guy blocking in his truck, a physical disturbance, a shot being fired. Wolf was just glad it had taken the man so long. Obviously, he had enjoyed watching the show through the window as it had progressed.

Maybe I should've sold tickets, Wolf thought.

Hitting the remote button, Wolf unlocked the Escalade and shoved Luth into the left rear seat.

"Stay there and behave," he said, slamming the door.

Luth immediately rotated onto his back and began using both of his feet to kick at the glass window in the door, which buckled outward. Wolf sprang out to rip the door open before the glass shattered, but he was too late. The shards flew into his face, and he instinctively closed his eyes and whipped his head to the side.

Luth's filthy tennis shoes hung out the broken window.

Wolf opened the door and delivered two punches into Luth's side. The man gasped with each blow.

"You through playing around now?" Wolf asked.

He could hear the sirens getting louder.

Shit, he thought. *Just what I need. To go a couple of rounds with the cops.*

Grabbing a nylon dog leash he kept on the front seat, he looped the noose around Luth's feet, pulled it tight, and then slammed the door on the excess. It would prevent any more movements or kicks. Wolf opened the door of the Escalade and hopped in.

"Hey," the Hispanic man said. "Who's gonna clean up all that glass on the lawn?"

"Sorry about that," Wolf said, resisting the urge to retort, *Whose lawn is it?*

But time was of the essence. He shifted into reverse and backed out, hearing the tires making popping sounds as they rolled over the broken glass.

***

Office of Emmanuel Sutter
Bail Bondsman
Phoenix, Arizona

"Jesus," Manny said. "This fucker stinks."

"Yeah, well, I would've run him through the car-wash," Wolf said, "But he kicked out the window in Mac's car."

Manny's mouth twisted into a grin. "No shit?" He glanced at the handcuffed figure of Luth, whom Wolf had deposited in the chair opposite the big bail bondsman's desk. "Were you a bad little boy, Timmy?"

"Come on, Manny," Luth said. "This asshole broke down the door at my girlfriend's place and dragged me outta there with no explanation of who he was or what."

Wolf knew better than to get into a verbal confrontation after all he'd been through with this idiot.

Besides, he thought, glancing at his watch, they were almost out of time.

"He took a shot at me, too," Wolf said.

Manny's eyebrows rose like twin caterpillars on his wide face. He probably weighed about three-fifty and had an old-fashioned bob-style haircut. A chrome snub-nose revolver rode on the belt next to his enormous belly, which stretched the material of his short-sleeved Hawaiian shirt to the max.

"He miss ya?"

Wolf shook his head and pointed to the black stain and hole on the right side of his shirt.

"Hey, that was your fault," Luth said. "You grabbed my hand, and the gun went off. How was I supposed to know who you was?"

"Shut up," Wolf said. "I want any shit out of you, I'll squeeze your head."

"It was an accident, Manny," Luth said. "Honest. And I didn't mean to miss court. It just sorta slipped by me."

He'd calmed down with the realization that he was going back to jail and facing the bleak prospect of not getting bonded out again after skipping his court date.

"Is that a fact?" Manny grinned and plucked another donut out of the box on his cluttered desk. "Good thing I gave that extra vest to Mac." He bit into the donut. "Now you owe me, big-time."

The office was small, and the two desks took up most of the room. A row of padded chairs reinforced with an excess of strategically placed duct tape was in front of Manny's desk. Three big filing cabinets lined the wall behind him. Dust mites swirled in the beams of sunlight that filtered in through the filthy front window, and the two air-conditioning units built into the wall hummed on overdrive. Wolf still felt the sweat trickling down inside his shirt from his armpits.

"No," Wolf said. "You owe me. I'll take my percentage of the bounty now if you don't mind."

Manny chewed a bite, swallowed, and then ran his tongue over his front teeth.

"You know the drill," Manny said. "Take him over to Central Booking and get your booking slip. Then you get your percentage."

Wolf glanced at his watch again. "The police should be here any second. They can take him."

Manny wiped his nose with his fingers and sorted through the box for another donut.

Manny's nephew, Freddie, was just coming out of the can. He was a thin guy, maybe a buck and half with an unruly crop of red hair and a pair of thick glasses perched on a hook nose. Freddie nodded and winked at Wolf, dropped the girlie magazine on the second desk, and plopped down in the chair.

"Hey, Sherman," Manny said. "Didn't I tell you to get me *two* Bavarians?"

Freddie didn't answer.

"Hey," Manny said. "You fucking deaf, or something?"

"No." Freddie adjusted himself in the seat and shrugged. "I'm just getting tired of you calling me that."

"Calling you what?'

"Sherman. That ain't my name."

Manny frowned. "It's what you call a term of endearment. So, next time, don't forget to ask for two Bavarians."

"That's exactly what I told them," Freddie said.

"Okay, *Sherman*." Manny grinned, wiped at his nose again, and grabbed a brown donut with white icing and green sprinkles.

Freddie's face scrunched, and he glared at his morbidly obese uncle.

Send in the clowns, Wolf thought, recalling the old Sinatra song. No, wait, they're already here.

"You ever remember the name of that law firm that hired us in Vegas?" Wolf asked.

He didn't want to mention Mexico in front of Luth.

Manny smacked his lips and shook his head, then his eyes narrowed as he looked through the front window.

Outside, two marked squad cars pulled up diagonal to the Escalade. An officer got out and eyed the damaged window, cocked his head, and said something into his radio mic. The other officer got out and approached the front door, placing one hand on the doorknob and the other on his weapon. The first spoke into his radio mic again, and then they both approached the door. Wolf kept his hands open and out in front of him. He made sure his bail enforcement agent badge was prominent on his chest. Manny edged his expansive gut closer to the desk and told Freddie to keep his piece out of sight.

The officer pulled open the door, stepped inside, and looked around.

"You the one driving the Escalade?" he asked.

Wolf nodded, still keeping his hands visible.

"You're the guy working for Big Jim McNamara," the cop said.

Wolf nodded again. He hoped it would be a plus to have a friend in high places. Or maybe low ones.

"He's working for me, Charlie," Manny said, lifting the box. "You guys want a donut?"

The officer glared at the big man, then back at Wolf, and pointed to the holster on his right side.

"You armed?"

"Just with a Taser." Wolf placed his hands on his head and stepped over to the cop, who did a quick pat-down. He paused when he came to the tear in the shirt. Wolf winced as the man's hand went over it.

"This what I think it is?" he asked.

"He shot me," Wolf said. "I was effecting an arrest. He's got a warrant out for possession and delivery, PCS."

"That wasn't me," Luth said. "And I shot him, but it was self-defense."

The cop finished his pat-down, clapped Wolf on the shoulder, and told him to drop his hands and relax. Wolf gave the officer his IDs, and the first cop ran a check on him.

"What's your version of what happened?" the other cop asked.

Wolf gave them a quick rundown, explaining he was working for Manny on fugitive recovery and had been staking out Luth's girlfriend's place, hoping to find him. He left out the part about her calling him.

"Bullshit," Luth said. "That bitch set me up. I know she did. She's gonna pay for it once I get out."

"You'd best keep your mouth shut," the first cop said. "Making threats in front of two police officers after you just shot someone's not real smart."

"I never shot him," Luth said. "Well, I didn't mean to."

"Yeah," the cop said. "Whatever." He turned back to Wolf. "How bad's your injury?"

Wolf shrugged. "Not real bad. It hit me a glancing blow on the vest." He pulled up the shirt and displayed a swollen red patch.

"Want me to call the paramedics?" the officer asked.

Wolf shook his head. "I'll go get it checked out, but I've been hurt worse."

In reality, he didn't have health insurance, and he didn't want to ask Mac to foot the bill for an emergency room visit.

The cop clucked his tongue. "We recovered a Glock seventeen at the scene. Is that the weapon?"

"Probably," Wolf said. "I left it there for you."

The cop smirked. "Knew we were coming, did you?"

"Figured as much. The neighbor was kind of pissed that I blocked in his truck."

"Why didn't you wait around to explain things?" the other cop asked.

"Well, like I said, the neighbor seemed kind of pissed off that I was blocking in his truck."

The questioning went on for several more minutes, with Wolf declining to sign a criminal complaint at this time and the officers re-cuffing Luth and agreeing to take him in for booking on the warrant.

"There'll be a detective following up with you," the younger cop said.

"I'll send Sherman here over for a copy of the booking slip," Manny said. "Okay?"

"Freddie. The name's Freddie."

Manny snorted and shrugged. "Yeah, well, you look like a Sherman to me." He grinned. "You guys ever watch that old Rocky and Bullwinkle cartoon show? Don't he look just like that kid that was with the dog? What's his name? Mr. Peabody?"

"And the Wayback Machine," the older cop said. laughing. "Yeah, he does."

Wolf remembered seeing the show on a nostalgia channel and had to admit there was a distinct resemblance.

Freddie slammed a drawer shut.

After they'd left, Manny went to his safe, opened it, and took out a wad of bills. He glanced over his shoulder periodically as he counted out the fee, then stuck the rest back in the safe and closed and locked the door.

"Here you go," Manny said. "Ten percent recovery fee. Wanna count it?"

Wolf did as he stood there, then said, "How about tossing in a little extra for the broken window?"

Manny snorted. "You're joking, right? That's the price of doing business."

Wolf didn't feel like arguing or admitting that

Trackdown, Inc. needed the money after their disastrous trip to Mexico. Instead, he asked Manny what else he had open.

"I gotta call the clerk's office later on this afternoon," he said. "See who skipped out on me. I'll get you something."

"We could use something substantial."

"Yeah, yeah, I know," Manny said. "But with Mac being out and you working by yourself and seeing as how you can't pack no heat, I got to be very selective." He opened the lid of the box and began perusing what was left of the donuts. "After all, I wouldn't want you to get hurt or nothing."

"Yeah, right," Wolf said. The sting in his side was getting worse by the minute.

"I'm serious," Manny said, deciding on a chocolate frosted. "You and Mac are two of my favorite people. The best of the best."

Wolf said nothing.

Manny shrugged and picked off what appeared to be a hair on his donut. "I feel bad enough at what happened to you two down in Cancun, even though it wasn't me that sent you guys down there." He brushed his fingers on a corner of his shirt. "I mean, I kinda had a hand in it."

Wolf nodded. It wasn't a trip he was likely to forget. "Manny, look. We need the work. We never got paid what we were owed on that one."

"Yeah, well, that ain't *my* fault." He bit into the donut and raised the index finger of his right hand. It was stained with chocolate frosting.

"Hey," Wolf said. "I asked you before if you remembered the name of that law firm that hired us to go down there."

"Yeah?"

"Well," Wolf said, "*do* you remember the name of it?"

Manny shook his head. "Sure don't. All's I remember is that Teddy said they was from New York. But they mighta give me a card or something. I'll look around for it." He stuffed more of the donut into his mouth and chewed. "Too bad we can't ask him. He was the one that actually sent you down there. Hey, I tell you he got killed at the conference?"

"Yeah," Wolf said. "You did. Several times."

"Fell down a flight of stairs right there in the hotel." He shook his head again. "Who'd a thunk it? You just never know." Manny took another bite and continued talking with his mouth full. "Tell you what I'll do. I got a couple simple cases that should be like a walk in the park for you." He opened another drawer and removed two manila envelopes. "Here, work on these."

"Thanks," Wolf said, accepting the files.

"I might have something in the works for you as soon as Mac gets back in action, though. Got a call from a pal of mine in Vegas. He posted bond for a big-time slimeball. A fucking attorney, no less. Rumor has it the dude might be hiding out around here somewheres."

"Who is it? What's his name?"

Manny shook his head. "Huh-uh. I'm still looking into it."

Which means, Wolf thought, *that you're still angling for a piece of the pie.*

"But in the meantime." Manny popped the remainder of the donut into his mouth, then brushed his hands together, sending a shower of powdered sugar and flecks of chocolate over the sea of paperwork littering the top of his desk. He pulled open a side drawer, looked in, frowned, and slammed it shut. What he saw in the next drawer made him smile.

"Here you go," he said, reaching downward.

He straightened up, his padded chair groaning in protest with the movement, flashed a grin, and tossed a roll of duct tape on the desktop.

"For fixing the window on the Escalade."

"Thanks," Wolf said.

He had started to walk away when Manny said, "Hey, wait."

Wolf turned and watched the huge man scoop the last remaining donuts from the box, shake the crumbs into a wastebasket, and hand the empty box across the desk.

"What's this for?" Wolf asked.

"Tape it in the window," Manny said, picking up a donut with an array of red and green sprinkles.

***

The hot air rushing in through the broken window made a hell of a racket on the drive back to McNamara's place, not to mention letting the air conditioning out, but Wolf was barely cognizant of it. Instead, the memory of the Mexico disaster of three weeks ago and the names involved kept playing over and over in his mind like an unpleasant tune he couldn't forget: Eagan, Cummins, Nasim, and Zerbe. Four of the men he'd crossed paths with south of the border.

And the one he hadn't: Von Dien.

It was unfamiliar, but it was the most ominous.

Who's Von Dien?

He asked Eagan that question as his foe lay dying at the base of a Mayan pyramid. Eagan's cryptic answer had troubled Wolf for weeks. *Your worst nightmare.*

What the hell did that mean?

He and Mac had traveled down south to apprehend a fugitive child molester and ended up getting in way over their heads. There had been much more to it than they'd been told, and even now, Wolf still wasn't sure what all was involved. Ironically, it was also tied to the incident in Iraq four years ago that had robbed him of his military career. He'd started that day as Staff Sergeant Steven Wolf, decorated US Army Ranger, and ended up accused of murdering three Iraqi civilians and charged with dereliction of duty for causing the death of one of his squad members. The pisser was that the head injury Wolf had sustained had robbed him of the memory of what had happened.

Five, ten, maybe as much as fifteen minutes were a total blank. He wasn't sure exactly how much, so he'd settled on eight. Eight missing minutes that held the key. He could remember events up to a certain point: going back into that house and seeing Eagan, a member of a PMC group called the Vipers, and Cummins, a fat-ass first lieutenant from military intelligence, interrogating the Iraqis. The three of them on their knees with their hands tied behind their backs, chanting *Allahu Akbar*, "God is great," over and over. The poor fuckers must have known they were on their way to meet their seventy-two virgins.

Then the pain from getting hit, and the rest of it was a blank. Nothing. Just a solid white wall with nothing on it.

Sometimes in his dreams, an unknown hand would begin scrawling graffiti on that wall, but he could never read it, like it was in Arabic or some other language that was undecipherable.

The rest was history, and a sad history at that.

The incompetent JAG lawyer urging him to take the Alford plea—pleading guilty while maintaining your innocence because the prosecution had overwhelming evidence against you, the four years at Leavenworth, and emerging as an ex-con with a dishonorable discharge. It was that last one that stung the most. Wolf had stepped off the reservation and entered the Army at eighteen, intent on making something of himself. He had excelled in Basic, AIT, jump school, and Ranger training. Not bad for a half-Indian with an alcoholic father who'd crashed his pickup truck into a cement porch at ninety miles per hour. The decorations he'd earned—the Silver Star, his jump wings, his stripes—had all been stripped from his now-slick-sleeved uniform.

It had seemed like a new start when Mac, his Green Beret surrogate father and mentor, had picked him up outside the prison that day and offered to tutor him to become a full-fledged Bail Bond Enforcement Agent. Mac had spent his whole life in the Army, then started Trackdown, Inc. as a way of filling the action void in retirement.

But they'd gotten more than they'd bargained for on that Mexico trip. It had turned into a brutal array of shootouts, dead bodies, and betrayal, with Mac getting shot and Wolf coming full circle to once again meet the bastards who'd set him up in Iraq.

Eagan and Cummins.

He could still remember seeing Cummins and Zerbe, another of the duplicitous crew that betrayed them down there, hovering over the slanted stones of the pyramid in that helicopter before disappearing into the night sky.

Who's Von Dien?

Your worst nightmare.

What did that mean, and how did it all tie together?

He didn't know much, but he decided to concentrate on what he did.

He knew some of the players. Zerbe, that private dick who'd met them down in Mexico. What was his first name?

Jim? Jonas?

No, Jason, he decided.

Jason Zerbe, private investigator. South African transplant, based out of where? That was still a mystery.

Wolf allowed himself a cynical smile as he recalled the man's box-like physique in that white Panama hat and dirty light-colored sports jacket. He'd worn what appeared to be prescription sunglasses even at night, and when they were inside, he had smelled like a combination of body odor and motor oil.

A private dick, all right. A dick in every sense of the word.

He'd mentioned being from South Africa but not where he was based now. He'd purportedly been hired by that law firm that was supposed to be representing the victim's family in a child molestation case. That one guy, Reynolds, had given them a card with the law firm's name and address. Mac had lost it in the confusion of his emergency room visit, and Manny, who'd made the introductions that had gotten them involved, said he couldn't find his either.

Alls I remember is that Teddy said they was from New York.

Some help he was, and his buddy Teddy the human scarecrow was no longer among the living to be consulted.

A law firm, Wolf thought. Cummins had been in military intelligence in Iraq. A reservist, but wasn't he a lawyer in civilian life? Could he be connected to the same law firm?

It was a tenuous connection, considering the fat coward had turned up next to Zerbe in that departing helicopter, but the connection was worth looking into. The three principal players from Iraq, Eagan, Nasim, and Cummins, had all shown up for round two four years later, and that was too great to be a coincidence. Wolf had never believed in those anyway.

But how did it all fit together?

It was a conundrum, all right. A mystery wrapped in a riddle inside a conundrum.

Wasn't that what Churchill had once said?

Wolf felt like a masculine Dorothy stumbling around in a violent and perverse version of *The*

Wizard of Oz. Teddy, the scarecrow, had tumbled face-first down a flight of stairs, Zerbe, the Tin Man, was wearing prescription sunglasses and a white Panama hat, Cummins, the cowardly lawyer, was no lion—that was for sure. And the man behind the curtain, Von Dien, was turning out to be a real wizard at staying hidden.

The familiar gas station and strip mall popped into view, ending his reverie.

Wolf saw the turnoff that ran perpendicular to the highway, and he activated his turn signal. The wheels of the Escalade crunched over the stones, and it brought back more unpleasant memories. Mexico had been full of gravel roads. Wolf was dreading showing Mac the damage to the Escalade. The big SUV was his pride and joy.

"After all them years of riding in jeeps, Humvees, and helicopters," Mac had said, "I figured I deserved something nice."

Now he was in danger of losing that something nice. The company was in trouble, and the repo man was looming. So was the mortgage.

And Wolf still felt like a freeloader, not pulling his weight in Trackdown, Inc.

Well, the fee he'd earned today would help.

The house was a two-story ranch-style with a circular drive and an attached garage. Across the expansive cement driveway, another garage sat adjacent to the house. It was two full stories as well and had once been the original the occupants had used. When McNamara had bought the land and had the ranch house built, he'd used the substantial garage mostly for storage but had converted part of it into a mini-gym with a small apartment on the second floor. Wolf occupied that place now, and he found it more than adequate for his purposes. It was only two rooms, a small kitchen and bedroom/living room. There was a bathroom too, but Wolf had to go downstairs to use the shower. Regardless, it was a hell of a lot better than an eight by twelve cell in Leavenworth that he had to share with another man, and McNamara had yet to charge him any rent.

Maybe I am that son he always wanted, Wolf thought, remembering the first words Kasey had muttered when Mac had introduced them.

He pulled up next to her tan Honda Civic. Mac's daughter ran the office and the computer investigation end of things, and she was good at both. It would have made for a smooth working relationship except for one factor; she didn't like Wolf.

In recent weeks, it had gone from mere dislike and resentment to sheer hatred. She blamed him for her father getting shot in Mexico.

And for their dire financial straits.

And for the strained relationship she was currently having with her fiancé.

Wolf grinned as he got out of the Escalade.

And probably a hundred other things she hadn't even thought of yet.

He wondered if she'd had time to run a check on those names he'd given her.

Zerbe and Cummins. The others, Eagan and Nasim, were dead but still worth checking into. And then there was his worst nightmare to wonder about.

Von Dien.

When he got out of the Escalade, he slammed the door a little too hard, and some residual shards tinkled down inside the rear door.

Mac is not going to be happy when he sees this, Wolf reminded himself and went in to face the music.

***

Catskills, New York

Jack Cummins started to sweat as he looked out the tinted window of the limousine speeding through the late afternoon. Almost three weeks had passed since he'd returned to New York for the debriefing. Then he had been driven to a remote cabin in the Catskills and told to chill out until they were ready to talk to him again.

Three weeks of isolation with a phone with no calling capability, no Internet, no car. At least clean clothes, toiletries, and his meals had been provided three times a day, along with a polite inquiry asking if he had any special requests. Cummins always asked when this imposed isolation would end, but none of the delivery boys would answer his question. There was a big flat-screen TV, a DVD player, and a book-case case full of movies, but he'd basically been held incommunicado. To make things worse, a security patrol periodically came by in a four-wheel-drive vehicle, but they wouldn't talk either.

It had been almost like being in prison, except there were no bars.

It had to be Von Dien's idea. The rich man was calling the shots, and he was one paranoid son of a bitch.

When the phone rang earlier in the day, it had shocked him.

"Get yourself ready," the voice said. It sounded familiar. "We'll be picking you up shortly."

The knock on the door had come soon after, and the limo had been waiting outside for him. After climbing inside the commodious space, Cummins had longed for a drink, but this limo had no booze. All it did have was that foul-smelling PI, Jason Zerbe, he'd met back in Mexico. It looked like the son of a bitch was wearing the same clothes, too. Zerbe acknowledged him with a nod and asked if he'd enjoyed his stay in the cabin.

"What do you think?" Cummins said. "Where you been?"

"Around," Zerbe said. "Working on a few things."

Cummins asked more questions, but Zerbe just shrugged and said they'd all be answered soon.

"You know what this is all about?" Cummins asked.

"What do you think?" Zerbe said with a smirk. "Mexico. It's the price of failure. Hopefully, we'll be offered a chance at redemption."

Cummins tried to engage the prick in further conversation, but he just sat there and shrugged, smoking one cigarette after another. Plus, he was wearing that same filthy jacket, hat, and dark sunglasses he had in Cancun. Cummins wondered if he'd changed his underwear. From the smell of him, he doubted it.

But the questions lingered.

Was Zerbe as nervous as he was? He obviously knew more about what was going on, but like the closed-mouthed delivery boys who'd brought him his food, Zerbe wouldn't say shit even if he had a mouthful.

As far as Cummins knew, Zerbe was another of the bit players, just like him, but apparently, he hadn't been benched after the first string had dropped the ball.

The price of failure.

It had been a total clusterfuck, and he hoped he wasn't going to be blamed for the disaster. It hadn't been his fault. Sure, he was initially supposed to be in overall charge of the operation, more or less, but that hotshot Eagan had taken over. He had been the one running the show down there.

Technically, Cummins told himself again, *what happened wasn't my fault.*

Some of the things Eagan had done had been wrong. Very wrong. Like underestimating that guy, Wolf.

Who would have thought a half-breed Indian ex-con would turn out to be Captain America, capable of besting Eagan and his vaunted Viper team?

Some bunch of Vipers.

They'd had Wolf outgunned and outnumbered, and he'd still killed them all. Or at least, he figured he had. Eagan had looked like a dead man as he slid down that old Mayan pyramid, and then Wolf had taken potshots at the copter.

It had been time to leave, and all they could do was beat feet back to the States.

Cummins tried to convince himself that it was a good sign. That although he and Zerbe had been interviewed and housed separately, they were being brought back into the game together.

Maybe the old man wants to keep the remnants of the team together, Cummins thought.

But they could hardly be considered a winning team. Eagan and his raghead buddy Nasim had both ended up on the wrong side of a bullet down in Mexico. At least, that's what Cummins had been led to believe during the debrief. And the Lion Attacking the Nubian, that precious fucking artifact Von Dien was so hot to get, was nowhere to be found. The guy who'd had possession of it, Thomas Accondras, was most likely dead as well. Cummins had spilled everything he knew about it, including that he'd overheard Accondras say the artifact was concealed in a plaster statue of a Mexican bandito. Where it was now was anybody's guess, but that wasn't what the old man had wanted to hear.

What the hell, Cummins thought. Did the old bastard think we were all gonna fall on our swords if we couldn't get the thing for him?

It was just a thousand-year-old piece of art, for Christ's sake.

He wondered if it had been cursed. A dozen bodies lay in its wake this century alone.

CHAPTER 2

THE MCNAMARA RANCH
PHOENIX, ARIZONA

"Aw, hell," McNamara said, looking at the broken window in the Escalade. "This poor baby's taken more hits than a long-range recon patrol. Had to drop the insurance to just liability, and I still ain't got that damn seatbelt fixed yet, either."

He was wearing a black t-shirt with US ARMY printed in white block letters across the front, a pair of gray sweatpants, and gym shoes. The multicolored metal cane he leaned on had an L-shaped handle that Wolf knew was connected to a knife blade on the inside of the tubing. It only took a quick half-turn and a jerk to free it.

Except this time, I'm the jerk, Wolf thought.

Mac's daughter, Kasey, stood next to him, arms

crossed, a frown on her pretty face. But her gaze wasn't fixed on the window. She was glaring at Wolf and not saying anything. As usual, her silence was deafening.

This couldn't have come at a worse time, he thought. *Just when I needed her to check on those names for me.*

"But I'm more concerned about you," McNamara said. "You ought to go to the ER. Get checked out."

Wolf shook his head. "I'm fine."

"You sure?"

Wolf nodded.

Not having insurance toughened you up, he thought.

But he didn't want to say that.

McNamara clucked his tongue and winked. "Ranger-tough, all right."

Chad, Kasey's five-year-old son, came running up to them and skidded to a stop on the asphalt driveway.

"Grandpa, what happened to your car?"

McNamara reached out and tousled the boy's unruly crop of chestnut hair.

"When are you going to take this little guy in for a haircut?" he asked.

"When we can afford it," Kasey said, her frown deepening. "And I like his hair longer."

"Never make it in the Army with a mop like that," McNamara said.

"Which is why I like it," Kasey shot back. "Come

on, let's at least get out of this heat."

She grabbed her son's arm and steered him toward the front door.

McNamara watched her go and braced his cane on the ground, gesturing for Wolf to follow him.

"Well, at least this'll make it easier for the repo man." McNamara said with a wry grin. "Maybe we ought to consider clearing out your place so we can hide it in there."

My place? Wolf thought, glad that Kasey hadn't heard that.

The garage was separate from the two-story wood-frame house, which Mac always referred to as "the Ranch," and he'd filled the bottom half where the cars were supposed to be stored with a ton of old furniture, assorted boxes of military gear, photograph albums, old filing cabinets, tools, a generator, and just about everything else he'd acquired over a lifetime of traveling the world and accumulating memories.

One corner, however, had been left bare and transformed into a quasi-gym. A narrow corridor between stacks led to a haphazard assortment of benches and weights. Once Wolf had moved in, they'd hung a heavy bag from one of the cross-beams in the ceiling. They'd also erected a speedbag platform and an over-under bag that spanned the distance between the thick overhead beam and the wooden block that had been nail-blasted to the floor.

A plastic-coated jump rope hung on a nail on one of the beams near the bags, and a small kitchen timer sat on a shelf next to the rope.

Above this area, on the second level, was the apartment Wolf had called home since his release from Leavenworth. All things considered, it was a good deal, and he was satisfied and grateful.

Which was not to say he didn't long to get back on his feet and find something better. But first, he had to start paying McNamara back. He just didn't know when that was going to be.

And now, the broken window had popped up like an unexpected punch to the gut.

The repo man?

Wolf grimaced. He knew things were bad financially, but he hoped Mac was only kidding.

"Thing's really that bad?" Wolf asked.

"Well, I've been trying to decide." McNamara sighed. "You know that old saying: if you only have enough for your car payment or your house payment, you need to remember that you can always live in your car, but you can't drive your house." He looked askance at Wolf, then laughed.

Wolf forced a chuckle because he sensed that was what Mac wanted, but he felt like he'd been gut-punched.

"Anyway, even if we lose the Escalade, we'll still have Kasey's car. And I figure it'd get pretty damn crowded with all five of us living in the Escalade anyway."

"Maybe this will help." Wolf handed him the envelope with the cash from Manny.

McNamara jammed it into his pocket and nodded. "He give you anything else?"

"Two easy ones," Wolf said. "Or so he says."

"Well, I'm riding shotgun on them two."

Wolf had figured as much, but he'd also been afraid that was what Mac would say. He'd been shot in the abdomen in Mexico, and the damage had been significant. Their rush to get back Stateside to get better and more affordable medical treatment had been costly for Mac's health. The torn bowel had resulted in peritonitis, which had required more hospitalization and heavy doses of antibiotics. Getting into the VA hospital had proven next to impossible, and by the time all was said and done, the medical bills from both here and Mexico had eaten up all their profits from the mission. Not to mention, it had put them at the center of a federal investigation to boot.

"I don't know if that's such a good idea, Mac."

"Hell," McNamara said with a chortle. "You wouldn't know a good idea if it snuck up and bit you on the ass."

Wolf stepped ahead and opened the door for McNamara. The big man shuffled through the door slowly, placing the rubber tip of the cane down prior to each new step. The muscles of his right arm bulged with the pressure of the movements. Despite his age, he was a powerhouse. Wolf noticed Mac was striving to cover the grimace of pain with a wide smile.

Covering pain and discomfort and bad times with a mask of bravado, Wolf thought. That was Mac, all right. The toughest and finest man Wolf had ever known.

They stepped into the air-conditioned coolness. Kasey had resumed her position at her desk and was clicking keys on her keyboard. She didn't look at them as they entered. Chad had grabbed his rubber AR-15 rifle and was running from cover point to cover point in the living room and dining room. Adjacent to the front door was a long stairway leading to the upstairs bedrooms. The boy paused by the banister and said, "I'll cover you guys."

"You do that," McNamara told him.

The house was very large and decorated in a Western motif. It had traditional wood trim and floors, with beige walls and a large stone fireplace on the far wall. The mantle above the fireplace had a shadow-box display of Mac's Green Beret, along with his CIB and the other decorations he'd been awarded over his long career. His time in the military had been more than double that of most Army lifers, and he'd amassed enough ribbons to fill virtually the entire case. Now all his past glories resided behind a small pane of glass within a larger wooden box. Next to the shadowbox, the Mexican bandito, their souvenir from their ill-fated adventure south of the border, seemed to stare back at Wolf with a taunting insolence. Mac had insisted on keeping it when they'd left Mexico.

"I've grown kind of attached to that *hombre*," he said. "Kind of sums up our whole trip down there."

They passed the couch, which had McNamara's sheets, blanket, and pillow neatly folded with military precision in the center. He'd been sleeping downstairs in the den since his return, having found the nightly trip up the staircase a bit too challenging.

Kasey was still busy at the computer. Wolf set the new files on the desk. She glanced at them but didn't say a word.

"Kase," McNamara said, "me and Steve are gonna run over to the body shop and get an estimate on that window. We'll hit the bank, too." He pulled out the envelope and tossed it on the desk. "You need to take anything out of this right now?"

She didn't reply but grabbed the envelope, rifled through the sheaf of money, and tossed it on the desk. "Put it in the company account. I'll make the notation later."

Wolf wanted to ask her about the list of names he'd been ruminating about since Mexico and if she'd found anything. She was a wizard at finding information, but so far, she hadn't given him squat.

"Say," Wolf said, trying to flash an ingratiating

smile, "you have time to check on those names I gave you yet?"

"I haven't had time," she said. "I've got a paper due."

The brusqueness was obvious in her tone. Besides running the office part of their bounty hunting company, she was going to grad school to pursue a degree in English. "If I'm going to go after a worthless degree," she'd often say. "It might as well be in something I like." Mac harbored hopes that she'd continue on to law school after graduation, although at this point, motherhood and the company took precedence over everything.

"Aw, come on, Kase," McNamara said. "We been hearing that for the past month. Those are some important leads we gotta follow up on."

She continued typing and didn't look up from the monitor.

Important is putting it mildly, thought Wolf. *It's the only lead I've got.*

"Leads that are going to net us zero in terms of income and profit." Her fingers were flying over the keys now. "Do I need to remind you of that?"

"Well, when you gonna get to it?" McNamara asked.

"When I have time," she said.

McNamara frowned and glanced at Wolf.

Wolf knew it would do no good to badger her. She was holding all the aces. He had no computer and limited skills for searching on the free ones at the library, not to mention the time factor. Plus, he could hardly expect her to devote her time to his personal Easter egg hunt when Trackdown, Inc. was in such dire financial straits.

McNamara sighed and snatched the envelope off the desk. He turned, and Wolf could read the anger and frustration on his face.

"We'll put it all in the checking account then," McNamara said. "Let's get outta here. A might too cool in here right at the moment."

Wolf shot a quick look at Kasey, but she showed no sign of having heard what her father had just said.

"Yeah," McNamara said as he strode toward the door. "Frigid in here, all right."

Chad curled around the wall and pointed the rifle at them.

"Any bad guys around here?" he asked.

McNamara stopped and grinned.

"Just one," he said, turning to point at the foot-high plaster statue of the Mexican bandito on the mantle above the fireplace. "But his guns aren't loaded."

The boy grinned and dashed away.

Wolf saw a cloud of dust stirring on the drive that led to the house. He was about to mention that they had visitors, but Mac beat him to it.

"I'm sure glad the county didn't have that road paved yet." He limped to the tall grandfather clock next to the front door, hooked the cane over the top of it, and pressed two sections in a child-proof lock sequence on the frame that held the clock face. A drawer slid out of the left side of the case, and McNamara reached in and took out a Glock 43 9mm pistol. After retrieving the cane, he moved to the window and pulled the edge of the curtain away to view the progress of the approaching vehicle. Wolf saw that it was a white Ford van.

"Look familiar?" Wolf asked."

"No, but there's only two things that arrive in vans. Good deliveries and bad deliveries." McNamara continued to peer out the window.

The vehicle slowed to a stop and parked next to the Escalade after pulling onto the concrete slab between the house and the garage. Wolf could see that two people sat inside. The passenger appeared to be male. A big bastard, from the breadth of his shoulders. The driver looked like a woman. The glare of the sun made it impossible to discern more, but when the passenger-side door opened, he recognized the man.

It was Reno Garth. The elevated section of his mohawk had been trimmed down to little more than a half-inch, and his face looked drawn and weak. The t-shirt hung loosely on his powerful frame.

"Looks like this one has the makings of a bad one." McNamara took three steps back to the clock, replaced the Glock in the drawer, and pressed it back into place.

Pulling open the door, he stepped outside onto the porch. Reno stood beside the open door of the van and eyed the broken window on the Escalade, then glanced at McNamara and Wolf and nodded hello. Before slamming the door of the van, he removed his own cane from the vehicle.

His steps were slow and laborious as he approached them.

"Big Jim," Reno said. "Wolf."

"What you need?" McNamara asked. His tone was far from cordial.

Reno didn't reply. Instead, he took a series of hobbling steps that brought him within a few feet of the porch. He took a deep breath and compressed his lips.

Whatever he's come to say isn't coming out easily, Wolf thought.

Finally, Reno spoke: "I wanted to stop by and thank you, both of you, for saving my life down in Mexico," he said. After another deep breath, he shifted the cane from his right hand to his left and extended his open palm.

Wolf waited to gauge Mac's reaction. They'd been harassed and betrayed by Reno and his partner Black Hercules in the past, especially on the Mexico trip, but the way things had turned out, Reno realized that he and his partner had been on the short end as well. Reno had ended up wounded, and Herc was dead. McNamara, although wounded himself, had driven

Reno to the hospital while Wolf had faced down the killers and emerged victorious, but it had been Pyrrhic victory. Wolf had few answers and a lot of pressing questions.

McNamara shifted his cane as well and shook Reno's hand.

Wolf did the same.

"How's the leg?" he asked.

"Well, I ain't gonna be getting back in the octagon anytime soon." He raised his eyebrows. "Not sure I want to anyway. My bounty hunting career's on hold, too. We're in negotiations on the TV show, but that movie deal they were talking about seems like it's fallen through."

"That's too bad," Wolf said.

He caught a sideways glance from Mac.

"But I still got my gym," Reno said. "And you two are more than welcome to come and workout there anytime. Especially you, Wolf. You'd be a natural for MMA."

Wolf mumbled something that sounded like an appreciation for the offer and felt an idea forming. It might be a way to make a few bucks.

"Good luck, Reno," McNamara said, turning back toward the door. "Thanks for stopping by."

"Wait," Reno said.

McNamara turned back to him with a questioning expression.

Reno reached into his pants pocket, removed an envelope, and handed it to McNamara.

"Here."

"What's that?" McNamara asked.

The other man shrugged.

"It's a check," Reno said. "For the seatbelt and the tire Herc cut. Back when we…ah…done that stuff we shouldn't have."

In one of their previous encounters, Reno and his partner had stolen an arrestee from McNamara and Wolf and damaged Mac's vehicle. It had occurred before the Mexico trip.

McNamara accepted the envelope without saying anything.

"It's blank, so you can fill in the amount you need to get it fixed," Reno said. "What happened to the window?"

"We had an unruly arrestee," Wolf said.

"Kicked out the window because the seatbelt wasn't working," McNamara added.

Reno looked at the ground.

"Well," he said, "if you want to put fixing the window on my tab too, I won't blame you."

"Now, that's mighty neighborly of you," Mc-Namara said. "You and your friend want to come inside for a glass of iced tea or something?"

Reno's face twisted into an unexpected smile, but he shook his head.

"Nah. I appreciate the offer, but me and Barbie gotta get back to the gym. I'm training one of my guys for a fight coming up." He paused, and his smile faded. "There's one more thing."

"What's that?" McNamara asked.

Wolf caught the faint sound of a car's tires turning onto the gravel road from the highway and looked at the road. A navy blue sedan was making its way toward the house.

"The FBI," Reno said. "They come to see me at the gym this morning. Asking me all kinds of questions about what happened down in Mexico. They know all about that guy that got killed, Accondras, and they wanted to go over what happened to Herc again."

McNamara's face tightened. "And what'd you tell 'em?"

"Nothing. Honest. I stuck with that same story, like you told me to do down in Mexico. That some bandits hit us, and after that, CRS. Can't Remember Shit."

"You sure that was all you said?" McNamara's eyes zeroed in on the other man.

"Yeah."

"They believe you?"

"I think so." Reno reached in the pocket of his pants and withdrew a business card. "One of them give me this. Said I should call him if my memory improves before they have to convene a federal grand jury."

The sedan was getting closer, and Wolf caught a

glimpse of US government plates.

"Looks like they've come to ask us the same questions," Wolf said.

***

The Law Offices of Fallotti and Abraham
New York City, the borough of Manhattan

The trip had taken less time than Cummins expected, but what really surprised him was the state of the offices upon their arrival on the fourteenth floor of the Manhattan skyscraper. Electronic shredders were humming in every room, and files and equipment were being boxed up. He looked at the window of his office and saw that his computer and monitor were both gone.

What the hell was going on?

He got his answer several minutes later when he and Zerbe were ushered into the main partner's office. Anthony Fallotti sat behind his big mahogany desk, the arrangements of degrees, accolades, and fine oil paintings on the wall to the right of him untouched. On his left, Dexter Von Dien, looking like a full-size version of an American Buddha without the epicanthic fold to his eyes, sat in one of the two leather chairs, his girth substantially overlapping the arms. Cummins didn't offer to shake hands with him. In the intervening three weeks, Cummins had almost forgotten what a physically enormous individual Von Dien was, but not that he detested most physical contact.

A big guy with very broad shoulders and wavy blond hair that looked like it had been styled like a movie star's stood at the rich man's side, alert and formidable. Cummins remembered him from the last time they were in this office. It had been right before he and Eagan left for the cluster fuck in Mexico.

Fallotti remained seated and gestured for Cummins and Zerbe to take the seats at the opposite end of the desk.

"Gentlemen," Fallotti said, smiling. "Thank you for coming."

As if we had any choice, Cummins thought.

He wondered where this was going. Surely Von Dien, or VD as Cummins secretly called him, couldn't blame him for the fiasco south of the border. But the fact that he had been held in virtual isolation for the past three weeks seemed to indicate that, as Zerbe had said, neither of them had been brought here to be given a commendation. From the look of things, Cummins wondered if he was still going to have a job with the firm.

"Mind if I smoke?" Zerbe asked as he plopped down in the chair and began reaching into the breast pocket of his jacket.

"Don't be ridiculous," Von Dien muttered.

The big bodyguard snapped his fingers and pointed at Zerbe, who withdrew his hand.

Good, Cummins thought. *He's got no more clout than I do with the rich son of a bitch.*

Fallotti cleared his throat.

"We've had time to do a thorough review of the recordings of your debriefs," he said. "I'm happy to say that they both match with what we've been able to find out about the Mexican operation."

Recordings?

Cummins felt a sudden surge of panic. He hadn't known he was being recorded during that thing.

There has to be enough on those things to incriminate me all the way back to Iraq, he thought.

He'd told them everything, freely admitting to being a party to kidnapping and murder, and mentioned they'd been shot at. What else could he have done? Of course, he'd explained it all in such a way as to place all the blame on Eagan for the failures, but as a lawyer, Cummins knew what he'd said made him an accessory after the fact.

"You didn't tell us we were being taped," Zerbe said.

That must have meant the PI had spilled his guts, too.

Great, he thought. *At least I'm not in this alone.*

But this gave them a big hold over both of them.

They had them by the short hairs, but the worst thing would be to appear weak right now.

"What's going on with the office?" Cummins asked, resisting the temptation to demand why he'd been under the isolation order. "We moving?"

Fallotti cast a quick glance at Von Dien, then said, "The firm's being liquidated."

"What?" Cummins was stunned.

"Yes," Fallotti said. "Mr. Von Dien's made a very generous offer to buy us out. All of the employees are being given generous 401Ks and offers of employment with one of his corporations."

He's tying up the loose ends, Cummins thought.

"What about me?" he asked.

"Especially you, Jack," Fallotti said. His smile didn't look genuine. "You're one of our most valuable employees. We always take care of those."

Those? Cummins thought. He's already talking about me like I'm some kind of commodity—one of those loose ends.

His mouth went dry, and he could feel the sweat trickling down the back of his neck.

Zerbe was sitting to his left, not saying a word, but Cummins knew the PI was sweating too from a sudden increase in his body odor.

Von Dien made a huffing sound like he'd smelled the unpleasant odor as well.

"Tell me again what was said about the artifact," he

said. "His exact words."

Cummins tried to swallow, but his mouth was still too dry. When he spoke, his words sounded hollow and brittle.

"He said that he'd hidden it in a plaster statue."

"And this statue." Von Dien leaned forward, the bags under his eyes tightening. "Where was it?"

Cummins shook his head. "He said something about a backpack."

Von Dien transferred his gaze to Zerbe. "Was this the same backpack he'd been in possession of when you apprehended him?"

The PI shrugged. If he was intimidated by the big man, he wasn't showing it. Cummins hoped that wouldn't make things worse.

"He was wearing a backpack when we grabbed him," Zerbe said. "At the time, Wolf and McNamara had him in the back of the van while we transported him. They searched it, found no weapons. I didn't see what was in it, but the thing did seem to have something substantial inside."

Von Dien hissed, ending with his lips drawn tighter than a miser's silk purse.

"That was it," he said after a few moments. "It had to be. He wouldn't have trusted anyone with it and had to keep it handy. Hiding it in plain sight. And you let it slip through your fingers." He spat the last words and stared at Fallotti. "What else have you got?"

"Well," Fallotti said, "as soon as we got this information, we sent Jason here back to Cancun to try and locate the backpack."

Von Dien transferred his gaze to the PI. "And?"

"And," Zerbe said, "I managed to apply quite a few bribes to the Mexican authorities. This was a bit of a delicate task, I might add, since I had to be very circumspect in letting them know what I was looking for and what my interest in it was lest they recover the item or one purporting to be it and try to negotiate a new deal. Not to mention the arrival of the FBI to investigate the matter."

Von Dien waved his hand dismissively. "I don't want to hear those details. Cut to chase."

"Of course, sir," Zerbe said. "Accondras' backpack was not listed in any of the accompanying property inventory sheets. I know this because I obtained copies of them, which I faxed to Mr. Fallotti."

The lawyer nodded.

Zerbe waited a few seconds before continuing. "I also obtained copies of the personal property inventoried by the hospital for both James McNamara and Reno Garth. A backpack was listed as being on Garth's property inventory list."

Von Dien's eyes widened within their layers of fat.

"Was the statue in it?" He sounded breathless.

"It was only specified as '*con articulos*,'" Zerbe said. "Which means, with contents."

Von Dien made another huffing sound.

Fallotti picked up the conversation. "I was able to call in a couple of discreet favors from my connections in Customs. It seems McNamara listed a statue on his declaration form."

Von Dien's face froze. "Was that it? *The* statue?"

"If it wasn't," Fallotti said, "it's one hell of a coincidence."

Von Dien leaned forward, gasping for breath. The bodyguard reached into a backpack, withdrew a small unmarked bottle, and handed it to the rich man.

He twisted off the top and took a quick sip, then sat there staring blankly.

Several seconds passed.

"So they must know," he said. "Accondras must have told them."

"I doubt that," Zerbe said. "I was with them the whole time after they grabbed him. He talked a lot, trying to get us to let him go, but never mentioned the artifact.

"And you didn't say anything either?" Von Dien's tone was harsh.

"How could I?" Zerbe said. "At that point, I had no idea what we were looking for."

"That was the way we set the operation up, Dexter," Fallotti said. "Remember?"

"Shut up." Von Dien took another sip from the bottle, replaced the cap, and handed it back to the bodyguard.

Fallotti's neck reddened, but he said nothing.

"And where is this statue now?" Von Dien asked.

No one spoke.

Finally, Zerbe said, "It's a good bet that Wolf and McNamara have it. They live together."

"Live together?" Von Dien's face registered disgust. "Are they gay?"

"No," Zerbe said. "McNamara runs a bounty hunting service in Phoenix. Wolf's his partner, but the relationship's more like a father and son. McNamara's Wolf's mentor from the military, so to speak."

"Wolf, Wolf, Wolf," Von Dien said. "He's the cause of all of this. Damn him. We'll need someone formidable to deal with this Wolf person."

Cummins felt relief at the big man's rant.

At least he's focused on someone else, he thought. *And not on me.*

Then he noticed Von Dien staring at him.

"You've underestimated him time and time again," Von Dien said. "First in Iraq, then with that prison fiasco, and then once more in Mexico."

"What can I say?. The man's a…"

He was about to say "marvel" but stopped himself. Luckily, Zerbe took over.

"He's a *meerdere vegter* as we used to say in South Africa. A highly capable combatant." He placed a cigarette from his pack between his lips but didn't light it. "And if I may be so bold, I may know someone who can handle him."

Von Dien raised an eyebrow.

Zerbe removed the unlit cigarette and held it between his fingers.

"Of course, I'll have to make a call to see if he's available." He looked at his watch. "There's a time zone difference."

Von Dien regarded him with hooded eyes. "He's foreign?"

"An Afrikaans," Zerbe said. "South African. He's used to working internationally, he's discreet, and he has his own mercenary team. But…" Zerbe smiled, "he's expensive. Very expensive."

Von Dien nodded. "Do it. Money is no object. Just find out if Wolf has that statue. Then bring it to me."

***

The McNamara Ranch
Phoenix, Arizona

Wolf recognized the pair when they pulled up in the navy blue Crown Vic. They were the same two who'd questioned him at the embassy in Mexico. What were their names again? Franker was the younger one. He reminded Wolf of a cherry jumper and probably didn't even shave every day. The older guy, Turner, had flecks of gray in his hair and stayed in the background. Franker had shot his load, trying at first to be friendly, and when that didn't work, he'd switched to what he thought was a show of authority. That hadn't worked either, and Wolf had left the embassy after claiming he hadn't been with Mac or Reno when the robbery incident had occurred.

"Why don't we say *allegedly* occurred?" Franker had asked.

"Say whatever you want," Wolf told him. "After all, you're the FBI."

They'd parted on less than friendly terms, but if there was anything six years in the Army and four years in Leavenworth had taught him, it was never to overlook an opportunity to keep his mouth shut.

"God gave you two ears and one mouth," his father always said. *"That means you should always do twice as much listening as you do talking."*

It was one of the few good pieces of advice his old man had given him.

The younger FBI agent had been driving, and he was grinning when he stepped out of the car. He glanced at his partner and pointed at Reno. The other fed nodded. His expression was blank.

"Well, well, well," Franker said. He reached into the breast pocket of his blue suit jacket. "Mr. Garth. Interesting that you raced right over here after we spoke to you. Isn't it?"

Reno sneered at the man.

"I don't know what you're talking about."

The feds exchanged another set of glances before Franker pulled out a black badge case and flipped it open, displaying his credentials along with a small gold shield.

"You're still having those memory problems, eh?" His smile broadened. "To refresh things then, I'm Special Agent Franker, and this is my partner, Special Agent Turner. We're with the FBI."

"I know that," Reno said, his face still harboring a scowl.

Franker made a show of snapping his badge case closed and replacing it in his pocket.

"Misters McNamara and Wolf," Franker said. "Nice to see you again as well."

"Wish we could say the same," McNamara said, flashing a smile of his own. "But your appearance brings back a lot of bad memories. The kind of stuff we'd like to forget."

"You're all pretty good at forgetting things," Franker said. "Aren't you?"

McNamara started to answer, stopped, and affected a confused look. "What was that you just asked me?"

He followed that with a grin.

Franker seemed stunned, then exhaled a short breath.

"Do you know it's a felony to lie to a federal

agent?" Turner said.

McNamara widened his eyes, then turned to look at Wolf. "Well, what do you know? He talks."

Wolf saw a flush of red appear under Turner's swarthy complexion.

"We need to re-interview you both," he said. "Would you mind coming downtown with us?"

"As a matter of fact," McNamara said, "I would mind. I mean, I would love to talk to you, but I've got something to do."

"And what's that?" Turner asked.

"Oh, gosh darn it," McNamara said. "Now I'm having that memory trouble again. I plum forgot."

Wolf didn't like the way this was going. Mac was being way too coy and confrontational with these two federal jokers. He was used to dealing with authority figures in the military who would always back off when he puffed up his big chest with all those combat ribbons, silver jumpmaster wings, and the green beret on his head. Back then, it was obvious, despite the chain of command, that he was the king of the jungle. These guys played by a different set of rules, and this was a different jungle.

"You caught us at a bad time," Wolf said. "Maybe we can make an appointment to come to see you or something."

"Ah, Mr. Wolf," Franker said. "Your parole officer been by to see you lately?"

"I'm not on parole."

Franker raised an eyebrow. "You know, Otis. Maybe we need to take another look at Wolf-boy's prison file. Maybe we should go over the transcript of his court-martial in case they missed something the first time."

"Wolf-boy?" McNamara said, taking a step forward. "That's about enough. This man's a decorated veteran and won the Silver Star, which is more than I can probably say for the two of you. Either of you served?"

"No, but neither of us have a dishonorable discharge, either," Franker said.

McNamara turned toward him. "Get off my property."

Wolf stepped in front of Mac to block him, their faces inches apart. He didn't think Mac was going to take a swing at the fed, but he didn't want to give them any justification for saying they felt threatened.

"Mac, cool it," he said. His years in Leavenworth had taught him an icy coolness in the presence of authority. Stand your ground, show proper respect, but don't let them bait you.

Franker snorted. "Look, why don't we drop the shenanigans here? We've got new information that we need to discuss with you regarding the murder of several American citizens down in Mexico. Are you going to cooperate or not?"

"American citizens?" McNamara said. He seemed

to have cooled down a tad and nodded at Wolf to signal this. "Who you talking about?"

"Henry Preen, for one," Franker said.

"Who's that?" McNamara asked.

This time Wolf felt that Mac's question was genuine. The name rang no bells with him either.

"That's Herc," Reno said. "His real name."

"Things starting to come back to you now, Mr. Garth?" Franker asked. "Don't you want to help us find out who killed your friend?"

For a moment, Wolf was afraid the sentiment might make Reno fold, but he didn't.

"I wish I could," he said. "I just can't remember nothing."

The expression of sadness on his visage was unmistakable, and the twin tracks of tears wound their way down his cheeks. He turned, saying, "I gotta go."

They watched his limping hobble to the van, the pretty face of the woman behind the wheel exhibiting concern. He slammed the door and the vehicle backed up, making several stops and forward and backward movements before negotiating around the FBI sedan.

"He appears pretty upset," Franker said.

Wolf thought so too, and it worried him. The feds had picked up on Reno being the weak link. If he broke, the whole sad tale they'd constructed about Mexico would come tumbling down like a house of cards.

"We already gave our statements down in Mexico," McNamara said. "And we're not saying anything more unless we have our attorney with us."

"Your attorney?" Turner said, a smirk forming under his dark mustache. "Why do you need an attorney? You're the victims, aren't you?"

"I'll bet that's what you told General Mike Flynn, ain't it?" McNamara said. "I know how you federal snakes operate, and I don't want nothing to do with you."

He started walking back to the house. Wolf looked after him and saw Kasey standing in the doorway with a distressed look. Her eyes locked with his, and her expression hardened.

Great, he thought. *I guess I won't be getting any of that info I asked for anytime soon.*

He glanced back at the FBI agents.

"He just got out of the hospital for his second surgery," Wolf said. "He's been having a rough go of it."

"It'd go a lot easier if you two would cooperate," Turner said.

"We did," Wolf said.

"Bullshit," Franker said. "Do you really want to go head to head with the FBI?"

Wolf didn't. He kept silent.

You can't get in trouble for what you don't say, he thought.

"We were in the middle of something," he said.

"If you have a card, we'll give you a call and set up an appointment."

The two special agents said nothing.

Apparently, this hadn't gone quite the way they'd hoped.

Franker reached into his shirt pocket and pulled out a business card.

"Listen, Wolf," he said as he handed over the card. "Anytime an American citizen gets murdered on foreign soil, it becomes a Bureau case. We're going to get to the bottom of who killed Preen and the others. It would be in both your and Mr. McNamara's best interests to cooperate."

"We know you both know more than you're telling," Turner added.

You got that right, Wolf thought.

But once again, he said nothing.

CHAPTER 3

NEW YORK CITY

They watched as Von Dien laboriously rose from the chair and trundled out of the office, followed by his huge bodyguard. The rich man stopped by the door and tilted his head slightly.

"Find that bandito statue," he said. "Get it for me. Soon. And tidy up those loose ends we discussed."

Without waiting for a reply, he waved his hand at the door. The bodyguard reached over and pulled it open, his face as emotionless as marble.

Loose ends, Cummins thought.

He'd heard that before and didn't like the sound of it, not after being kept incommunicado for three weeks. He knew the big son of a bitch could very well be referring to him as one of those loose ends.

As the office door pneumatically closed, Fallotti

took a deep breath, then his nose wiggled.

He must have gotten a full whiff of Zerbe, Cummins thought.

It amused him, although he struggled not to show it.

Serves the prick right for keeping me stowed away for so long, he thought. *After all I went through in Mexico.*

Cummins caught a whiff of his own BO and knew he smelled bad too, but the South African PI smelled worse, like he hadn't showered or changed clothes in a week.

I'm not looking forward to working closely with him, Cummins thought.

"Okay, gentlemen," Fallotti said. "Let's brainstorm a bit. We're going to need some heavy-duty backup on this to deal with this Wolf character." He opened a manila file on his lap. "This McNamara fellow shouldn't be taken lightly, either. He was a Green Beret."

"The man I have in mind will make mincemeat out of both of them," Zerbe said.

"You're sure?" The lawyer raised his dark eyebrows. "Eagan and his Viper unit came equipped with a pretty impressive résumé, and Wolf took them all out singlehandedly."

"He's no pushover," Cummins said.

Zerbe smiled. "Apples and oranges. Believe me."

"All right," Fallotti said. "Tell me more about this guy."

Zerbe leaned forward in his chair.

Cummins tried to edge away from him and breathe through his mouth.

"His name's Luan Preetorius," Zerbe said. "Ran a counter-terrorist squad in South Africa until the new *swart* prick of a president took over. Things started to go to hell in a handbasket, so he got the hell out. Formed his own team. They call themselves the Lion Team. Do mercenary work all over the continent now. The world, too."

"The Lion Team, huh?" Fallotti said. "That's appropriate. They operate out of South Africa?"

"For now, they do," Zerbe said. "Johannesburg's pretty much of a mess now, thanks to the fucking *basters*. They're slaughtering white families all over the country and stealing their farms and property. Pretty soon, the country's going to be another Rhodesia."

"Don't they call it Mozambique now?" Cummins said.

He couldn't resist sticking the knife in this asshole and twisting the blade a little. Why the hell hadn't they locked his ass up, too, and why was Fallotti, for whom Cummins officially worked, listening to this smelly cretin?

"Zimbabwe, actually," Zerbe said. He looked irritated.

Fallotti looked at Cummins and frowned.

Oh, shit, Cummins thought. *I'd better keep my mouth shut, at least for the time being.*

But he also knew that he had to reinsert himself into the plan or risk being discarded—and being discarded by Von Dien or his proxies wasn't a pretty thought.

"As I said, he and his team operate internationally. Special assignments." Zerbe put the cigarette back between his lips. "You mind?"

Fallotti shook his head.

"They ever do anything in this country?" Fallotti asked.

"Well, they've been here but not doing what you'd call wetwork." Zerbe took out his lighter, lit the cigarette, and blew two plumes of smoke out of his nose. "Mostly to teach seminars on warfare techniques, urban combat, and weapons."

"Weapons…" Fallotti looked at him. "In the event they needed equipment, would that be a problem obtaining it here?"

Zerbe grinned and pulled back his jacket lapel, exposing a gun in a shoulder holster.

"Does it look like it'd be a problem?"

Fallotti nodded quickly, and Cummins wondered if the gun had shaken him up. Apparently, it hadn't.

"Okay," Fallotti said. "Get hold of him."

Cummins was wondering how he was going to fit into this. He had to figure out something, but then again, he was the one who'd helped smuggle the other half of the artifact out of Iraq. Plus, he was also the only of the three of them who'd seen that half, and he'd given them the information about the artifact being concealed in the bandito statue. That had to count for something, even if they had flubbed up and not recovered it, which hadn't been his fault.

Blame that fuck-up on Eagan, he thought.

There was another angle he could play, too. They seemed to think he knew more than he did about the bandito. That amused him. He'd never even laid eyes on the fucking thing.

But at this point, it was one of his main bargaining chips, and he intended to make the most of it. It was time to get back into this card game.

"So," he said after clearing his throat. "Are we operating under the assumption that Wolf doesn't know what he's got?"

Fallotti stroked his chin. "What do you think?"

Cummins tilted forward in the chair, trying to make himself appear to be in charge.

"Since I've been isolated up in the Catskills for the past three weeks," he said. "I'm not as well informed as the two of you."

"That was by order of Mr. Von Dien," Fallotti said quickly. He waved his arms. "Christ, look around. He ordered that the whole firm be dissolved, for Christ's sake."

Eliminating those loose ends, Cummins thought, more convinced that he too was on the dissolution list.

"Be that as it may," he said. "It did give me a lot of time to think. It would seem logical that Wolf knows something but is not privy to all the details. He hasn't approached anyone about a making deal or trading for information."

"Good point, Jack," Fallotti said.

Ah, Cummins thought. He called me Jack.

He was starting to feel a bit more secure, but he wanted to press whatever advantage he could muster, make them think he was on the ball despite the mess south of the border. Convince them it was due to their placing too much faith in that incompetent asshole Eagan.

"Don't you mean 'as far as we know?'" Zerbe said. "Is it possible he just doesn't know who to contact about the thing?"

The prick, Cummins thought. *I trust this asshole about as far as I could throw him.*

Fallotti shrugged. "I suppose that's a valid point. It does seem significant that they brought something like that back with them and even filled out a Customs declaration for it." He looked at Zerbe. "You're sure Accondras didn't spill the beans to them?"

Zerbe pursed his lips contemplatively, then shook his head.

"No, I was with them practically the whole time.

He alluded to having some kind of ace in the hole but never specified what it was, only that it was valuable. Very valuable."

"Maybe they kept it because they know it's the key to something," Cummins said, trying to reinsert himself into the conversation. "That had to be obvious. Why else would that asshole Accondras have been carrying it with him when he went to his... assignation."

"Maybe he was going to give it to the kid to play with while he got his rocks off," Zerbe said. He emitted a husky laugh.

Cummins laughed too when he saw Fallotti's grin, but the imagined scene bothered him. He already knew about Zerbe's lack of scruples, but obviously, if Cummins' own boss shared a lack of repulsion for the seamy side of things, how far could he be trusted?

"So why don't you contact your man in South Africa?" Fallotti said. "See how quickly he can respond."

"I'll probably have to leave him a message and have him get back to me," Zerbe said. "It's about ten at night over there now."

Fallotti nodded. "Let me know when he's available, as long as it's soon. I'm putting you two on a redeye to Phoenix tonight. Get on the ground out there and start checking things out."

"We're gonna need some cash," Zerbe said. He leaned his head back and blew out a smoke ring.

"Same arrangement as last time?"

"Already taken care of," Fallotti said. "My secretary's preparing a packet and some generic debit cards for you." He paused and turned to Cummins. "I'll have her do one for you too, Jack."

Cummins nodded but found Fallotti's wording troublesome. It was as if he were an afterthought. Like he hadn't been included in the original plan, and it wasn't until he had reasserted himself that he was brought back in.

He couldn't help but ponder the obvious unspoken question: what had they had in mind for him when they'd effectively had him on ice for those three weeks?

I'm going to have to be careful in this, Cummins thought. The assurances and promises came floating back to him from when he'd first been recruited into this operation. Christ, that had been over four years ago.

He'd been a young lawyer employed by what was then a credible law firm. When he'd gotten called up by his reserve unit, things had changed. He'd gone to his boss, Mr. Fallotti, the head of the firm and a well-known man of significant influence, and asked for help getting out of it. Fallotti had said he would look into it for him, and a couple of discreet favors later, Cummins had a cushy job in military intelligence in Baghdad with the condition that he'd take care of one small assignment over there for the firm. Then he'd be brought back early and be well compensated. That was how he'd gotten entangled in the whole morass involving the Lion Attacking the Nubian, Eagan, those murders in Iraq, setting up Wolf, and the esteemed Mr. Dexter Von Dien. And become another expendable loose end.

Well compensated... Yeah, right.

He had probably been on a one-way trip to oblivion until this second chance popped up. He was going to have to play it for all it was worth and be careful.

Very careful.

"And while you're out there," Fallotti said, "don't forget to deal with that other loose end I told you about."

"Not a problem," Zerbe said. He winked at Cummins and blew another smoke ring.

"Loose end?" Cummins asked.

"Shemp. That lawyer who was looking into Wolf's case," Fallotti said. "McNamara must have put him up to it."

Cummins nodded, recalling the inquiry that had sparked an unsuccessful attempt to eliminate Wolf before he got out of Leavenworth. The man was nothing if not redoubtable, but his time was coming. He'd almost bought it in Mexico, but he was indomitable. He was one major loose end that would need tidying up as well.

Loose ends. The rich man's obsession.

Cummins was also more convinced than ever that if he didn't play it right, he'd be on the chopping block as well.

What's another dead lawyer? he thought.

"One more thing." Fallotti leaned forward, looking at Zerbe and then at Cummins. "I don't have to stress how important it is that we handle this discreetly and successfully. No mistakes. In other words, we can't afford any fuckups. Not like Mexico."

No. Cummins almost shuddered. Not like Mexico.

***

Phoenix, Arizona

Mac had declined Wolf's offer to drive the Escalade to the body shop and said he wanted to take Kasey and Chad into town anyway to buy them some ice cream.

"Besides," McNamara said, "I got to get back in the saddle again soon. I want to get used to driving more."

Wolf figured it had more to do with Kasey not wanting to have to drive Wolf back from the body shop in her car. That suited him just fine. The friction between him and Mac's daughter was like constant sniper fire.

No, make that mortar fire. He could always see or hear her coming.

After the feds had left, he'd tried to caution Mac about playing it cool.

"They're the FBI," Wolf had said.

"What do you want me to do?" McNamara replied. "Genuflect?"

"No, but keep in mind butting heads with federal agents is like trading butts with a water buffalo. Just lying to them is a felony."

"Shit, we're already in hot water then."

Mac laughed, and Wolf smiled.

"Anyway," McNamara said. "You think I can't handle a couple of weak sisters like them two?"

"It's not you I'm worried about. It's Reno. He's the weakest link." Wolf paused and looked at him. "They had to see that this morning."

McNamara considered, then nodded.

"Yeah, I see what you mean. But what do you think we should do about it? We can't very well tell them what really happened down there, can we?"

"No, that would be a disaster. We already gave them statements down in Mexico. If we contradict what we said, they'll have us for lying to federal agents."

McNamara slowly nodded. "Guess one of us is gonna have to go see Reno and make sure he understands."

"I'll do it," Wolf said. "Think I can borrow Kasey's car when you get back?"

McNamara looked askance.

"I'll see if the body shop can give us a loaner,"

he countered.

"Yeah, I get it. She's not being real helpful on that Internet search, either."

"I know, I know. I been trying to talk to her. This thing wasn't your fault." Mac shook his head. "Don't know what's wrong with that girl lately."

Wolf did; she was resentful of her father's relationship with him. Her words from back when they were first introduced still rung in his ear: *He's finally got the son he's always wanted.*

"Aw, hell," McNamara said. "Maybe she'll end up marrying that damn Shemp and move the hell outta here."

"We'll miss her computer skills."

"Not really." Mac grinned. "I've been practicing."

"Yeah, right."

***

Kasey had shot him one of her standard *Everything is your fault* glares as she'd driven past him in her Honda, following Mac in the Escalade. He'd waved just to piss her off. Chad had waved back. At least her son liked him.

He hadn't even inquired if she'd had the time to run checks on the names he'd given her, not wanting to give her the satisfaction of letting her know he was anxious about it.

Jason Zerbe, Jack Cummins, and Von Dien, who-ever that was. He also tried to recall the name of the law firm that had hired them and realized he'd forgotten to check back with Manny to see if he'd found that card.

Maybe telling the FBI they couldn't remember shit wasn't far from the truth after all.

It was still too hot for Wolf to tackle the mountain, but he wanted more than anything to go for a run. Mac's place was close enough to the incline that he had made the daily ascents part of his workout routine.

Never skip on the roadwork, he told himself, remembering the legendary Joe Frazier's cryptic statement about the fighters' creed.

Nobody will know if you cheat on those morning runs under the nascent sky, Frazier had more or less said. *Until you show up in the ring and can't find your legs after the third round when you catch a blow to the liver.*

Those weren't Smokin' Joe's exact words, but they were close enough. The message was all that mattered. Staying in fighting shape was a daily battle waged over time. Skip the hard stuff now, and you'd end up regretting it later. One of the worst things about being in Leavenworth had been his inability to run. He'd compensated by doing pushups, chin-ups, using the weights, sparring in the prison's boxing ring, and taking an occasional trip or two around the exercise yard. It wasn't until he'd resettled out here that he began the runs again and found challenge and pleasure in going up the mountain.

He usually accomplished those runs at first light, but today he'd been on that bounty surveillance since the middle of the night out of necessity.

And it had been a half-assed workout taking down that asshole, Luth. He was bone-tired and his side was still a bit sore, but the solitude and release of a lengthy run were tempting him as he went to the mini-gym. After pounding out two easy rounds on the speedbag and two more on his suspended sand-filled duffel bag, he assessed his condition. The place on his side where Luth's bullet had grazed him stung but wasn't what he considered debilitating. Stripping off the bag gloves, Wolf grabbed a bottle of water from the refrigerator and held it against the bruise. The coolness eased the pain.

Maybe a run *was* in order, he thought and headed out the door.

The prospect of being alone with his thoughts as he went up the mountain was attractive.

After smearing his face and ears with sunblock, Wolf tied a handkerchief over his head, doused it liberally with water, and fitted the two water bottles into the nylon belt he always wore, making sure the bottles were nowhere near the bruise. The belt was equipped with a fanny pack, and he dropped in his keys. Mac had offered to give him the two-shot Bond Arms derringer to carry for self-protection, but Wolf had declined. An ex-con, even one in the bounty hunting business, getting caught carrying a gun was a sure-fire way to get an all-expenses-paid one-way trip right back to the joint. And Wolf had no intention of going back.

Ever.

Clearing his name was another matter.

The unexpected visit by the feds had reinforced that.

He knew that somehow this whole convoluted mess was tied to that incident four years ago in the Sandbox, but the particulars still evaded him. It was like a big jigsaw puzzle with some of the pieces missing.

But he was going to find them, no matter how long it took.

He made sure he'd locked the garage door and started his run, heading down the cement slab to the gravel road and then turning left onto the highway that wound through the mountains. The jarring made his t-shirt feel like sandpaper rubbing his ribcage.

Wolf gritted his teeth and continued, hoping the pain would vanish when the endorphins kicked in.

Back to the jigsaw puzzle.

Cummins. Eagan. Nasim. They'd all been in Iraq four years ago, mixed up in something, and they'd reappeared in Mexico for the finale. Toss in Zerbe, who'd met them down there, supposedly as the point man for that law firm looking for Thomas Accondras, who was also somehow involved.

But how?

And who the hell was Von Dien?

My worst nightmare, Wolf silently repeated to himself, remembering Eagan's last words.

Eagan had been a closed-mouthed prick to the last. He'd probably laughed all the way to hell.

If only there were some answers forthcoming to all these damn questions.

Maybe cooperating with the feds would give him some. They could certainly find out more than he could.

No, he thought. They're in the business of getting information, not giving it out.

Especially to ex-cons under a cloud of suspicion.

The heat was fading, but it was still hot enough to make him feel like he was running barefoot on a sizzling frying pan, and the pain in his side continued to escalate. Every step brought a new level. If he'd been in Iraq or Afghanistan, he would have pushed through the pain, but this was getting too intense.

He slowed down, glanced up and down the highway, and did a wide turn so he'd be facing any oncoming traffic on the way back.

On the way back to what?

Even though he was running outside, it felt like he was on a big treadmill, going through the motions as fast as he could but not getting anywhere.

And scrounging for a buck.

Which brought him back to Reno Garth.

Maybe *he* could remember the name of that law firm.

It would be worth the time to ask him.

And maybe, Wolf thought, *I can also ask him about getting me an MMA fight.*

It would be a pleasure to be in a situation where he could strike back for a change.

After a few more steps, the pain in his side was so bad that he slowed to a walk.

He wondered about stepping into that octagon with his side like it was.

I guess I could always take a dive, he thought with a smile as the pain continued to grind that sandpaper over his ribcage.

The questions and the names kept bombarding him with each step like an invisible opponent giving him a systematic beat-down.

CHAPTER 4

NEAR BELI
REPUBLIC OF THE CONGO

His BDUs were black, and with the dark camo paint smeared over his face, Luan Preetorius could imagine himself being one of those big jungle predator cats he had stalked in his youth in the game preserves. The mission was a simple one: *Vinnige inskywing, vinnige uitgang.* Quick entry, quick exit. Rescuing the hostages would hopefully fall somewhere in between. So would the recovery of the ransom money. But it was in CFA Francs anyway, so not that it mattered much. Just so the Lion Team was paid in Euros or dollars so they could spend their R and R time in the best of places.

Preetorius adjusted the volume on his radio and surveyed the scene before him.

The house was one of those old colonial-style mansions on a former rubber plantation. It was a remnant from the bygone era when the Europeans—the French, most likely—in the last century had exploited the natural resources of the continent. Back before the Africans had managed to kick the imperialistic white assholes out. Not that Luan sympathized or felt any kinship with the Congolese. They were just more *negers* to him, the same kind of lowlife fuckers who had ruined his country when they seized power and were now slaughtering the South African whites and stealing their land with alacrity, just like they'd done in Zimbabwe after their transition to "majority rule." He had yet to hear any protest about that from the sanctimonious Americans or their hypocritical European cousins. Everything the *blankes* built up in Africa, the *swarts* were hell-bent on stealing. Pretty soon, even Cape Town would be ruined.

Back to the task at hand, he told himself.

Vinnige inskywing, vinnige uitgang.

"They're almost here now," Rensburg's voice said over the radio.

He was operating a drone with a telescopic infrared camera, a nifty little gadget Preetorius wished they'd had when he was in the military. Of course, these eyes in the sky made things a little less challenging.

A pair of headlamps glowed in the darkness on the road leading to the palatial structure. It was a two-story wood-frame multi-room house with four once-majestic pillars lining the porch, each with a gable. A balcony was recessed over the front doors, with French-style windows on either side. Of course, the paint was now peeling badly, and using the rangefinder function on his night-vision viewfinder, Preetorius could ascertain that dry rot had afflicted several places along the front walls. He had no doubt the inside of the place was a decaying mess.

Much like an aging countess with a bad case of gonorrhea, he told himself, amused by his metaphorical wit.

The vehicle came to a stop in front of the place. It was a dandy black SUV. The light extinguished as it turned from the main road onto the drive that led up to the house.

I wouldn't mind having one just like it to ride around in, Preetorius thought. Too bad we're going to have to blow it up.

But given their location, he'd never be able to get it back to Cape Town. Not without a C-130 at his disposal. Besides, these M23 fuckers had most likely stunk it up.

Maybe someday, he told himself.

"Commo check," he said, depressing the key button for the mic.

"Lima Charlie," De Jager answered.

Henrico was a stickler for proper radio etiquette.

The others responded with unintelligible grunts, but Preetorius was certain of each of them.

Down the line for his squad: De Jager on point about forty yards ahead of him in the thick shrubbery, Mulder and Loots on the left flank, Engelbrect and Haarhoff on the right, Coetzee and Moolman on the rear and Rensburg, his appointed sniper, with the Denel 14.5.

Amiri Moolman was the only *swart* on the team but not a bad man for one of them. He was well-trained and knew how to follow orders, and why not? His Christian name meant "the prince." A good *soldaat*, and after all, they were both members of the new South Africa.

Two men got out of the SUV, slung their rifles— cheap-looking Kalashnikovs—over their shoulders, and headed for the front door. One of them carried a briefcase.

Ah, Preetorius thought. The ransom has been paid, as agreed.

"Get ready to move in," Preetorius said into his radio. "They're taking the money inside and will probably be killing the hostages next."

Another round of muddled acknowledgments echoed in his earpiece.

Preetorius pushed himself erect, his muscular form accomplishing that task with ease. He adjusted the cross-sling so his Heckler and Koch MP5 hung diagonally in front of his chest. That was the way he liked it, with the barrel canted upward and the pistol grip accessible so he could grab and fire it in an instant.

Faster than one of those gunslinger cowboys in those stupid American movies of old.

What was that big fucker's name?

John Wayne? Yeah, that was it.

Totally overblown and ridiculous, but the big son of a bitch had style.

Preetorius was a big guy too. Not as big as the legendary actor, and not bulky either. He was streamlined but still all corded muscle, and he had a preternatural quickness. At one time, he'd considered a career as a professional boxer. Then he'd entered the military and found his true skill was killing, and it was an enjoyable one. Only Loots and Haarhoff were bigger than him, but they both had German heritage.

Say what you want about those fucking Krauts, he thought, but they came from good breeding stock.

Not like the *swarts*.

Preetorius crept through the dense underbrush with the ease of a big jungle cat and came up next to De Jager.

The two men paused in front of the house, and Preetorius hit the button to activate the long-range portion of his viewfinder again.

One of the men took out a pack of cigarettes and offered a smoke to his partner. The second one slipped it between his lips, and the flickering flame of a lighter danced like a burning spark in Preetorius' viewfinder. That would make an easy target for Rensburg with the big rifle, but the noise would tip off the others in the house.

He keyed his mic.

"Francois, are you close enough to take them out silently?"

"Affirmative," Loots answered.

Preetorius said, "Do it. The rest of you move in after we hit the front door. Johannes, stand by."

The muted replies came through his earpiece.

"Henrico, let's go," he said to De Jager.

De Jager rose from his prone position, and they started down the embankment toward the house.

The two men by the vehicle laughed, and both inhaled deeply on their smokes.

Three seconds later, both of them twisted to the ground, the cigarettes tumbling like mini-glowsticks lighted at only one end.

Preetorius and De Jager met Mulder and Loots. A wisp of smoke trailed from the circular end of the sound suppressor attached to the end of the barrel of Loots' Vektor R4 rifle.

They quickly pulled the bodies around the SUV, leaving them lying on the side opposite the house. Mulder had recovered the briefcase and snapped open the catches.

He lifted the lid only enough to verify that it was the ransom money and closed the catches again. He looked at Preetorius, who smirked and said, "Leave it with our two friends for now. They aren't going anywhere."

Mulder tucked the briefcase between the two bodies and straightened.

"We'll go in as planned," Preetorius said. "Henrico and I up top."

He adjusted the sling of his MP5, making sure it was clipped and remained close against his vest and reaffirmed the snug fit of his fingerless black leather gloves.

After a quick check of the front of the house, the four of them rushed to the left side of the door, away from the view of the shuttered windows but in line with the far edge of the balcony.

Preetorius stepped back as the other three quickly formed a human pyramid. Once again feeling like his jungle cat namesake—his Christian name "Luan" meant "Lion"—he scrambled up the backs of his teammates. As his hands reached the rail of the balcony and gripped it, evidence of the decay of the mansion came to the forefront: the rail broke off in his fingers.

Shit, Preetorius thought, managing to maintain his balance. Using his powerful leg muscles to spring upward, the upper half of his body thrust through more rotted wood, and he pulled himself all the way onto the balcony. The floor seemed none too sturdy, but it held when he pressed down on it as a durability test. Satisfied that it would support his weight and that of another, he spun and removed the coil of rope from his shoulder pack.

"Henrico," he whispered as he lowered the rope.

De Jager was the smallest of the three below. He was also the most agile. When Preetorius felt the rope go taut, he braced himself and pulled as De Jager's feet skipped up the wall. He dropped the line as soon as his compatriot was on solid footing, then drew his Vektor Z88 from its holster. After screwing on the sound suppressor, he pressed the button and sent the red laser dot onto the wooden framework.

All charged up and ready to go, he thought.

Just like him.

He withdrew the KA-BAR knife from the sheath on the left side of his body armor. While he preferred the knife for up-close-and-personal killing, they were here on a mission. A paid assignment, so he resheathed the blade once more.

Business before pleasure, he thought. *Perhaps I'll have an occasion to combine both.*

De Jager was loosening the closed shutters on the window facing them with his knife, and Preetorius knew Mulder and Loots were already on either side of the front door and the others were positioning themselves for a dynamic entry on his signal.

The anticipated thrill of the next few moments

swept through him like a sexual climax. This was when he felt most alive, knowing the big cat was about to strike and other men were going to die.

De Jager popped the shutter loose, and Preetorius saw the pane behind it was long gone. He motioned for De Jager to enter first, and the smaller man slid through the opening with the ease of a black mamba. Preetorius followed, his much larger body slowing his movements slightly. They paused on the floor, testing its resilience with toe-pressing caution. It wouldn't do to plummet through a weak spot, but neither would it be apropos to alert their adversaries with noticeable tapping.

Letting his eyes become accustomed to the darkness of the room, he studied the dimensions. It was vacant, as was the doorframe. Light spilled in from below. Preetorius flipped down his night-vision glasses, and the crystal-clear green images took form. Keeping the Vektor in a ready position close to his chest, he moved to the edge of the open doorway and took a quick peek. On the first floor, music played, and the smell of burning cigarettes, hard liquor, and sweat lingered in the air. Masculine voices drifted upward, speaking what sounded like French mixed with Kituba. Men talked in low murmurs, occasionally laughing as a woman moaned. He moved with cautious stealth to the upstairs banister and took another quick peek.

There was enough light from the half-dozen or so electric lanterns down there that he switched off and pushed up his night-vision goggles. Seven hostiles were below, one of them in a chair holding a naked woman. He was naked as well. She was white. Two more women, both black, lay in twisted heaps in the center of the floor, surrounded by three more men in various positions around the room. These women were nude as well, but the men were partially clothed. Two of them were shirtless but wearing pants. Another shirtless man reposed on a decrepit sofa, his pants around his knees, and another was taking a swig from a bottle, his head tilted back, a good portion of the liquor spilling down his dark cheeks. Three AK-47s were carelessly stacked on either side of the sofa, and the drinking man's weapon was leaning against a wall. The other two held theirs haphazardly.

The principals at the oil company had informed them that seven of their personnel were missing and believed kidnapped, according to the ransom demand. Four men and three women. Preetorius had inquired about the ages of the women and been told they were young. He informed the principals that time was of the essence because there was a strong possibility that the women would be severely mistreated. Norton, the controller, had grimaced.

"Do you mean they'll be molested?" he'd asked.

Preetorius had nodded. It was a given, considering who they were dealing with.

The man had grimaced. "Even if we pay the

ransom?"

"There's a good chance of it. They will most likely be killed as well. I would recommend we act quickly."

"Bastards," Norton had said.

It had come to pass, at least the rape part. The client would not be pleased by this development.

At least I prepared them for the worst, Preetorius thought.

But was this the worst?

None of the male hostages were visible.

That meant they were either secured in another room or dead.

Preetorius hoped for the former. He had the reputation of the Lion Team to think about.

Maybe the males were still alive. Maybe these *negers* didn't want an audience for their debauchery.

He edged back and keyed his mic, whispering a quick description of the scene below and advising Coetzee and Moolman in the rear to assume cover so as not to get caught in a crossfire. He assigned the zones of fire, stating the ones he would take out personally.

"Leave at least one or two alive. We need to find out where they've stashed the other hostages."

The rest of the Lion Team acknowledged. Preetorius then said, "Go."

Stepping to the edge of the second-floor landing once again, he extended his arms and fitted his index finger through the trigger guard. The Vektor had a double-action pull on the first round, then transitioned to single-action. He constantly trained for that first long trigger pull, careful not to allow the adrenaline rush to cause him to drop the first round. That was always a danger, especially with the heavy silencer. But as usual, his aim was perfect, punctuated by the plink of the suppressor.

The head of the man standing by the wall, the one holding his rifle at port arms, jerked back, and his knees bent in unison as the rest of his body wobbled back and then forward.

Like he was doing a dance, Preetorius thought as he completed target acquisition of the man next to the falling one.

This one glanced around as he grabbed for the Kalashnikov leaning against the wall.

Preetorius' second shot hit him in the left temple, and he crumpled.

There was one more shot he wanted to make before leaving the remaining crew for Loots and Mulder to deal with as they came through the front door.

The man holding the woman dumped her on the floor and stood, surveying his collapsed cohorts. Preetorius leaned over and sent a round through the man's meaty right buttock. He fell on top of the woman he'd just dropped.

Sounds of the front door being breached echoed in the room as Preetorius swung his legs over the banister, which was surprisingly sturdy, and made the fourteen-foot drop to the room below. As he landed, he peripherally saw another of the hostiles drop, accompanied by the plunking suppressed rounds. The last hostile standing was in the process of bringing his rifle into a firing position, but Preetorius shot the man through the right bicep and then the abdomen. Before the weapon had tumbled out of the man's hands and hit the floor, Loots surged forward and delivered a quick butt-stroke with his Vektor R4. It had a metal folding stock and packed enough punch to knock the dirty *neger* silly.

"Two clear the other rooms," Pretorius said into his comm as the rest of the Lion Team moved through the room. "Henrico?"

"Second floor clear," De Jager said from above.

The naked man below him groaned, and Preetorius put his boot on top of the man's back and bore down.

"I'll be with you in a moment," he said.

The naked black women were starting to stir. The white one was still underneath her tormentor, so Preetorius pulled the man off her. The white woman's chest heaved. She was breathing. A trail of blood snaked down her cheek from her hair.

"Section Alpha clear," Loots said.

"Bravo clear," Coetzee reported.

Moolman chimed in, signaling the final quadrant. "Charlie clear."

"Johannes?" Preetorius said.

"All quiet on the western front, boss," Rensburg said. "Sounds like I missed all the fun."

Preetorius smiled. "Next time, Gerhardus will be the sniper. Keep watch while we do interrogations." He glanced at his watch: 2150 hours. Not bad for a night's work so far. But they still had a ways to go.

Miles to go before I sleep, Preetorius thought, re-calling a favorite line of poetry from some obscure American poet he'd read in grammar school. Perhaps when this was over, he'd look up the quote and see who it was. But in the meantime...

He was cognizant of the rest of the team drifting into the room, checking the bodies.

"Check the women," he said to Engelbrect and Haarhoff, then motioned to Mulder and Loots. "Bring that one over here."

They brought over the last man Preetorius had shot. Blood was spilling out of the wounds on his arm and abdomen. He appeared to be going into shock.

Preetorius grabbed the naked man who'd been shot in the ass and threw him to the side.

He would be the most likely squealer. The other one wouldn't last that long.

Loots dumped the other one on the floor a yard or so away.

"The women are all alive," Engelbrect said. "Looks like they've been beaten and raped."

"See if you can find some clothes for them," Preetorius said as he unscrewed the silencer from the end of his Vektor. "Strip those fuckers of theirs if you can't."

After slipping the suppressor into his pants pocket, he re-holstered his pistol and withdrew the KA-BAR. The light was bright enough to make the silver blade gleam as he rotated it. Loots grabbed the arms of the man with the ass wound and twisted them behind his back. He screamed in pain.

Sounds like a little girl, Preetorius thought, knowing he'd made the right decision about which one would break first. Mulder held the man with the abdominal wound. His gut was swollen and distended from the blood welling up inside. After making sure ass-wound was watching, Preetorius gripped the ear of the gut-wounded man and jerked his head up so their eyes locked.

"You've been some bad little *negers*," Preetorius said, smiling. "Where are the other hostages?"

"*S'il vous plait*," the man said.

Preetorius repeated his question. "Where are the other hostages?"

The man mumbled something in French that Preetorius assumed was either a plea for help or profanity. Either way, all that mattered was that the one with the ass wound was watching.

Preetorius stuck the tip of his knife under the wounded man's chin.

"One more time, asshole," Preetorius said. "And I don't speak French or Kituba. Where are the other hostages?"

Again the man mumbled something, so Preetorius swiped the blade downward, opening a long but shallow cut from the man's chin to the pulsing hole in his side. The blood poured out.

"Please, boss," Ass Wound said. "He no speak English."

"But you do, eh, boy?" Loots said, exerting more pressure on the man's bent arms.

"*Oui, oui*," the man said. "Yes. Me have English."

"You certainly don't look it," Preetorius said. "The male hostages. Where are they?"

"They in rubber shed out back, boss."

"Alive or dead?"

"They alive, boss. We no kill 'em. We good. Only wants da money, boss."

"We saw something that looked like an old rubber drying room back there," Moolman said. "About a hundred yards back."

Preetorius checked with Rensburg. "You see anything that looks like a shed in the rear?"

After about fifteen seconds, Rensburg replied, "Old wooden shack. Can't see anyone near it."

Preetorius told Coetzee and Moolman to check it out. They slipped out the back way. After they'd left, Preetorius looked down at Ass Wound.

"You know what happens if you lie to me," he said. It was not an interrogative but a statement.

"I no lie, boss," Ass Wound said. "I no lie."

They stood in silence for about three minutes before Coetzee's voice came over the com.

"They're here. All four of them. Badly beaten but alive."

"Bring them to the house," Preetorius ordered.

Ass Wound's eyes widened. "See? See, boss? I no lie to you. I no lie."

"True," Preetorius said. "But you're still going to hell, asshole."

Drawing back his arm, he smiled right before he drove the knife forward.

He had gotten to get to use it up close and personal, after all.

***

LaGuardia International Airport
New York City

Cummins settled into the seat of the redeye, grateful that Fallotti's reservations had been for first-class. It gave him precious breathing room and a bit of distance from Zerbe. After they'd left the office, it had been hectic. Cummins had barely had enough time to visit his apartment, empty his mailbox, and toss some clothes in a suitcase. He hadn't been surprised when Zerbe announced he had no luggage to speak of, just a carry-on.

"It's best if you just travel light and buy whatever you need in this business," he explained.

Cummins hoped that would include a change of underwear. The man's pungent odor was sickening.

After they'd reentered the limo and departed for the airport, Zerbe removed his phone, looked at it, and frowned.

"He hasn't called me back yet," he said, then shrugged. "Of course, it's getting on toward the wee hours over there."

Cummins knew that meant South Africa. They were seven or so hours ahead. He'd been surprised Fallotti had approved the use of a foreign team as backup to neutralize Wolf, but if these guys were as good as Zerbe had said they were, that poor son of a bitch wouldn't stand a chance.

Of course, that was what they'd figured in Mexico.

Zerbe punched in some numbers on his cell and waited.

Cummins could tell it rang several times before going to voice mail.

"Hello, Luan," Zerbe said. "*Hoe gaan dit?* It's your old comrade in arms, Jason. I've got a particularly good assignment in mind for you. Right up your alley. Give me a call back as soon as you can. Oh, by the way,

I'm in the US. *Gesels later.*"

He removed the phone from his ear and pressed another button to terminate the call.

"My guess is he's out somewhere on assignment," he said. "Keeps pretty busy, that one. He's in demand all over Africa and Europe and the Middle East."

"So you said. What makes you think he'll fly all the way here to take this job?"

Zerbe smiled. "For one thing, the money will be right. Also, once I tell him what happened in Mexico and who he's going up against, he'll be chomping at the bit."

"Why's that?"

"He won't be able to resist." Zerbe slipped his phone back into his pocket and pulled out his pack of cigarettes. "He loves a challenge."

Cummins mulled that over for a few seconds.

That was exactly what Eagan had said, he thought.

"What makes you so sure he'll be able to handle Wolf?" Cummins asked.

Zerbe scoffed. "I told you. He's the best."

CHAPTER 5

MCNAMARA RANCH
PHOENIX, ARIZONA

With the new dawn, Wolf had decided to tackle the mountain again. This time he'd used a neoprene wrap around the bruised area and dumped a half-dozen ice cubes inside it. The numbness helped for the first part of the run, but about halfway through the first mile, the ice had all melted and dribbled away, and the sandpaper returned and started rubbing his ribcage again. Each jolting step exacerbated it.

Shit, he thought as his feet inexorably slowed to a walk. This ain't working.

Even though it was barely light, the heat was already enveloping him.

But it's a dry heat, he told himself.

Of course, that was what they used to say about

the Sandbox, too. Luckily, this place wasn't as deadly.

He started walking back, the sweat pouring down his face and neck onto his saturated t-shirt. After covering half the distance back at what he felt was a snail's pace, Wolf sucked it up and started a slow jog toward the gravel road that intersected the highway. Once he rounded it and began the final leg, his side had started to ache again.

Damn that idiot Luth for shooting me. And damn those idiots, Reno and Herc, who'd cut the rear seat seatbelt in an obnoxious show of machismo back before Mexico. If the seatbelt hadn't been damaged yesterday, he could have secured Luth in the seat properly, and he wouldn't have been able to break the damn window, adding to the chaos.

For want of a nail, he thought.

Then he recalled the scene yesterday with the despondent and capitulating Reno, who'd arrived to shake their hands and offer reparations for damaging the Escalade.

Poor Herc had paid for his transgressions and then some south of the border.

Wolf remembered the AK-47 rounds that had ripped through the big man's chest. He'd been one powerful son of a bitch, capable of breaking out of a pair of steel handcuffs. But all the muscle in the world didn't stand a chance against a 7.62-caliber opponent. At least the guys who'd killed him were dead.

Small consolation, Wolf thought as Mac's place came into view.

The confrontation had damn near killed all four of them and had left Mac and Reno wounded. It wasn't the first time Mac had been shot. He had three Purple Hearts on that plaque in the shadow box. But the lower right side was a lousy place to take one, and Reno's leg had been severely impaired. Nerve damage. Wolf had been telling himself it couldn't have happened to a better guy until yesterday when the humbled, broken figure had stood there offering his thanks and extending his hand.

Shared combat makes strange bedfellows, he thought.

As he got nearer, he saw a flicker of movement at the end of the driveway.

It was Mac, leaning on his sword cane, waiting for him.

It gave him an incentive to ignore the pain and quicken his pace.

Finish strong, he told himself as he kicked it up a notch and managed to sprint the last fifty yards or so.

Well, maybe it was twenty-five.

McNamara was grinning from ear to ear as Wolf shot by him.

"Damn," McNamara said, clucking his tongue. "Getting shot one day and out doing wind sprints the next. You are one tough son of a bitch. Ah, no offense intended to your mama."

"None taken," Wolf said, slowing to a stop and leaning over with his hands on his knees. Normally, he liked to walk it off to cool down, but today it hurt to move.

"You're up pretty early," Wolf said. "What's the occasion?"

"Two things," McNamara said. "One, I got a text from Manny last night. Says he wants to see us first thing about something. Something big."

Wolf nodded. Picking up a hefty bounty would mean more money to help Mac stay one step ahead of his creditors.

"And two." McNamara's smile faded. "The feds. They left me a message on the business answering machine. They want to see us down at the Federal Building this morning at ten."

"Ten?" Wolf said, managing to straighten. "Well, at least that's not too early."

McNamara's face remained solemn.

"They also accidentally and conveniently let it slip that they were fitting us in after they spoke to *Mr. Garth.*"

Mr. Garth? Wolf thought. Reno?

It made sense. The feds were going to try to break the weakest link first, or at least give the impression they had when the time came to talk to them.

***

The Federal Building
Phoenix, Arizona

Wolf sat in the small room and reflected that it was still larger than his cell had been at Leavenworth. Standard setup: an empty table and two chairs, nothing else. And his chair, the one he'd been directed to sit in, had a slant. The front legs were probably a half-inch shorter than the rear ones. It was designed not only for discomfort but to constantly convey the feeling that you were slipping forward, requiring constant readjustments. Make the subject feel as uncomfortable as possible in little ways while you make him wait. There was a mirror on the wall on his right. One-way glass, no doubt, so they could stand in the darkened room and watch the person squirm.

He and McNamara had arrived together and been ushered into separate rooms. Mac had protested, saying their lawyer was on the way. The agent who'd escorted them into the interior office section of the building assured them that as soon as the attorney got there, the SAC would let them know. In the meantime, someone would be with them shortly.

That was pretty much what Wolf had expected. The casual mention by Agent Franker earlier about their interviews being after Reno's session was meant to be a scare tactic. It was Interrogation 101: have them relate their story, then hint that there are inconsistencies between the various accounts.

Wolf pictured it in his mind. *"Your story doesn't quite match up with what Mr. Garth told us. How do you explain that?"*

He wondered how long it would be before one of them added, *"Do you know it's a felony to lie to the FBI?"*

Yeah, Wolf thought. *I know that, all right. That's why we're not saying shit unless we have a lawyer sitting next to us.*

A lawyer...

Rodney F. Shemp, Attorney at Law. "Rod" to his friends.

Also the fiancé of Mac's daughter. He remembered the first time Mac had disclosed that fact.

"I'd appreciate it if you wouldn't call him Rod," Mac had said. *"After all, he is dating my daughter."*

Actually, Wolf didn't think Shemp was a bad guy. Mild-mannered and soft-spoken, he wasn't a macho type, but he seemed like a decent sort. And he'd taken a look at Wolf's case, investing a lot of time and effort in going over the trial transcript and requesting reports. He'd done it all pro bono, albeit at the behest of Mac.

Wolf smiled. The prospect of having Mac as a father-in-law was daunting enough, much less not complying with the favor that had been asked.

Shemp's review had yielded little Wolf didn't already know about his chance for a new trial. Unless there was new evidence, he would remain an ex-con with a DD forever.

He glanced at his watch and saw it was nearing ten-forty. When they'd stopped at Shemp's office at nine, he'd told them he had court commitments until at least ten.

"That's good," McNamara said. "Our appointment's not scheduled till then. We'll see you there."

Shemp looked like he'd just been kicked in the shins, but he forced a smile and said he'd be there as soon as he could after court.

"And I'd advise not answering any questions without me present," he'd added.

"Don't worry," McNamara said. "I ain't planning on it."

Wolf hoped that was true. Mac was the ultimate alpha male, even though he was a bit past it and suffering from a healing abdominal wound. He'd been around long enough not to let a pair of pretty-boy assholes like Agents Franker and Turner bait him.

Franker and Turner... That sounded like a comedy team, but they were far from it. He got the feeling they knew what they were doing. Exactly what they were doing.

But so did he, compliments of the school of hard

knocks. Going through his court-martial and getting "schooled" by the jailhouse lawyers on the inside had hardened him to the unprincipled aspects of the federal government.

So he wasn't worried about himself or even Mac.

Reno was another matter.

If he were running the investigation, that was where he'd concentrate. His only hope, and Mac's too, lay in Reno's claim of total amnesia. Hopefully, he'd been smart enough and tough enough to stick to it in one of those small rooms down the hall, like this one.

The door opened and the two agents walked in wearing their standard white shirts, dark neckties, and blue suits.

They both held Styrofoam cups of steaming liquid.

Coffee, Wolf assumed.

Franker held two.

"Sorry to keep you waiting, Mr. Wolf," he said as he moved to the chair on the opposite side of the table, taking the time to set one of the cups down and extend the second one toward Wolf. "I didn't know if you'd want cream or sugar, but I figured most of you Ranger guys probably like it black."

He flashed a smile.

Wolf made no move to touch the cup after Franker set it in front of him, nor did he say anything.

"Was I right?" Franker asked, the friendly smile still on his face.

"The Army already has my DNA on file," Wolf said. "In case my corpse was too mutilated to identify."

Franker raised his eyebrows and snorted a laugh.

"Yeah, you're right," he said. "We do. Mr. Mc-Namara's too." He sighed. "Man, that guy's got more medals than a casino's got chips."

"He earned them all, too," Wolf said.

Franker's smile returned. Apparently, he felt that he'd bridged a gap by getting Wolf talking. Wolf wondered if that meant the Mac had told them to go pound sand. He also wondered if Shemp had arrived yet.

"I'll bet he did," Franker said. "You've got quite a few, too."

"Not as many as Mac," Wolf said. In a strange way, he was enjoying this interchange. If it had just been his ass on the line going up against the FBI, he would have been more relaxed, but not knowing what Mac and Reno had said was like playing poker.

"I see you were awarded the Silver Star," Turner said. He'd opened a manila file that was full of papers.

Wolf nodded.

"Wow," Franker said. "What was that all about?"

"It was about trying to stay alive," Wolf said. "Combat."

"I can imagine," Franker said. "Thank you for your service."

"It was pretty hairy over there, I bet," Turner said. "Huh?"

"It had its moments," Wolf said.

"So, what was it like?" Franker leaned forward and drank some of his coffee, motioning for Wolf to drink his.

He didn't touch the cup. "It was combat."

"You got three stars for valor, too," Turner added.

Wolf nodded again, and they sat in silence for a few seconds. The agents glanced at each other.

Finally, Franker's smile faded, and he blew out a slow breath. "All right, let me put my cards on the table. We work what's called the flyaway squad. Any time an American citizen gets killed in a foreign country, it becomes a Bureau case."

Wolf thought the guy looked boyish. He was probably in his late twenties and appeared to be in good shape, but he reminded Wolf of Opie Taylor in a blue suit.

Wolf had loved that old show, which was in constant reruns on the nostalgia channel. Too bad these guys lacked the sincerity of good old Sheriff Andy Taylor.

"You were a friend of Henry Preen, I take it?" Franker asked.

Wolf shook his head.

"You're denying you knew him?" Turner this time.

"No," Wolf said. "I met him a few times. I wouldn't call us friends."

"Where did you meet him?" Franker asked.

Wolf considered his answer. They'd succeeded

in getting him talking, which he hadn't intended to do, but the questions seemed innocuous. Score one for their side.

"I met him here in Phoenix," Wolf said. He almost added that they were both in the same business but remembered that it wasn't a good idea to offer information.

"You were both in the bounty hunting business?" Franker asked.

Wolf shrugged.

"I didn't catch that," Franker said.

"I didn't throw anything," Wolf replied.

Franker flashed a grin.

Maybe this isn't going as smoothly as I'd hoped, Wolf thought. *Score one for me.*

"When did you next meet him?" Franker asked.

Wolf considered his answer and tried to anticipate how they intended to trip him up. They were trying to take the roundabout way to the final meeting in Mexico when Henry Preen, aka Black Hercules, was killed.

"Can't say as I can recall," Wolf said.

Franker looked at Turner, who held his Styrofoam cup in his mouth while he used both hands to shuffle through the papers in the manila file. After acting like he'd found what he was looking for, he reached up and retrieved the cup, then said, "Does Las Vegas ring a bell?"

Wolf took his time answering. Had Reno mentioned the incident at the Shamrock Hotel where he and Mac'd had their second confrontation? Had Mac said something? Did they have surveillance video from the casino?

"It rings a lot of bells," Wolf said. "Ever been there?"

"It's better if we ask the questions," Franker said. "Do you recall meeting him in the Shamrock Hotel and Casino or not?"

First they'd succeeded in getting him talking and now they'd backed him into another corner. The score was now two to one, their favor.

"What does Las Vegas have to do with your case?" Wolf asked. Tossing a question back at them would hopefully throw them off balance.

"As I said," Franker leaned forward slightly, "it's better if we ask the questions here."

"Better for who?" Wolf said.

He tried to lean back in the damn chair but couldn't. It would require effort and make it look like he was straining or nervous. Instead, he leaned forward, placing both forearms on the table.

Franker's face twitched.

"Would it surprise you to learn that we know that you did, in fact, meet Henry Preen in Las Vegas?"

"If you know that," Wolf said in a calm, measured tone, "why are you asking me?"

Franker's lips compressed.

"What did you two talk about?" Turner asked.

Wolf shook his head and tried to affect an expression of concentration.

"Was that the last time you saw him?" Franker said. "Before you met down in Mexico?"

Backed into another corner, Wolf thought. These guys weren't the lightweights they appeared to be. Score another one for the G.

Wolf said nothing. Without knowing what Reno and Mac had said, he was walking a tightrope without a net. He'd been there when Herc was murdered and loaded his body into the back of the van before Mac and Reno drove off. Could they have recovered his DNA on any of the bodies? Was that why they were trying to get him to leave some in the coffee cup?

No, Wolf thought. That coffee cup thing was a tool to unnerve him. Something they could hold up and jiggle like they did on TV, making him think he had something new to worry about. As he'd said, the Army already had his DNA. They didn't need to fish a coffee cup out of the garbage.

Little by little, they were boxing him in, and all they had to do was catch him in one lie. They hadn't even taken the gloves off yet.

It had been a mistake to talk to them.

"Did my lawyer get here yet?" Wolf asked.

When in doubt, take yourself out of the game.

The agents exchanged glances again.

"Why do you need a lawyer?" Turner asked. "You

got something to hide?"

Wolf was tired of this game, of their coyness, their duplicity. He wanted to lash out and tell them to go to hell, but he couldn't afford to do that.

"I don't know," he said. "Do you think I do?"

"What we think isn't the question," Franker said. "We're investigating the homicides of several American citizens in Mexico, and you know more than you're telling."

Several American citizens. That told Wolf a lot. They'd found the bodies of the others: Eagan and his Viper team, Accondras, the Mexicans Paco and Jose. It had been a bloodbath, but trying to explain it would put him right back in prison, either here or in Mexico, even though he had killed only in self-defense.

It was just like being in Iraq, fighting under rules of engagement that were stacked against him.

A knock on the door broke the silence.

Turner slipped the file under his arm and opened the door. A man, obviously another FBI agent, said something *sotto voce*. Wolf hoped it was good news.

Turner nodded and turned back.

"It seems an attorney is here. A Mr. Shemps, claiming to represent you?"

"That's Shemp," Wolf said. "And he's my lawyer all right."

Game over, Wolf thought. And not a moment too soon.

**

When they walked outside the Federal Building, Wolf saw Mac waiting for him by the rental car the body shop had arranged for them. It was a small, cramped Toyota Corolla, and Mac was leaning against the front fender. The white van Wolf had seen Reno in yesterday was pulled up next to the Toyota, and Wolf saw the familiar high-and-tight buzzcut hair style and knew Reno was in the passenger seat. As they approached, Mac shifted his body off the car and strode over to meet them. He was using his regular aluminum cane today rather than the sword cane.

"How'd it go?" he asked, his expression a mixture of worry and concern.

"Smooth as a cherry jumper's first drop," Wolf said. He patted Shemp on the back. "Rod here came in and rescued me just like the cavalry in those old John Wayne movies."

Mac flashed a look of disapproval at the nickname but nodded his thanks to the lawyer.

"We don't owe you anything for this," McNamara said. "Do we?"

Shemp smiled nervously and shook his head.

"No, no, That's all right, sir." His lips drew back in a smile that vanished as quickly as it had appeared. "Well, I'd better get going. Got to work on a brief."

Wolf extended his hand toward the lawyer.

"Rod," he said. "Thanks again."

Shemp stared down at Wolf's open palm for a moment as if he weren't sure what was being offered, then shook it. McNamara leaned forward, keeping both hands on his cane, and made no motion to offer his hand. After a few awkward moments of blasé conversation, the lawyer got into a Buick LeSabre. He waved as he drove off.

"Well, at least he's driving an American car." McNamara frowned as he looked at Wolf. "I thought I told you not to call him 'Rod.' Not with him dating my daughter."

"Come on, Mac. He did us a solid, and he didn't even charge us anything."

"He's lucky I ain't charging him," McNamara said. "For all the times Kasey's had him over to Sunday dinner and such. Come on."

He ambled toward Reno's van.

"Hey, Steve," Reno said. "How'd it go?"

"My lawyer got there in the nick of time. How about you?"

Reno laughed. Wolf could see that the dynamite chick who'd driven the van yesterday was once again behind the wheel.

"I laid it on so thick, they'll have to use a fire-hose to wash the place down." He cocked a thumb toward the rear of the vehicle. "I came and went in my wheelchair, along with my doctor and my lawyer, a guy in a four-thousand-dollar Armani suit, and stuck to my guns. PTSD causing total CRS."

"Sounds like an expensive lawyer."

"The six-figure kind. He's the TV company's lawyer. They don't want to take no chances now that the show might get picked up for syndication."

"Syndication?" Wolf said.

"Yeah," Reno said. "You know, them endless repeats that run all the time on cable channels? Like *Walker, Texas Ranger* and *Law and Order*. Puts a lot of money in my bank account every time one of them is broadcast."

Wolf raised his eyebrows. It was good to know that somebody in this business wasn't hurting for money. Also that Reno had gone in with an elephant gun instead of a BB gun.

"You need a wheelchair?" Wolf asked.

Reno laughed again.

"Nah. Not once I got out of rehab. But I kept the van and the chair just for shits and giggles. Figured when I start fighting again, I can use it as a publicity gimmick. You know, saying I was getting it ready for my opponent because they're gonna need it."

Wolf nodded and wondered if Reno's shot-up leg would allow him to step back into the octagon again. Perhaps this would be a good time to ask him about setting up an MMA match so Wolf could get his feet wet.

Reno snorted. "If I ever get back to fighting, that is. Anyway, it came in handy today. I used it to keep them federal idiots off my back, and it's also how I met Barbie here."

The gorgeous girl behind the wheel flashed a dazzling smile.

Wolf was leery about discussing too much about this FBI matter in front of her, but if she and Reno were close, he'd probably confided everything to her anyway. That could be a problem down the road.

"Well," Wolf said, "all's well that ends well, I guess. We'd better get over to Manny's. He said he had something pressing, right?"

"He did," McNamara said. "But you ain't heard the best part yet. Reno's gonna let us drive the Hummer until we get the Escalade back."

Wolf was stunned.

"The Hummer?"

"Yeah," Reno said. "I ain't been driving it anyway. You guys might as well get some use out of it, least-ways until you get yours back."

About twenty-five minutes later, in the parking lot of Reno's gym, McNamara and Wolf gazed at the massive jet-black Hummer with its heavily tinted windows. The vehicle was a modified and scaled-down version of the Humvees they'd driven in Iraq and Afghanistan. It didn't have any armor plating or exhaust pipe extension, but it was impressive even without the combat accessories.

"Reminds me of the ones we drove in the Sand-box," Wolf said.

"It's a kissin' cousin, that's for sure," McNamara said. "And it sure beats the hell out of that damn rental." McNamara was still walking with the assistance of a cane, but he made a beeline for the Hummer. Wolf strode beside him, unsure if his friend was going to be able to ascend into the high seat, but when they got there, Wolf saw the footrails.

Hitting the remote to unlock the big vehicle, McNamara made a show of walking around it and checking out the interior.

"Hot damn," he said, opening the rear door. "Will you take a look at this?"

Wolf stepped over and saw that two sets of manacles had been welded to floorboards and to a bar running horizontally across the back of the front seats. Reno had also installed a metal cage behind the rear seats so the back could be used to transport prisoners. Wolf wondered how much this decked-out vehicle had cost with all the bells and whistles. The memory of Reno's buddy Herc taking three 7.62 rounds in the chest also lingered in Wolf's mind. The reconciliation between Reno, Mac, and him had come at a high price.

"Pretty impressive," Wolf said.

"Impressive, hell," Mac said. "It's ingenious. Reno's

smarter than I thought."

Wolf chuckled, glad Reno had elected just to give them the keys and not accompany them to inspect the vehicle.

"This way, we can make multiple pinches in one fell swoop," Mac said. "We can leave one guy trussed up in the handcuffs while we go grab another one."

Wolf nodded, wondering how Kasey was going to react to her father putting himself back into the game.

"Let's not get too far ahead of ourselves," Wolf said. "You've still got a ways to go on your recovery, don't you?"

"Shee-it," McNamara said. "I'm feeling better and better every day. Why, I was even tempted to join you on your run this morning."

"Well, you don't want to overdo it."

McNamara snorted and slammed the rear door. He opened the driver's door, angled himself next to the footrail, and lifted one foot and then the other onto it.

"Let's go see what Manny's got for us," he said, shifting his bulk onto the seat and situating himself behind the wheel. "I'm itchin' to make an arrest, and I'm even more itchin' to make some money."

Making money, Wolf thought. That was the name of the game right now.

As they drove to Manny's in tandem, with Wolf in the loaner, he assessed the aftermath of the morning sessions with the feds. Mac's interview had apparently gone reasonably well. He said he'd managed to stick to the story he'd used in Mexico: that he, Reno, and Herc had met down there, hired a driver, some Mexican guy whose name Mac couldn't recall, to take them around Cancun to do some sightseeing and maybe meet some pretty *señoritas* on the sly. Then this group of *banditos* stopped them somewhere; he didn't know where and couldn't remember when due to their imbibing. The *banditos* had tried to rob them and had shot them up. Their driver pulled a gun and started the firefight. Herc got shot, as well as Reno and Mac, who'd managed, by the grace of God, to drive all of them to the hospital. All except the Mexican driver, who vanished.

"When they asked me for a description," Mc-Namara had said, "I described our little *bandito* fella on my mantel."

"You got to be careful about shoveling too much bullshit at them," Wolf had cautioned.

McNamara had derisively blown out a breath. "Those FBI pussies couldn't find their asses with both hands and a flashlight. They typed out a statement and wanted me to sign it, but Shemp got there and told me I didn't have to sign nothing." He'd grinned. "He asked if I was under arrest, and when they said no, we walked right on out, slick as could be. Then he went back in to fetch you."

"Sounds like *Rod* made a double play," Wolf had

said, stressing the lawyer's name.

"Rod?" McNamara had frowned. "I thought I told you not to call him that."

Wolf saw the flicker of the Hummer's left turn signal up ahead, and it jarred him out of his reverie. He flipped his down and reflected he'd been so lost in his thoughts about the federal investigation that he hadn't even realized they'd driven across town and were at the bail bondsman's office.

I wonder what was so pressing that he had to see us right away? Wolf thought.

He'd said it was big.

Of course, that was how the last mess had started.

CHAPTER 6

OFFICE OF EMANUEL SUTTER
BAIL BONDSMAN
PHOENIX, ARIZONA

"I got a call from the Pope," Manny said between chews after biting into a foot-long Subway sandwich.

Wolf and McNamara were seated in the two unpadded metal chairs in front of Manny's big desk. As usual, it was awash with paperwork. Freddie, aka Sherman, was seated off to the side, talking into his cell phone. His side of the conversation consisted mainly of a lot of yeahs, uh-huhs, and an occasional crack of laugher.

Manny yelled for his nephew to keep it down.

"We're trying to have a conversation here, for Christ's sake."

Freddie swiveled in his chair, turning his back

on them.

Manny took another bite.

Wolf's stomach growled. He'd been in such a rush to shower and get prepped for the interview that he'd skipped breakfast. He was sure Mac had too.

"The Pope?" McNamara said. "I didn't know you were Catholic."

Manny held up his finger while he chewed the substantial portion down to a reasonable enough size to resume the conversation.

"Not *that* Pope," he said after shifting a portion to his right cheek. "Alexander Pope. He's a bail bondsman in Vegas. Calls himself the Pope of the Strip."

"What's up with him?" McNamara asked.

Manny didn't answer immediately in favor of clearing out more of the masticated food. Finally, he swallowed once, grabbed the extra-large soft drink, and took a hefty swig.

After exhaling in satisfaction, he belched and made a move to devour more of the sandwich.

"Why don't you wait on that until you tell us what's up?" McNamara said. "We missed breakfast."

Manny's eyebrows rose. "Heck, I didn't know that. Want me to send Sherman here out for a pick-up for youse?"

Freddie's head bobbed around at the mention of his unwelcome nickname, but he kept talking into the phone.

"No," McNamara said. "Watching you has spoiled my appetite. What I do want is for you to tell us what's so damn important that you had to see us right away."

Manny nodded and drank more of the soda. He set the remainder of the sandwich on the waxy wrapper that was spread out on his desk.

"Okay, first things first." He reached into a desk drawer and pulled out two files. "The Wolfman here's been pushing for some quick pinches, so I'm gonna give you two. Both paper tigers, so you shouldn't have no trouble with them." He handed the files across the desk to McNamara. "You can thank me later."

Wolf felt like saying he'd buy him dessert, but he didn't think his bank account could handle the strain.

"Second," Manny said, "like I told ya, I got a call from the Pope. He's gonna be out a big one to the tune of a hundred and fifty Gs if he don't get this guy in by the next court date next Wednesday."

"Standard recovery fee?" McNamara asked.

Manny nodded, then grinned. "Plus a nice big bonus."

Wolf noticed that Manny had copious amounts of food stuck between his teeth.

McNamara whistled softly. "What exactly is he offering in the way of a bonus?"

Manny grinned. "Don't get too excited just yet. There's more. First of all, he ain't even sure the skip's in Phoenix. The only thing he is sure of is that he beat feet outta Vegas in a hurry."

"Who is this guy?" Wolf asked.

"His name's Willard Krenshaw."

Something clicked in Wolf's memory, but he wasn't sure what.

Manny was still grinning and shaking his extended index finger at Wolf.

"Yeah, I figured the Wolfman would know that name," Manny said. "Been in the news plenty the last couple months."

Then it clicked for Wolf. "The attorney?"

"Right. The guy that was suing that congressman a year or so ago for allegedly playing hide the salami with that model."

It was a male model who'd made the claim that the married congressman had forced his attentions upon him after slipping him a roofie or something like that. Wolf remembered hearing it on the news while he was still inside. It had gotten a big laugh from his cellmate, who never missed a news broadcast. Wolf didn't remember the case going much farther than the news cameras, but the lawyer had subsequently gotten into more trouble.

"Then old Willard stepped on his dick," Manny said. "Big-time."

"He got indicted for something," McNamara said. "As I recall."

"Yeah, for witness tampering." Manny laughed out

loud. "The dumb fucker got caught on a wiretap."

"Wasn't the mob involved in some way?" McNamara asked.

"Sure was. The Bellotti family. Krenshaw was their standard mouthpiece."

"So, the feds were tapping an attorney?"

"No, it's more complicated than that." Manny picked up the sandwich again but didn't take a bite. He just fingered it lovingly. "He's been the Outfit's lawyer for years. The case where he got his dick in a wringer was for insurance fraud. He was pressuring this company to offer a cash settlement or something and hinted that his friends the Bellottis were in his corner." Manny laughed again. "The company went to the feds, and they started recording everything. Got poor old Willard on tape being a greedy asshole."

"And the feds grabbed him," McNamara said. "Hoping to use him as leverage to build a case against his *other* clients?"

"Exactly," Manny said. "Which is why the Outfit wouldn't post bond for him. They figured they could get him iced in jail easier than they could on the outside, and it wouldn't look all that suspicious."

"So he called the Pope," McNamara said.

"Everybody always does in Vegas," Manny said. "But in this case, it was his girlfriend that called."

"And the Pope posted bond for him?" McNamara shook his head. "Didn't they have to put up some collateral?"

"Yeah. She put up some of her jewelry, and the shitbird put up his Mercedes and his house in Palm Springs." Manny chuckled. "Turns out the jewelry's quality paste, the car's a beat-up piece of junk, and he's so upside down in his mortgage that the equity won't even cover your bar bill for a month."

"I'm liking this more and more," McNamara said.

Wolf wasn't.

"So, why'd he skip out?" he asked.

Manny shrugged. "He probably knows they got the goods on him. This milquetoast wouldn't last a New York minute in the joint, and his only other choice is to play ball with the feds and to roll over on the mob boys."

"Which means the Outfit's looking for him too," Wolf said. The picture was getting darker all the time.

Manny's head canted to the right, and his fingers continued to trace the loaf of bread.

"Well, yeah. That's always part of the picture."

"Hell, we ain't scared of no goombas," McNamara said.

"I don't know, Mac," Wolf said. "We might need substantial backup on this one if the mob's involved."

McNamara huffed and was about to speak when Manny broke in.

"And you got some," he said. "The Pope's already got Ms. Dolly and the P Patrol on the case, and they're heading this way."

McNamara smiled broadly, looked over at Wolf, and winked.

"Now, that is good news," he said.

Wolf remembered the three beautiful female bounty hunters with a lot of fondness as he recalled their liaison in Las Vegas, but he couldn't speak to their professional talents. His contact with them had been purely social and extremely pleasurable as well, as had Mac's. But he'd said they were consummate pros, and he and Mac could certainly do worse for partners on this one. It was a given that Mac was going to jump on it.

"And Ms. Dolly seems to think Willard's heading for Phoenix?" McNamara asked.

"Right. His sister lives here."

"So, in addition to the feds and the mob," Wolf asked, "is anybody else looking for this dude?"

"Just Ms. Dolly and you guys," Manny said, then shook his head. "I'm sorry, I wait any longer, I might turn into a pumpkin." He brought the sandwich to his mouth and took an enormous bite.

You don't have too far to go, Wolf thought.

"So, the Pope's gonna be out a hundred and fifty large," Manny said, shifting the food to his cheek. "He specifically asked who the best bounty hunters in Phoenix were, and I told him you guys."

He took another bite, then reached for the large

paper cup containing his soft drink and sucked up a copious amount.

"What's our cut if we grab him?" Mac said.

"Well," Manny said, "like I told you, the P Patrol's involved too, so I'd say you guys could be in for maybe a third or even half, depending on how things go."

Mac grinned. "Ordinarily, we'd do it for free for Ms. Dolly, but we got some financial issues at the moment. We'll settle for half."

"That's for you to work out with her. Or work in." Manny's grin was lascivious. "But one other thing. The clock's ticking on this one. He's due in court in four days."

"Hell," McNamara said. "Anything else?"

Manny flashed a lips-only smile and replied with a shrug.

At least he kept his mouth closed, Wolf thought.

He was ready to get out of there and started to stand up when the big bail bondsman leaned forward and held up his index finger.

"Hey, you know what else is funny?" Manny said, shifting the masticated sandwich to both cheeks. "After you asked me about that law firm thing yesterday, I found that card they give me."

Wolf's interest was piqued. It could be a solid lead as to who had betrayed them in Mexico and possibly a tie-in to what had happened in Iraq.

"Where is it?" Wolf asked.

Manny held up his index finger again and winked. He obviously had bitten off more, as they say, than he could comfortably chew. Wolf hoped the bail bondsman didn't choke because it would probably take both him and Mac to get their arms around him to do the Heimlich maneuver. He set the sandwich down, pushed back his wheeled chair, which squealed in protest, and opened the center drawer of his desk.

After several moments of searching and chewing, Manny swallowed. He shifted his bulk to the right and spoke to Freddie.

"Hey, Sherman, where'd I put that card I told you about?"

Freddie, who was off the phone and busy clicking keys on his computer, turned and rolled his eyes.

"Will you quit calling me that?"

"Calling you what?"

"Sherman," Freddie said. "It ain't my name, for Pete's sake."

"Whaddaya want me to call ya?" Manny asked. "Pete?"

"How about Fred? You know, they used to call me Freddie the Fox when I was in high school."

"That's a pussy-sounding name," Manny said, cocking his head toward McNamara and Wolf as if the three of them were all sharing a dirty joke.

Wolf felt sorry for the maligned nephew and wondered if the worm would one day turn.

"You stuffed it in the bulletin board," Freddie said. "Didn't ya?"

Manny snorted and nodded, swirling another half-turn in the chair. A bulletin board, replete with thumb-tacked printouts, flyers, and wanted posters, had been affixed to the wall next to him. He reached up and pulled a business card out of the padded triangular corner guard.

"Yeah," he said. "This is it. New York, New York."

He swirled the remaining thirty degrees to full circle.

Wolf looked at him expectantly. Manny leaned forward, his chest mashing part of the half-eaten sandwich, and handed the card to him.

Fallotti and Abraham Law Firm

John H. Cummins, Attorney at Law.

Cummins... Finally, things were starting to come together.

A Manhattan address and phone number were along the bottom edge.

Wolf stood and reached for Manny's landline.

"Mind if I use your phone?" he asked.

At last, something tangible to go on, he thought.

McNamara looked expectant too.

"Help yourself, why don't ya?" Manny brushed mayonnaise off the front of his shirt. "But it ain't gonna do you no good."

Wolf already had the receiver in his hand. He paused.

"Why not?"

"Cause I tried to call them yesterday," Manny said. "Just to confirm that they were the same one, but the number's no longer in service."

"Figures," Wolf said.

Was he ever going to catch a break?

***

Wolf drove the Hummer while McNamara sat in the passenger seat and perused the two files Manny had given them. The GPS map on the dashboard illuminated their chosen route to their first stop, the car dealership.

"There's way more to this whole thing that we gotta find out," McNamara commented.

"The pinch?" Wolf said. "I thought Manny said they were a couple easy ones?"

"I'm talking about that law firm card he give you. We gotta look into that more."

Wolf heaved a sigh. Truth be told, he would much rather be trying to track down information on this Fallotti and Abraham Law Firm than be out with Mac trying to run down a couple of pathetic losers who'd skipped out on their court dates, but Wolf's computer skills were sorely lacking. He didn't even have a laptop or a tablet. Most of his research was done on one of the computers at the public library, which for him was like trying to traipse through the jungle blindfolded while carrying two buckets full of water. But it was still easier, and ultimately faster, than relying on Kasey to help him.

"I'm gonna lean on her some more," McNamara said as if reading Wolf's thoughts. "She never got back to you about those names, huh?"

"Well, she's been kind of busy with Chad and all."

"Bullshit," McNamara said, shaking his head. "She's spending too much time with that damn Shemp. I tell you they're talking about getting married?"

"I figured they were pretty serious."

McNamara bit his lip. "You don't think she's sleeping with him, do you?"

Wolf almost chuckled but suppressed it.

When he didn't answer, McNamara answered for him.

"You do, don't you?"

"Look, Mac," Wolf said. "She's not sixteen years old anymore. She's already been married, had a kid, and gotten divorced."

"That was back before we reconnected," McNamara protested.

"Yeah, but still…"

McNamara rubbed his fingers along the sides of his mouth. Lately, he'd been growing a Fu Manchu mustache.

"But to me," he said, slapping the files shut, "she's still my little girl."

"And she always will be," Wolf said, thinking that given how intimidated Shemp was by Big Jim McNamara, the lawyer's abstinence was a distinct possibility.

"Pull over there," McNamara said, pointing to a McDonald's parking lot with a couple of empty spaces. "I need to call in."

"Call in?"

"Yeah." McNamara glanced at him. "What's the matter with you?"

Wolf raised his eyebrows. "I guess I'm a little worried about what Kasey's going to think."

"Aw, hell, she's got to get used to it." McNamara's attention shifted to the cell.

Wolf pulled into the lot and parked, taking up two spaces.

McNamara grinned.

"I can see why Reno liked this thing so much," he said, taking out his cell phone. "Commands attention. Conveys authority. Now, let's see if this Bluetooth thing works." He pressed a button on the dashboard, and the ringing of the phone became audible inside the vehicle.

Kasey answered after the first ring.

"Dad? Where are you?"

McNamara's brow creased. "Something wrong?"

"Yes," she said. "You left this morning without telling me where you were going, and then Rod called and told me you were interviewed by the FBI."

McNamara compressed his lips and clenched his big hands into fists.

Poor Rod doesn't know how lucky he is that he's not here, Wolf thought.

"He called you?" McNamara said.

"Yes, well, actually, I called him, and he told me all about it. Now, where are you?"

"Me and Steve are running down a couple of easy pinches," McNamara said. "I need you to check on a couple of guys for me."

"What?" she said. Her voice was shrill. "You and—" She stopped, hesitated, then began again. "Put *Steve* on the phone."

The way she said "Steve" made Wolf wince.

"He's right here, and you're on speaker," Mc-Namara said. "Go ahead."

After a pause of several seconds, she said, "I said, put *him* on the phone. And *turn off* the speaker."

Wolf reached over and took McNamara's phone, then pressed the button to disconnect the Bluetooth.

"Yeah, Kase," he said.

"Don't *you* call me that." The way she said "you" was venomous. "My name's Kasey, and what are you doing dragging my father with you on an arrest?"

"Well, I—"

"Shut up. You listen to me. You bring him home right now. Then you can go off gallivanting if you want to, but you're not going to drag my father along when he's recuperating."

She was shouting, and it was obvious McNamara could hear the conversation. He swore, reached over, and grabbed the phone, his fingernails scratching Wolf's ear.

"First of all," he said, "Steve didn't drag me anywhere. *I* dragged *him*."

Wolf could still hear her voice. "Dad? What are you... Put him back on."

"I'm your father, dammit."

"I told you to turn off the damn speaker," she said.

"I didn't need the damn speaker to hear, you're yelling so loud. Now cool it!"

Wolf could hear her giving it right back to him. McNamara swore again, pulled the phone from his ear, pressed the button to terminate the call, and threw the phone down. It bounced off the floorboard by Wolf's feet.

They sat in silence for a moment, then Wolf laughed.

"Were you that hard on the US government equipment you were issued when you were in?"

McNamara continued scowling.

Wolf smirked. "No wonder our defense budgets were so damn high."

"Horseshit," McNamara said. "I was in the Army kicking ass and taking names before you were even born, and then some."

After a few more moments of tense silence, Wolf looked at him and said, "Mac, she's just worried about you because she loves you."

Mac's frown deepened. "Yeah, I know." He blew out a heavy breath. "It's my own damn fault. I was always off fighting some damn war someplace when she was growing up. It's like she said. I missed all the important milestones in her life, and now she's worried I'll miss them in my grandson's life too."

"Maybe it'd be better for you to sit this one out."

McNamara shook his head. "I'll be all right. I'll just be in the car to pull it up when you call me. What could go wrong?"

"Wasn't that what we thought about Mexico?" Wolf said.

***

Cummins slouched in the seat of the rented Lexus RX350 and pulled the brim of the baseball cap farther down on his forehead. Behind him, in the rear passenger-side seat, Zerbe had a pair of binoculars pressed against the heavily tinted window. After the Hummer had pulled into the McDonald's parking lot, Zerbe had directed him to go around the block and set up on the street so they'd have a good vantage point.

Cummins had done so, petrified he'd pull up to the place while Wolf was exiting. Locking eyes with that one-man gang was the last thing in the world he wanted. Well, aside from being on Von Dien's expendable loose ends list. As it was, when he rounded the turn and slowly approached the McDonald's, the Hummer was parked haphazardly in two spaces on the far side. He was able to find a spot down the block that allowed Zerbe to use the expensive binoculars he'd bought, along with a ton of other equipment.

"Don't let them see you watching them," Cummins cautioned.

"Relax," Zerbe said. "This isn't exactly my first rodeo, as they say."

"Yeah, well, if Wolf sees us, it'll probably be your last. Remember, he knows what both of us look like."

"Which is why I got a rental with appropriately darkened windows." Zerbe kept the lenses focused on the restaurant.

"Maybe they're just eating lunch," Cummins said. "Anyway, what good is it going to do us, just following and watching?"

"I told you, we're trying to establish a pattern of behavior. See what their routine is."

Cummins decided to shut up, but the growing tension in his bladder was making him very uncomfortable. After arriving at McCarran in the middle of the night, they'd been going almost nonstop. From the airport, they'd gone to the car rental place, then to check in to their hotel. He'd only been able to grab an hour or two of sleep before Zerbe had banged on his door at seven, and after a lousy Continental breakfast, they were on the road again. Zerbe had hit several ATM machines along the way, withdrawing cash from the special account Fallotti had set up for them. Then it was a long shopping spree at several sporting goods stores and an electronics shop.

"What's all this shit?" Cummins asked.

"Surveillance equipment," Zerbe told him.

After that, they'd staked out that bail bondsman's place. Cummins had provided the guy's name from their Vegas meeting, and Zerbe had pressured him to remember which of the players from the bounty hunter conference knew his face from there.

"Just that bail bondsman guy," Cummins told him. "Manny Sutter. McNamara's never seen me."

But Wolf had. In fact, he would recognize both him and Zerbe. McNamara had also seen Zerbe up close. The bail bondsman knew him but not Zerbe, who had been certain Wolf would show up there eventually, and he was right. Maybe the sleazebag wasn't an idiot after all.

It had surprised Cummins that Wolf and McNamara arrived in two cars, but Zerbe made a few calls and ran checks on the license plates. The guy had some interesting connections, that was for sure. Wolf was driving a car with dealer plates, and his partner got out of a big Hummer registered to that Reno Garth character. This bothered Cummins because he'd been under the impression that Garth didn't like them. But then again, they'd all been betrayed together down in Mexico and were supposed to be dead, so maybe they'd somehow become friends.

It was just another sign that he shouldn't be involved in thing damn thing. Not after the Iraq screwup, and especially not after the Mexican fiasco.

Cummins wasn't happy that Fallotti had sent him here with Zerbe, but he understood why he'd done it. The sleazy PI evidently now knew the value of what they were after—the Lion Attacking the Nubian—and that the rich bastard Von Dien was willing to pay just about any price to acquire it.

The real irony was that stupid Wolf and his partner McNamara had it but didn't even know what it was. It was imperative they didn't find out, either.

Cummins had done some checking on James Mc-Namara. Retired Army, Special Forces, a chest full of medals, Vietnam vet, Desert Storm vet, Somalia, Afghanistan, Iraq, and veteran of numerous deployments in every shithole part of the world, clandestine and otherwise, in a military career that had lasted almost forty years. The guy had six Bronze Stars, three Silver Stars, the Army Commendation Medal, and four Purple Hearts. He purportedly had so much shrapnel in him that he could set off a metal detector just walking by it.

And now the son of a bitch had a bounty hunting business. Cummins was just as leery of running afoul of McNamara as Wolf. Luckily, McNamara hadn't seen him in Vegas or in Mexico, so he had that going for him, but there was always the possibility that a picture of him had surfaced. Fallotti had done a good job of scrubbing as many computer references to Cummins as he could find and had eliminated him from the law firm's website, and that was being dissolved, too. Von Dien was erasing them all, and he had the money to do it.

But my military pictures are still around, and with McNamara's connections to the Army, he and Wolf could probably get hold of one.

"Looks like they're getting ready to pull out," Zerbe said. "Don't take off too fast, or they might notice us following them."

Cummins lowered himself in the seat some more, which wasn't easy for a man of his size and bulk. Plus, it had been several hours since they'd taken a break, and he badly had to urinate.

He told Zerbe that.

"Christ. Suck it up," Zerbe said. "You want to know how many times I had to piss in fucking bottle when I was on a surveillance?"

"Not really." Cummins felt a momentary flash of panic as he contemplated the possibility that Wolf would turn left out of the parking lot and catch a glimpse of him. "Look, Wolf's driving. All he has to do is glance this way and catch a glimpse of us. He knows what we both look like."

"Well, scrunch down then, for Christ's sake."

Easy for you to say, Cummins thought. You're ensconced in the back seat.

He suddenly wondered if Zerbe was armed. He'd carried a snub-nosed revolver in Mexico but hadn't fired it, not that a little gun like that would do a lot of good anyway. That Wolf was a madman. If he ever caught sight of them, it would be all over, snub-nose or not.

"You got a gun?" Cummins asked.

"No. I didn't want to take mine through security at the airport. Why?"

"If Wolf sees us…"

"Oh, Christ. Just get ready to slip in behind them when they pull out," Zerbe said. "Let them get a few car lengths ahead."

"You know," Cummins managed to say, "I don't think that's such a good idea."

"What?" Zerbe tone was laden with irritation. "I told you we need to plant this tracker on his car."

"*We* need to be cautious. Like I said, he knows what we both look like. If he sees us, it'll all be over, and we'll have to answer to VD."

"Who?"

"Von Dien." Cummins realized a moment too late that he probably shouldn't have used his pet nickname for the big man in front of Zerbe, but the sleazy PI laughed.

"Good one," he said. "I'll have to remember to tell him you called him that."

"Don't," Cummins said.

Zerbe laughed again, and Cummins realized he'd inadvertently given the damn South African more leverage over him.

"Besides, I've got to go bad."

"All right, all right," he said. "We'll cut it off. I had hoped to plant that tracker, but it doesn't seem to be their car, anyway. We can pick them up tomorrow. I've got to make a few more calls in any case."

Cummins could tell by the way he said it that Zerbe was pissed, but that was just too goddamned bad.

I shouldn't be expected to do fieldwork, he thought. *That's his department.*

"Oh, Christ," Cummins moaned. "Here they come."

He pulled the hat down more and worried that his efforts at concealment would make him stand out, but Wolf turned right and headed down the street. Cummins heaved a sigh and straightened, then shifted into gear and pulled away from the curb. The sudden urge to vomit overwhelmed him, so he put a hand over his mouth and goosed the gas pedal, roaring into the parking lot their quarry had been in. He slammed on the brakes and spun into a vacant parking space. Throwing open the door, he struggled to unfasten the seat belt, threw the door open, and leaned partially out the door, spewing vomit on the ground. The asphalt seemed to sizzle in the oppressive late morning heat.

"Nervous Nellie." Zerbe laughed. "Just like Mexico. How'd you ever make it through a tour in Iraq?"

Cummins ignored him and continued to lean out of the car, occasionally spitting to clear the acidic taste from his mouth.

"Can I help it if I've got a medical condition?" he said between expectorations. "An *acute* medical condition."

"Do you now?"

"Yeah. A sensitive stomach. And I told you, I've got to go to the bathroom, too."

"The *bathroom*?" That made Zerbe laugh even harder.

Shit, Cummins thought. *How did I get myself into this?*

More importantly, how would he get himself out?

Just then, Zerbe's cell phone chirped, and he glanced at the screen and smiled. After pressing the button, he said, "Ah, Luan, *hoe gaan dit*?" He paused, then said, "Yeah, it pays very well, and it's right up your alley, *maat*."

The Lion Man, Cummins thought. *I hope he's as*

good as Zerbe says he is.

He spat once more, but the sour taste still was present.

"Hold on," Zerbe said and turned to Cummins. "You might as well go inside and take your piss. Just make sure you don't step in the vomit. We still need this car."

Cummins wiped his mouth and shot him a dirty look.

Zerbe ignored him and went back to his conversation on the cell phone.

"We'll need your team. How soon can you get here?" Zerbe listened, then smiled. "Outstanding. Come on over right away, and I'll reimburse you for your airfare when you get here."

Cummins did his best to lower himself from the running board so as not to step in the puke, but that wasn't easy for a guy his size. He realized he'd have a hard time getting back in when he returned.

Just like this damn assignment; it had seemed easy at first but had then gotten problematic. Now he was going to have to deal with additional players—a team of them and foreigners to boot. Zerbe had mentioned that these guys were mercenaries. At least he would have some protection against Wolf, and if this guy was bringing a team, it should be enough.

Then again, hadn't Eagan had a team with him in Mexico?

CHAPTER 7

NEAR HAPPY HOWARD'S TOYOTA
PHOENIX, ARIZONA

Wolf listened to McNamara review the first file on the drive over. Lonnie B. Coats, a forty-three-year-old black man, had an outstanding bond-forfeiture warrant for missing his last two court dates. He'd been arrested for driving under the influence, his third offense, and faced jail time, which might have been the reason he'd skipped out and was hoping to fly under the radar.

The guy was married and had two young teenage kids, and despite a drinking problem, he'd somehow managed to hold on to his job as a salesman at Happy Howard's Toyota. The dealership was in an auto mall housing several car dealerships in a broad semi-circular formation. The Toyota lot was full of shiny new cars, gleaming in the noon sun.

"Should be an easy one," McNamara said. "And put much-needed money in our pockets."

Your pockets, Wolf thought. But that was okay.

To Wolf's way of thinking, Coats had all the ear-marks of a functional alcoholic, dragging his feet and his family through the downward spiral. Not that different from Wolf's own father, who'd gone off to war and come back a broken man who found refuge from his demons inside a bottle. Wolf had seen way too many men like that in the Army. They were able to do their jobs during their shifts, sweating it out in between with the booze. Interestingly, they had seemed to be able to function in the desert once they'd sweated the stuff out of their systems and knew they'd have to do without while they were on Muslim-owned sand.

Guests of the nation, he thought. Just like he'd once been.

But it was just like Joe Louis once said. You could run, but you couldn't hide, especially from yourself.

Maybe Mr. Coats would have that same realization after he had been ensconced in jail for a time. Then again, maybe not.

"Pull up over there," McNamara said, cradling his cell phone on his big shoulder as he paged through the sheaf of papers in the first file. He pointed at an open space in front of a car dealership. "I got to call base."

By "base," he meant calling Kasey again, which he wasn't eager for Mac to do at the moment.

"That might not be such a good idea," he said.

McNamara waved him off, pressed a button on the phone, and waited.

Mac glanced at him. "What's the matter with you?"

Wolf raised his eyebrows. "You sure you're ready for round two?"

"Aw, hell, she's had enough time to cool off by now." McNamara's attention shifted to the cell. "Kase, it's me."

Wolf heard her voice coming from the phone again. It wasn't overly loud or shrill this time, but it was still a bit elevated. Mac listened, mumbled a few monosyllabic replies, and then said, "Yeah, I know, honey. I will. Now, do a quick check on a guy named Myron D. Kites." He spelled out the name and gave her an address and phone number, then his brow furrowed as he paused and listened. "Yeah, yeah, I'll stay in the damn car. I promise. I'll call you back." He ended the call and grinned. "Man, it feels good to be getting back into it."

"Just remember to stay in the damn car," Wolf said.

"I will. Until it's time for me to get out." He slipped the cell phone into his vest pocket and jammed the file up behind the visor. "Let's go see Mr. Coats."

Wolf started to get out of the car, but McNamara grabbed his arm. "Remember, if the shit hits the fan, I ain't got my Glock, but I've got my sword cane."

He grabbed his cane before opening the door.

Wolf smirked. "I thought it was a knife?"

"It is, but it's a big one."

"Hopefully, we won't need it."

The car dealership building was tan stucco and had expansive windows. They walked over to the side door, and Wolf looked through the glass. The showroom had several cars parked inside, all brand-new models.

For a brief moment, he wondered if he was ever going to reach a state of financial security where he could afford to buy a new car. He was still relegated to using his bicycle when he couldn't borrow Mac's Escalade, and getting access to that was like a teenage boy asking his father for the keys to the family car on a school night. He'd never dared ask Kasey if she'd loan him her car.

"You go in and ask for him," McNamara said. "Get him to step outside, and we'll grab him."

"How about *I* grab him? You were supposed to stay in the car, remember?"

McNamara's head twitched. "I won't tell if you won't."

"If something untoward happens, Kasey's gonna—"

"'Untoward?' What the hell kind of word is that?"

"I learned it in that lit class you insisted I take."

"Must be a good one, then. Let's do it. I know this

ain't your first rodeo."

Wolf chuckled and began walking toward the building. McNamara angled toward the service department, which was adjacent to the big showroom.

Wolf pulled open the door and felt the coolness of the air conditioning envelop him. A white guy looked up from behind a desk in an open cubicle, smiled, and asked if he could help him.

"I'm looking for Lonnie Coats," Wolf said.

The white guy nodded and pointed to his left. "Third space down."

Wolf strolled past three cars parked at angles on the tile floor, each having the smell of brand-new vehicles. When he looked at the stickers on the windows, Wolf knew that he'd be riding the bicycle for a long time to come.

He stopped and looked at the man sitting behind the desk in the third cubicle. The guy didn't look as disheveled as in the booking photo in the file Manny had given them, and his face stretched into a salesman's smile. But the sagging jowls and droopy eyes of a perennial drunk told Wolf the man was strung out and just that one drink shy of marginal comfort.

"Hi, I'm Lon Coats," the man said, standing and offering his hand, the smile still frozen in place. "What can I help you with?"

Wolf shook Coats' hand, not so much out of courtesy as to test the guy's grip strength. He could smell alcohol on him, and not just his breath. The sour, boozy smell of someone who lives in the neck of the bottle was oozing out of every pore. He didn't expect this would be too difficult, but he remembered what Mac had said about using finesse instead of force.

"I'd like to speak to you outside, sir," Wolf said.

The man's mouth twitched. "What kind of car you interested in? We can look everything up on the computer here and stay in the air conditioning." The lips twitched again. "I mean, it's damn hot outside, right?"

Wolf considered his surroundings. He was in his opponent's lair, and there were plenty of people who might jump in and assist Coats if he yelled for help. Wolf had little doubt that he could fight his way out, dragging Coats along with one hand, but that would be the hard way. He smiled at the car salesman.

"We both know this isn't about a car, Lon."

Coats' smile faded. "You a cop?"

Wolf shook his head. From the look on Coats' face, Wolf might have said, "Your worst nightmare" instead of "Bail enforcement officer."

The sad eyes drooped even more. His voice was a whisper. "Look, man, you got to give me a chance here. I'll lose my damn job if you take me out now."

Wolf felt a twinge of pity for the man, but he'd been there before. Empathy was the enemy of the professional, so he ducked behind that emotional wall that had served him so well in combat. "What you tell your boss is up to you, but right now, you and I are going to walk outside. The bottom line is if you try to fight me or run, it won't be pretty."

Coats' face pinched into a frown. "Man, don't do me like this."

Wolf stared at him, then said, "Let's go."

Coats licked his lips, "How 'bout we tell the boss we're going for a little test drive, okay?"

"Tell him whatever you want," Wolf said. "Just remember the bottom line."

Coats compressed his thick lips, made a motion toward his back pocket, then stopped when Wolf grabbed the man's arm. "Hold it. Whatever you're thinking about reaching for better be a sandwich, 'cause you're going to have to eat it." He patted Coats' hip and removed a thin, curved hipflask. Still holding Coats' arm, Wolf did a quick pat-down. When he was satisfied that the man didn't have any weapons, he released him.

The look in Coats' eyes told Wolf that he hadn't been expecting the speed of the grab or the strength of the grip. The walk outside should go smoothly, but it was too soon to relax. He'd learned that the hard way the day before with his buddy Luth.

Wolf let Coats go first and stayed behind him as the man stopped and said to the white guy, "Hey, Fred, we're going for a little test drive. Be back soon."

"Whatever, Lon," Fred said, not bothering to

look up.

Coats smiled and nodded at Wolf like they'd shared a conspiratorial victory. Wolf kept his expression neutral.

Outside, McNamara was waiting and fell into step with them. He held a pair of handcuffs in his beefy left fist and his cane in his right.

"Let me introduce you to my friends," McNamara said as he drew Coats' arms behind him and ratcheted the cuffs over his wrists. "Iron bracelets."

"Please, man," Coats said. "Don't do me like this. I'll lose my job if they see me being taken out of here in cuffs."

"You should've thought about that when you missed your court date," McNamara said.

"Oh, man," Coats groaned.

"Quit your whining," McNamara said. "You know, my buddy here might need a deal on a car relatively soon. Tell you what. Once we get to the car, we'll let you call your boss and make some stupid excuse about where you are, and nobody'll be the wiser."

"Yeah, right," Coats said.

He was a defeated man.

"Best we can do right now," McNamara said. "But since you cooperated, we'll put in a good word to Manny about you. Maybe he'll post bond for you again."

Coats' mouth drew downward, and he nodded. When they got to the Hummer, they secured Coats' feet to the floor shackles, then re-cuffed him to the large metal ring fastened to the bar.

McNamara slammed the door and smiled. "See? Smooth as silk. Let's go get the next one."

***

Once they were rolling again, McNamara punched the second address into the GPS, opened the second file, and took out his cellphone.

"You gonna let me make that call to my boss?" Coats said from the backseat.

McNamara ignored him and pressed the call button.

"Think we ought to drop him off at detention first?" Wolf asked.

"Nah," McNamara said. "We're on a roll. Besides, I want to take full advantage of the War Wagon here while we still got it."

Wolf felt that was a risk, considering that Mac was still recuperating from the gunshot wound and the subsequent peritonitis, but he knew better than to mention it with them being one step ahead of the bill collector. Mac was one of the toughest men he'd ever known, and taking Coats to the county jail and waiting around for a booking slip would mean a loss of both time and momentum.

But Wolf worried anyway, especially when he saw

McNamara call Kasey again.

"Hey, man," Coats said again. "You promised you'd let me make that phone call."

"Shaddup," McNamara said, then into the phone, "Hey, Kase, do me a favor—"

He stopped and listened.

Wolf couldn't hear Kasey's voice this time, so he took that to mean she wasn't yelling.

"Yes, I'm all right," McNamara said. "Of course, I waited in the car. I let Steve handle the whole thing." He shifted in the seat to shoot a wink at Wolf.

"No," he said. "We got one more, so did you do that check on Myron D. Kites?" He frowned, spelled the name, and gave her the address and phone number again. "Yeah, yeah, I'll stay in the car. Promise. Now, whaddaya got?" He listened intently, then said, "Okay, put me on hold and call both places. Try his apartment first. Just use the usual."

Using the usual meant that if the phone was answered, Kasey would pretend to be a telemarketer or use some other ruse to fix the subject's location. She also had a special app that allowed her to enter any number she wanted as the calling number. It would register on the person's Caller ID as anything from the IRS to the person's grandmother if they had one. Manny required a ton of information before agreeing to post bond, but that was available in the file, which she didn't have. Wolf knew Mac was reticent to reveal trade secrets in front of Coats, however.

McNamara perked up and started talking into the phone again. "Okay, honey. That's great. Thanks." He stopped talking and was about to hang up when he stopped and listened again.

"Yeah, yeah, I promise. Don't worry. Like I said, Steve's very capable of handling things without me."

She apparently said something more, and Mc-Namara smirked before terminating the call. He turned to Wolf and shook his head.

"What'd she say?" Wolf said.

They were getting close to the destination Mc-Namara had punched into the GPS.

"Never mind that." McNamara patted the dashboard and the GPS map display. "She confirmed that he's at work, just like I predicted."

"Is that how you done me?" Coats said, shaking his head. "Mmm, mmm, mmm, that's cold-blooded."

McNamara heaved a sigh. "All right, Lonnie. Tell you what I'll do. I'll square things with your boss for you."

"How you gonna do that?"

"What's his name and number?" McNamara said.

Coats recited the information, then asked, "What should I tell him?"

"You ain't gonna tell him squat," McNamara said. "Let me do the talking."

"But—"

McNamara held up his hand. Coats fell silent.

After a few rings, someone answered, and Mc-Namara spoke in a loud voice infused with authority.

"Mr. Robert Goldsborough?" Pause. "This is Sergeant McGuffy of the Phoenix Police Department. I'm calling on behalf of one of your employees, a Mister ..." He drew out the pronunciation of the word, then said, "Lonnie B. Coats."

Goldsborough apparently said something, and McNamara continued.

"No, no, Mr. Coats didn't do anything wrong. In fact, it's just the opposite. Several months ago, Mr. Coats came upon an armed robbery in progress. The perpetrator, a well-known gang member, was armed with a handgun and was about to shoot numerous innocent civilians when Mr. Coats managed to disarm the man and hold him for the police."

He stopped and listened to whatever it Goldsborough was saying, then continued. "I'm not surprised that you didn't hear anything about it, sir. Because of the notorious and dangerous reputation of this gang, as well as the robber being under the age of eighteen, the matter was kept out of the local media." He paused and listened again, occasionally chuckling and offering a few mumbles.

"Well, needless to say, his testimony is crucial to the successful prosecution of this case. However, it has come to our attention that the gang was planning a retaliatory move to prevent Mr. Coats from testifying in court. The DA directed us to place him in immediate protective custody, which we have done. I'm afraid he won't be available to come back to work until the court proceedings are finished."

Wolf looked in the mirror again and saw that Coats' eyes were the size of saucers.

"I'm not sure at this point," McNamara said, still using his authoritative tone. "It could take a few days, or a few weeks, or perhaps even longer."

The conversation went on for a few more sentences and ended with McNamara giving Goldsborough a cell phone number that McNamara said was his "undercover line." When he ended the call, he peered over his shoulder and said to Coats, "Your job'll be waiting for you when you get out. Now it's up to you to get this matter straightened out and fly right after that. No more drinking and driving."

Wolf glanced in the rearview mirror and saw that Coats was all smiles.

"Man," he said, "that was great. Thanks, Mr. Mc-Guffy. Or should I say, Sergeant?"

"Either/or," McNamara said, shooting another wink at Wolf. "I was a sergeant for a lot of years."

"Po-lice?"

"Army."

"That cool," Coats said. "I'm a vet too. Navy."

"Well, I'm liking you better all the time," Mc-

Namara said. "And I wasn't kidding when I told you I'd put in a good word for you with Manny."

"Appreciate it."

"What's the B stand for in your middle name?" McNamara asked.

"Beauregard. Named after my grandfather."

"My middle initial's B too," McNamara said.

"But in his case," Wolf said, intruding into the conversation, "it stands for bullshitter."

They all laughed, but Wolf felt only a scant bit of merriment.

Seeing Mac in such a good mood was almost worth the price he was going to have to pay with Kasey once they got back.

And they still had one to go.

***

The Elegant Suites Hotel
Phoenix, Arizona

Cummins was more than a little bit perturbed when they pulled into the hotel parking lot and Zerbe, who'd spent the better part of the return trip talking on his phone, told him to go get one of those luggage carts and bring it out to him. He continued to talk in obscure code to some guy named Dill, who was apparently in LA.

"A luggage cart?" Cummins asked.

"Right," Zerbe said, covering the phone. "So we can bring all the equipment in."

He went back to his phone conversation, and Cummins caught what he took to be the end of it. "Give me a call when you get in town, and we'll meet you."

Zerbe hung up, and Cummins wondered what that call was all about.

"Who was that?" he asked.

"Our weapons supplier." Zerbe looked askance. "The cart?"

Exhaling loudly so the other man would know about his displeasure at being treated like a Sherpa, Cummins opened the passenger-side door and slid out. "I ain't no damn go-fer."

"True enough," Zerbe said. "But it looks like you could use the exercise."

His irritating little staccato laugh followed.

After loading the stuff onto the cart, Zerbe stopped inside the front doors and went to the front desk. He still had on those dark sunglasses that looked like they belonged on a washed-up celebrity from a 1950s movie clip.

"I need to reserve some rooms," he said to the clerk. "I've got some members of my organization coming in tomorrow."

That must be the Lion Team, Cummins thought.

He waited while Zerbe read off the names from

his smartphone.

"What kind of names are those?" the insipid clerk asked.

"South African," Zerbe said. "We'll be teaching a desert warfare seminar in the area for the next week."

If the clerk was impressed, she didn't show it.

After Zerbe rejoined him, Cummings waited until they'd reached the elevators before asking, "Was that wise to tell her that?"

"It'll head off a lot of questions if they see a bunch of rough men with rifles coming in and out at all hours of the day and night."

"Rough men with rifles?"

Zerbe frowned. "I was paraphrasing Orwell about who ultimately has to get things done. A good reminder of our task here."

And a grim one, too, Cummins thought. He could hardly wait for this to be over.

***

Swifty's Auto and Towing
Phoenix, Arizona

The area was a mixture of business and residential and looked like it had seen better days. They drove by Swifty's Auto and Towing and saw a trio of tow trucks sitting by a one-story white stucco building that was surrounded by a ten-foot cyclone fence with three strands of barbed wire running along the top. The front of the building had a solid door and a window, and the side, which was inside the fence's perimeter, had another regular door and two large overhead doors, all closed. The rest of the area was filled with cars in various states of disrepair. A big dog, a Rottweiler from the looks of him, sat by a dog-house inside the perimeter. The neon sign in front, now unlighted, advertised twenty-four-hour towing and listed a number underneath.

"Okay," McNamara said, perusing the file, "My-ron D. Kites, white male, thirty-eight, six feet, two hundred and eighty pounds. Three counts of un-lawful use of a credit card. Another paper tiger." He glanced over his shoulder at Coats and added, "No offense, Lonnie."

Coats was silent.

"I don't like the looks of this one," Wolf said. "Tow yards are dangerous places, and I don't want to tangle with that canine."

"Me neither," McNamara said. "He kinda reminds me of me." He took out his phone and told Wolf to drive past.

Wolf knew from experience that there was al-ways a danger in confronting a bail jumper on his own turf, be it at his place of employment or his residence. That was when most of the battles came about. The smartest thing to do would be to save this one for another day, but when he saw Mac take out his phone and punch in some numbers, Wolf knew the big guy had a plan.

"If we can't go to him," McNamara said, "we'll make him come to us."

The phone rang a few more times, then apparently was answered.

"Yes," McNamara said. "I need a tow." He glanced at the street signs at the next intersection, then snapped his fingers and pointed to the curb. They were three blocks from the tow yard.

Wolf slowed the Hummer to a stop.

"Yeah," McNamara said, letting a forlorn tone seep into his voice. "I think my water pump's out again."

He listened for a moment.

"It's a big one," McNamara said into the phone. "A black Hummer." He gave the location, which corresponded to the street signs. "You towed my other ride a while back, and the guy did a real good job. I think his name was Myron or something."

McNamara grinned and held up his hand, making an O shape with his thumb and index finger.

"Okay, yeah," he said. "But this baby's cherry. I want somebody that knows what they're doing. I'd very much prefer him, 'cause he did such an outstanding job the last time." McNamara paused, then added, "All right. Be waiting on him."

He terminated the call, grabbed the file on the subject, and opened the door.

"You guys are real cold-blooded," Coats said.

All the goodwill from the ruse phone call from Sergeant McGuffy had vanished.

McNamara shifted in the seat and glared at him. "What are you complaining about? I squared it with your boss, didn't I? Or do you have that short of a memory?"

"No, sir, Sarge," Coats said, flashing a smile. "I ain't forgetting."

"We might as well lift up the hood." McNamara shoved the door all the way open and grabbed his cane.

Wolf searched for the hood release and pulled it, then got out. He and McNamara walked to the front of the Hummer and raised the hood. The heat from the engine radiated toward them, and combined with the high temperature, made Wolf start to sweat. He looked at McNamara. He was sweating too, and he looked flushed.

"You feeling okay?" Wolf asked.

"Be a lot better once we wrap up this second arrest."

"I thought you promised Kasey you'd stay in the car?"

"I will," McNamara said. "As soon as we got this guy cuffed and locked down." He scanned the area behind them, as did Wolf. Presently, they saw a tow truck exit Swifty's and head toward them.

McNamara flipped open the file and showed Wolf the mug shot of Myron D. Kites, then flipped it closed and handed it to him. "Put this on the passenger seat and move off to the side there. I'll stay here looking nice and non-threatening with my innocent little cane here and strike up a conversation with him. Once we verify it's him, you can move in, and we'll make the collar."

"The collar?" Wolf smiled. "Where'd that come from?"

He placed the file under his arm.

"Been binge-watching *Blue Bloods* and *Law and Order* during my recuperation." McNamara grinned. "How do you think I keep up on all the latest?"

Wolf slipped the Taser out of its holster, snapped off the cartridge, and placed it in the lower left pocket of his BDU blouse. He put the Taser in his other pocket.

"Why'd you take the cartridge off?" McNamara asked. "We might need to shoot him."

"If we need it, I'll use a drive-stun. I'm not going to be shooting it with you standing next to the guy." Wolf didn't want to say he was concerned about Mac being able to move out of the way quickly if things went bad.

The tow truck was getting closer, and Wolf moved to the other side of the Hummer as it came abreast. The driver slowed, glanced out the window, and waved.

About all Wolf could tell was that the guy was white, heavyset, and smoking a cigarette. It was still too early to tell if it was Kites.

He watched the tow truck pull around and park in front of the Hummer. Wolf opened the door and placed the file folder on the seat, then eased the door closed. He moved over to the sidewalk and assumed the air of an interested onlooker. McNamara stood by the upraised hood.

When the driver waddled closer, Wolf thought he strongly resembled the photograph in the file. The tip of the man's cigarette glowed brightly, and he squinted and flipped open the cover of a tablet. He set the tablet down on the corrugated bed of the truck and began punching the keyboard.

"You called for a tow, right?" he asked.

McNamara took a step toward him and said he had. His eyes shot to Wolf with a look of semi-alarm.

Mac was trying to tell him something, but what?

"What kind of a gun is that?" McNamara asked in a loud voice.

A gun. That changed things substantially. They hadn't counted on this wrinkle.

The second time in two days I've brought a Taser to a gunfight, Wolf thought.

Mac had made a point of leaving his Glock at home this morning since they were going into the Federal Building rather than taking the chance of locking it in the trunk of the rental with the Taser.

"It's Colt Cobra," Kites said. He was busy putting information into the tablet. "I'm gonna need to see your driver's license and two credit cards."

Two credit cards for a guy who had outstanding warrants for credit card theft. It was a no-brainer how Kites was getting the account and CVC numbers. The tablet probably took excellent pictures of the fronts and backs of the customer's stuff.

Wolf began to walk toward the front of the tow truck, figuring Mac would keep the guy engaged long enough, and the safest way would be to approach the subject from the rear.

Actually, he thought, the safest way would be to cut their potential losses and abort this mission right now. They could come after good old Myron another day—good old *armed* Myron—but Wolf knew Mac wouldn't do that. Once he had the hook planted, he didn't want to let go of the pole, and he wasn't about to be intimidated by a pistol, even if he didn't have one himself.

Wolf walked past the front of the truck, then hung a left as if he were going to cross the street. He glanced both ways and saw a mean-looking revolver riding in a holster on the right side of a massive gut. It was virtually swallowed by a dollop of fat.

"I heard about them," McNamara said. "A kissin' cousin to the old Pythons, right?"

"They're bringing them back, too," Kites said. "Ah, the credit cards and driver's license?"

McNamara gave a "Sure thing" nod and hooked his cane on the grill of the Hummer. He shifted his weight as if going for his wallet in his right rear pants pocket, then stopped.

"Hey, mind if I take a look at it?" he asked, his face twisting into a smile. "I been thinking about buying one of those."

"Then go to a gun store." Kites stopped typing on the tablet and straightened up. "You said you know me, but you don't look familiar, and I sure as hell don't remember towing no Hummer."

"What's that old saying?" McNamara said, his brow furrowing. "My other car's a Mercedes."

With that, he pivoted and grabbed Kites' right arm, twisting it back.

Wolf ran toward them, digging in his pocket for the Taser.

Kites swore and tried to pull away, but McNamara put more pressure on the man's arm, and the pair shifted back and forth in a ludicrous two-step.

"Bail enforcement agents," McNamara shouted. "You're under arrest."

"Okay, okay," Kites said, but his left hand was fishing for something in the detritus in the back of the tow truck. He came up holding a three-foot-long metal crowbar and lashed out with it.

The hexagonal ridged tool struck the McNamara's forehead, and a spray of crimson droplets swirled in the air. McNamara shifted his body and leaned forward, roughly jamming the other man into the hard metal frame of the truck's bed. He used his left hand to ratchet Kites' right arm upward and reached down with his right to try to pluck the revolver from the holster.

The crowbar waggled menacingly as Kites drew it back, but Wolf was next to him and grabbed it. He twisted it loose as McNamara gained possession of the Cobra and slammed it into the struggling man's face. A stream of bright red blood burst from each nostril and sprayed outward.

Wolf dropped the crowbar into the truck and angled the man's left arm behind his back. Moving in unspoken unison, Wolf and McNamara lowered Kites to the asphalt, and Wolf knelt on the man's left arm. He ratcheted the hasp of one of his sets of handcuffs over the left wrist, then reached for the right arm, which McNamara still held securely.

Kites grunted in pain. "Stop. You're killing me."

"If I'da wanted to kill you, asshole," McNamara said, "you wouldn't still be breathing. Now quit struggling before I get real mad."

"Don't bend my arms like that," Kites said. "I gotta bad shoulder."

Wolf saw that he was going to need a second pair

of cuffs and reached over to grab McNamara's. He then cuffed one section of that set over Kites' right wrist and secured the two empty sections together.

He looked at McNamara, who now had a steady stream of blood flowing from a jagged cut on the upper left part of his forehead along the scalp line.

"You all right?" he asked.

Mac grinned. "Yeah. Luckily, he only hit my head."

***

Office of Emanuel Sutter
Bail Bondsman
Phoenix, Arizona

After dropping McNamara off at the emergency room, Wolf drove over to see Manny in the hope that he could enlist some help in squaring away the paperwork for the two bail jumpers. Mac had disapproved of that plan, wanting to demonstrate his toughness by foregoing a trip to the ER.

"This ain't nothing," he'd said. "Hurt myself worse shaving out of a steel pot with no mirror."

"Well, you're bleeding all over Reno's car." Wolf cocked his thumb back over his shoulder. "So is Mr. Kites. I'm going to have to take it to one of those deluxe car wash places."

"Yeah," Kites said. "And you'd better get me some

medical attention, too. I'm gonna sue your ass for hitting me."

McNamara turned in his seat. "Take a number, asshole. Just remember, you hit me first in the process of a lawful arrest, and you also resisted." He held the Colt Cobra in front of the screen. "Not to mention this."

"Hey, I got a permit for that," Kites said.

"Oh, yeah? Let's see." McNamara took out his cell phone and made a call to Kasey. "Yeah, I need you to run a gun for me and check on a CC permit for it."

Wolf could hear her voice on the phone. He was grateful the words were indistinct.

McNamara frowned. "Just do it. And I'm fine. It's all over but the crying." He waited and covered the speaker. "She says she's getting ready for a date. You think it's with you-know-who?"

Wolf resisted the temptation to say "Rod." "Who else is it going to be?"

"I don't know," McNamara said. "Anybody but him."

Presently Kasey came back on the line, and whatever she said made McNamara grin like a clown.

"Thanks, honey," he said and hung up. He shifted in the seat and looked at Kites. "Myron, when the cops see that you had this *pistola* on you, you're gonna be facing a bunch of new charges. Did I tell you my best friend's buddy is a lieutenant in the Phoenix PD?"

That had shut Kites up, and when Wolf pulled up at

the hospital, McNamara got out of the car and walked in, motioning for Wolf to drive on.

At least we avoided the cost of an ambulance, he thought, hoping Mac hadn't sustained any serious damage. That damn crowbar had been the size of a baseball bat.

Kasey was gonna flip. He decided to leave it to Mac to explain it to her.

At Manny's, they managed to get Kites cleaned up, and Manny told him in no uncertain terms that if he pitched a bitch when the cops got there, he could never expect any consideration again.

"Plus," Wolf said, holding up Kites' tablet, "they're going to be very interested in your little two-credit-cards-and-an-ID procedure. Is that how you're getting all those numbers and CVC codes?"

"I ain't saying another word." Kites settled back into the chair and let Freddie clean the residual blood off his nose.

He was true to his word when the marked unit arrived, and the officer seemed very interested in the Cobra. Unfortunately, the injury to the suspect's nose necessitated a call for a supervisor. A brief conversation ensued, with Manny stepping out and smoothing things over with the cops. That guy seemed to know everybody, and after a few minutes of discussion and cajoling, both Kites and Coats were re-handcuffed and placed in the back of a patrol car.

Manny handed Wolf his cuffs and smiled. "Ya done good, Wolfman. I'll have Sherman write you out a check."

That was welcome news, although Wolf knew he couldn't bask in his glory. He felt the pressure building to tie up loose ends, like cleaning out Reno's Hummer and figuring out how he was going to return it. The loaner car the body shop had given them was still sitting in the parking lot as well, and Reno's gym was too far for a long of a jog back here to get it once he'd dropped the Hummer off. He could hardly impose upon Reno to give him a ride back.

Looks like I'll get that roadwork in, after all, Wolf thought.

He decided to give Reno a heads-up about the return and dialed the cell number he'd given him. Reno answered on the first ring.

"What's up?"

Wolf explained the situation, and Reno surprised him with his concern.

"Mac's hurt? Is it serious?"

"Hard to say," Wolf said. "Didn't look too serious, but he's going to need some stitches. I dropped him off at the ER, so I need to figure how I can get your Hummer back to you."

"Hey, don't worry about it," Reno said. "Just drop it on by tomorrow at my gym. And you're welcome to stop in for a workout too, if you want."

Wolf was amazed at how accommodating Reno was being. Just a few weeks ago, he had pointed a gun at them and bullied them in a casino.

But Wolf wasn't about to look a gift horse in the mouth, so he thanked Reno and saying he'd see him tomorrow. It not only bought him some time tonight, eliminating the need to find a full-service carwash that was open late, but it was also a money-saver. This way, he could wash the Hummer himself at Mac's tomorrow.

Wolf was feeling satisfied with the day's accomplishments when his cell phone rang. He glanced at the number and knew his run of luck had come to an end.

"Hey, Kase," he said, answering it.

"I thought I told you not to call me that?" she said. Without giving him a chance to respond, she asked another question: "Where's Dad? I've been calling his cell for the past forty minutes, and he's not answering. Is he with you?"

Wolf reflected on the number of questions and the accusatory tone while he formulated the best way to explain the situation.

I'll break it to her gently, he thought. *If I can.*

"Well," he said. "We made two arrests—"

She cut him off. "You had problems? Is that why he wanted me to run that gun? Where is he? Is he hurt?"

So much for being gentle. He went for the direct

approach. "Yes, we had some problems, and it did involve that gun. Mac's at the ER getting some stitches."

"*Stitches!*" Her voice was one decibel below a shriek. "I told him to stay in the car. And *you* were supposed to keep him from getting hurt. *You* were supposed to watch over him. This is all *your* fault."

Wolf thought about saying, "Tell me how you really feel" but decided it was better not to say anything and to let her vent. She demanded to know what hospital Mac was at, and Wolf told her.

She hung up.

Guess I'd better head over to the ER myself.

***

The Elegant Suites Hotel
Phoenix, Arizona

They stood side by side in the parking lot, and Cummins watched as Zerbe flew the drone around the perimeter of the building again and again, a cigarette dangling from his lips. He was intently focused on the monitor and operated the controls with deft precision. He'd purchased the drone at the electronics shop, and he'd been practicing for the better part of an hour after taking the aircraft out of the boxes. And he'd insisted that Cummins accompany him and familiarize himself with the basic controls, but so far, all he had him doing was acting as a timekeeper, recording the exact length of battery life flying time.

"Aren't you getting tired of flying that stupid thing around in circles?" Cummins asked.

"Practice makes perfect," Zerbe said. "Besides, once we get these set up, we can follow them at a distance. You won't have to worry about taxing your nervous stomach or weak bladder."

He gave one of those irritating little laughs that Cummins had come to despise.

The lawyer frowned. It was low to be making light of another person's afflictions. He thought about telling the sleazebag about dyspepsia, the condition that caused his unexpected and sometimes excessive vomiting, but decided not to say anything. It would be wasted on a smelly creep like Zerbe, and he'd just use the knowledge for more inappropriate comments. It had almost been easier working with Eagan and his Viper team. At least they'd pretty much left him alone. Zerbe was always making little digs that got under Cummins' skin.

The drone circled the lot one more time, then disappeared around the side of the building.

"Aren't you supposed to be keeping that in sight?" Cummins asked. "Plus, it's getting dark out. You could ram into something."

"That's why I have an infrared feature on the camera." Zerbe held up the monitor and Cummins saw the clear image, just like he was looking through a pair of night-vision goggles.

It's a wonder he can see anything, wearing those dumb sunglasses, Cummins thought. But he'd never seen Zerbe without them, even in the helicopter that night as they flew away from the last firefight.

"What's the time?" Zerbe said. "How long we been flying?"

"Twenty-four minutes," Cummins said as he thought, We *haven't been flying anywhere*.

Zerbe smiled. "Watch this."

He took his thumbs off the two miniature joysticks, then held up the monitor. Cummins saw the image flutter, then the incessant buzzing became more audible. The drone descended as it appeared around the corner, then hovered in the darkening sky like an oversized mosquito, then zoomed toward them. Cummins was worried it might fly into them, but it sloped downward and hovered a few feet above the asphalt before dropping to the ground.

"It's got an auto-return feature," Zerbe said, the ashes from his cigarette fluttering onto the controls. "Once the battery is depleted, it comes back automatically."

"Big deal. I'm not impressed."

"You don't have to be. Just go pick it up. And be gentle about it."

Cummins snorted in derision. "What for? It's not

like you paid *your* money for the damn thing."

"No, but I don't want to waste any more time having to go back and get another one to break in." His smile stretched into a grin. "Now go fetch, boy."

Cummins pursed his lips and glared at the other man before heading over toward the drone.

"Okay, but I don't appreciate having to do all the dirty work," he muttered.

"You haven't even *seen* dirty work." Zerbe smiled. His smile broadened. "Besides, like I said before, you can use the exercise."

***

St. Regis Hospital
Phoenix, Arizona

The emergency room's waiting room was crowded, but Wolf didn't see Kasey, which he took as a good sign. At least he wouldn't have to endure any of her reproachful looks until later. The rows of chairs were arranged back to back, and several television sets had been mounted on brackets that descended from the ceiling. He went to the main desk, where a pair of young Hispanic girls in blue and white uniforms sat behind an array of computer monitors.

"Do you have a patient named James McNamara in here?" he asked.

The younger of the two perked up and tapped some keys on the keyboard in front of her.

"How's that spelled?" she asked.

Wolf recounted the letters, and the girl's fingers fluttered over the keys once more.

"Yes," she said, "but he's in back being treated right now."

"I need to see him."

The girl's voice strengthened with a tone of authority. "Are you family?"

Wolf was getting tired of this game and didn't feel like playing twenty questions, but there was no sense becoming argumentative and getting tossed out by hospital security. Instead, he pulled the Bail Enforcement Officer's badge off his belt and held it up.

"Official business," he said. "Mr. McNamara was the victim of a crime."

He dropped his hand with the badge and clipped it back on his belt. Usually, people react to the sight of a badge without questioning its authenticity or even reading the printing on it. This girl was no exception.

"Right through those doors, Officer," she said, pointing to a set of sliding glass doors on the left side of the room. "The nurses will be able to direct you to his cubicle."

Wolf nodded his thanks and went through the doors.

Inside was a huge, circular room with an oval

counter in the center. The oval was ringed by a series of open three-sided rooms with a floor-to-ceiling curtain where the fourth wall should have been. Most of them stood open, but several were pulled closed. Wolf walked up to the nurse's station and was about to inquire which room Mac was in when he saw Rodney Shemp stick his head out of the curtain of room number eight.

"May I help you, sir?" the nurse asked.

Wolf shook his head and held up the badge again, figuring there was enough distance between him and the nurse that she wouldn't be able to read it.

"Official business," he said. "I'm here to see Mr. McNamara."

The nurse's eyebrows rose, and she picked up the phone. Wolf continued on his way and Shemp stepped out into the corridor, offering his hand. He was wearing a gray suit and a blue tie. The handkerchief decorating the breast pocket of the jacket matched the tie.

"Hi, Rod," Wolf said. "How'd you get here?"

"Kasey and I had dinner reservations." A quick, nervous smile twitched his lips. "We were on the way when she, ah, called you about not being able to get hold of her dad."

"Where's she at?"

The curtain ripped open, and Kasey stood there glaring at him. "*She's* right here."

She was dressed in an elegant black low-cut evening dress that exposed her bare shoulders and some of her cleavage. Her makeup looked flawless. Wolf had never seen her dressed up to this degree and was struck by how pretty she was. Not wanting to stare, he smiled and nodded as politely as he could.

"How's your dad doing?" he asked.

"I'm fine," McNamara's voice bellowed from within the cubicle.

He lay on a bed on rollers. It was elevated to an oblique angle, and a green cloth partially concealed Mac's face. The cloth had a large hole in the center, and a heavyset black woman stood on the right side of the bed by his head. She was working with a pair of stainless steel tweezers and a hook-like tool. A nurse who barely looked out of her teens stood on the other side of the bed, holding gauze.

"Hold still, please," the black woman said.

McNamara grunted something and added in a normal voice, "Well, step on in here, Steve. You can watch while this pretty gal stitches me up."

There was a tray next to them with a hypodermic syringe, several bloody cotton balls, scissors, and a spool of what appeared to be black thread.

"Mr. McNamara," the woman said, "you're going to have to hold still." She looked around. "I'm afraid we're getting too many people in here."

"Yes, Doctor," the nurse said. "Want me to get

security?"

"Don't bother," Kasey said. "One of us will be leaving." She glared at Wolf. "You go wait in the waiting room."

Wolf took a breath and started to turn to go when McNamara yelled again, "Hey, Steve, don't go. We gotta talk."

"Sir, please don't move," the doctor said.

The nurse's neck tightened, and she glanced at the doctor.

"Out," Kasey said. "He shouldn't have to look at the person responsible for him being here."

"He ain't responsible for me getting...being here," McNamara said.

"You told me you were going to stay in the damn car," Kasey said, turning back to her father. "I'm sure you had to jump out to help him."

"That ain't so," McNamara said. "It's just the price of doing business."

"I hope you realize you're going to have an ugly scar," she said.

"Badge of honor," McNamara said. "Besides, I already got a ton of 'em to go along with this new one."

"You never used to get hurt," Kasey said. "Not until *he* joined us."

"I told you," McNamara said. "The price of doing business. And hell, I used to have to pull my gun out a helluva a lot more before I had Steve backing me up."

"All right," the doctor said, stepping back a bit and staring at Wolf and Kasey. "Am I going to have to call security here? You both need to leave."

Shemp abruptly pushed through the curtain and placed a tentative hand on Kasey's bare shoulder.

She'd been looking at her father and recoiled at the contact, apparently thinking it was Wolf who'd touched her.

"Kase," Shemp said. "Why don't we step out and get some air?"

She took a deep breath and glared at him.

Shemp dropped his hand from her shoulder and stood mute.

No question as to who's going to get the top position in that relationship, Wolf thought.

He felt like smirking but didn't. The fact of the matter was that he kind of liked Rod, or Shemp, as Mac always called him. The guy had always been nice to him and had even looked into his arrest and conviction at Mac's behest. He knew McNamara had never paid Shemp for that, either.

"I'll have you know that you ruined our dinner date," Kasey said over her shoulder toward her father. "I hope you're happy."

That probably made his night, Wolf thought.

He kept silent, not wanting to voice how much Mac disapproved of his daughter's beau, but McNamara said it for him.

"You talking to me?" McNamara asked.

"Yes, I am," Kasey said.

"Well, hell," he said, chuckling. "Looks like I accomplished something good tonight, after all."

"Sir," the doctor said. "If you're not going to hold still, I'll have a couple of nurses come in and hold you down."

"Make sure they're as pretty as this one," McNamara said, gesturing at the forlorn nurse by his side.

She glanced at the doctor, who said, "Oh, they'll be pretty, all right. Pretty big and pretty burly. Now, will you *please* settle down?"

"He'll settle down," Kasey said. "Because we're leaving. We had reservations at Charlie's Steakhouse, which I'm sure have been canceled by now."

"Charlie's," McNamara said. "I love that place. Maybe we'll join you after I get outta here."

"Don't you dare show up there," Kasey snapped.

Shemp tentatively reached out and touched her upper arm. She shook him off.

"Hey, who's watching Chad?" McNamara asked.

"I got a sitter," Kasey said. "You certainly weren't available." Turning, she shot Wolf a final mean glance and then brushed past him, her high heels clicking on the tiled floor. "*Steve* can give you a ride home."

Shemp looked from Mac to Wolf and back again. "Sorry, Mr. McNamara. I hope you—"

"Come on," Kasey practically shouted. "Let's see

if we can get our reservations switched to tomorrow night."

Shemp's mouth settled somewhere between a smile and a neutral expression before he nodded at Wolf and hurried out of the cubicle.

McNamara shook his head and snorted. "Maybe if they're still together next Christmas, I'll look into buying him a pair of damn balls."

For a moment all was quiet, then Wolf looked at the doctor. "I'd like to stay if it's all right."

The doctor rolled her eyes and turned back to McNamara.

"If you can just lie still for a few more minutes," she said, "I should be finished, and you can both leave."

"I promise, ma'am," McNamara said, motioning for Wolf to step around to the other side of the bed. When he spoke again, his voice was hardly above a whisper.

"I'm real sorry about the way she acted, Doctor," McNamara said. "She's my daughter, and, well, you know how it is. You got kids?"

"That's all right, sir." She was intent on the task.

"Apologies to you, too," McNamara said to the nurse, then to Wolf, "In fact, apologies all around. Sorry, Steve."

"No problem," Wolf said.

"Just how in the hell did she find out I was in here?"

Wolf didn't want to say that it was he who'd told her, but the answer was obvious. He figured a wisecrack might break the tension.

"Well, her father is a great tracker. It's probably in her DNA."

"Ha-ha. Why'd you have to go and tell her for?"

"She called me wanting to talk to you when I was getting rid of our two pinches. Which, by the way, was a bit complicated due to our buddy Myron's little nose injury."

"They took him?"

"They did," Wolf said.

"Good. The son of a bitch had it coming. Manny pay you?"

Wolf reached into his pocket and held up the check. "Right here. I'll deposit it first thing in the morning."

"First thing in the morning, hell. We probably should do one of them electronic deposits tonight to beat the bill collector."

Wolf chuckled, knowing Mac was joking.

Or was he?

He put the check back into his pocket.

"Reno said we could drop the car off tomorrow," Wolf said. "I'll get up early and clean and wash it. We'll also need to pick up the rental from Manny's."

"Damn straight. I'm going to have to lean on the body shop extra hard to get the Escalade back before fourteen-hundred."

"Fourteen-hundred?" Wolf said.

McNamara reached up and carefully lifted part

of the green cloth away from his face. His grin was obvious.

"Right," he said. "We gotta be at the airport."

"The airport?"

"Yep," McNamara said, slowly lowering the cloth. "We're picking up Ms. Dolly and the P Patrol."

Wolf felt a thrill at the prospect of seeing the three women again, especially Yolanda, but also wondered how Kasey was going to react. Their brief meeting after the Mexico fiasco had been anything but cordial.

"Ms. Dolly called me a little while ago," McNamara said. His tone was slow and mellow as if he were anticipating the pleasure of the coming reunion. "She's got a lead on that matter Manny was telling us about and wants to cut us in on it. So, we've got to get busy on that one tomorrow."

Wolf tried to recall the particulars... Mob lawyer on the lamb. His sister is in the Phoenix area. Big recovery fee, but they'd have to split it at least two ways.

"So, let's you and me plan on taking them out to dinner tomorrow night," McNamara said. "What do you think?"

"Sounds good," Wolf said.

As long as it was not at Charlie's.

CHAPTER 8

MCNAMARA RANCH
PHOENIX, ARIZONA

The next morning Wolf got up at first light and went running. As the nascent sky turned from gray to orange, he contemplated the events of the previous day and his current situation. They were making progress on the financial front, but they still had a long way to go. As far as his quest to find out what had really happened in Iraq and how it tied into Mexico, he still had more questions than answers. A disconnected phone number for the Fallotti and Abraham Law Firm in Manhattan, Cummins, Eagan, Nasim—two of whom were dead—and somebody named Von Dien, who was supposed to be his worst nightmare.

The whole scenario was the stuff nightmares were made of, that was for sure. And after the fiasco in the emergency room the night before, he doubted he was going to get much help or cooperation from Kasey in tracing down what meager clues he did have.

It's not like I've got a lot to go on anyway, he thought.

After finishing his run, he toweled off a bit and drank a bottle of water before going back to the Hummer, which was parked in the driveway next to his garage apartment. He grabbed a roll of paper towels, a couple of rags, a toothbrush, and some cleaning liquid and proceeded to give the inside a thorough cleaning. Mac's blood decorated the front passenger dashboard and door, and Kites had bled all over the back portion. After working for the better part of an hour, he'd managed to scrub and wipe away the telltale blood splatters.

Wolf was still ensconced in the rear seat area, putting the final touches on the job, when McNamara came out of the house in a t-shirt, jeans. He carried two cups of steaming coffee and handed one to Wolf. The ER crew had shaved some of the hair on his forehead, and he sported a trimmed gauze pad that was secured by three Band-Aids. Despite the injury, he walked with a spring in his step.

Wolf wiped the floor with a crumpled paper towel and sat up. "Where's your cane?"

McNamara shook his head. "I'm retiring that damn thing unless I need to look distinguished or use the blade. I hung it on the clock."

By "the clock," he meant the grandfather clock by the door where he kept his pistol secreted.

"Besides," McNamara said, taking a sip from his cup, "I can't be looking old and infirm in front of Ms. Dolly and the P Patrol."

Wolf sampled some of the brew, which turned out to be hot, strong, and black. He straightened his legs and slipped out of the vehicle.

McNamara looked in and gave the Hummer an appraising once-over. "You got the War Wagon all cleaned up, I see."

"Yeah. I figured I'd top it off and then drop it at Reno's gym."

"Good idea. But first, we gotta go back to Manny's to get that loaner. They promised me they'd have the Escalade ready by noon so we can go pick up Ms. Dolly."

Wolf recalled the airport commitment.

"I thought you said it was at fourteen-hundred?"

"It is," McNamara said. "But I want to run the Escalade through the car wash and get one of them pretty-smelling dandies to hang from the rearview mirror. You know, maybe mint or something."

"Or something." Wolf sipped more of his coffee and smiled.

"You think I oughta get 'em some roses, too?" McNamara grinned. "I mean, just for Ms. Dolly and Brenda. You can get Yolanda's."

"Why don't we just get an extra couple air fresheners and call it even?" Wolf drank more coffee and tossed out the remainder. After handing the cup back to McNamara, he went toward his apartment.

"I got to hit the shower," he said.

"Sounds like a good idea. You want me to have Kasey put on a couple of extra eggs for you?"

Wolf recalled the drama of the night before. "No, thanks. I'll grab something later. Reno invited me to do a little working out in his gym this morning."

"Okay," McNamara said. "See you in a bit."

Wolf pushed open the side door of the garage and walked past the workout equipment spread out over the cement floor, pausing to give the hanging duffle bag a couple of kicks and punches. He stopped almost immediately.

Better save some energy for the gym, he thought as he proceeded to the shower next to the staircase and stripped off his clothes. It made little sense to shower since he'd be getting sweaty at the gym in a couple of hours, but he hoped the flowing water over his skin would revive him a bit. Besides, he hadn't showered last night after the fracas, and he needed to shave, too. The downstairs bathroom was small, consisting of a shower, a sink, and a toilet. Luckily, Mac had put a second toilet on the second floor, so it wasn't necessary to negotiate the stairway for any middle-of-the-night calls.

He splashed hot water on his face and lathered up, staring at his reflection in the small mirror fastened to the wall. It reminded him of his Army time. Usually, the camps had adequate facilities but nothing elaborate. Shaving in Leavenworth had been more complicated, not to mention always having to watch his back.

He took a deep breath and wondered how much longer he would be stuck here at Mac's. Not that he minded, nor could he afford much more. McNamara didn't even charge him rent, so the price was right, but the price was also steep and growing steeper. He couldn't shake the feeling of being a freeloader and wondered how much longer he should sponge off his mentor and friend.

It can't go on forever, he thought as he pulled the safety razor across his cheek. The blade made a scraping, bristling sound. No, not forever, but for the moment, for better or for worse.

At least until he could get things unraveled, whenever that might be.

***

The Elegant Suites Hotel
Phoenix, Arizona

Cummins watched as Zerbe loaded the drone into the rear of the Lexus and pressed the button to lower the tailgate. At least, he thought it was Zerbe. The man had changed his appearance substantially, shedding the prescription sunglasses for contacts and dumping the worn, filthy white sports jacket for a tan polo shirt and brown slacks. He'd even slicked down and combed back his hair, so it looked almost presentable. Perhaps Cummins' admonishment that Wolf knew what they both looked like had struck a nerve with the sleazebag.

He didn't know, but one thing Cummins was certain of was that he didn't want to cross paths with Wolf again unless it was with a small army. He hoped those South African mercs were as good as Zerbe said they were.

They'd better be, he thought.

They hadn't eaten yet, and Cummins was feeling that familiar gurgling in his abdomen. Zerbe walked around to the driver's side and motioned for Cummins to get in. The lawyer adjusted his baseball cap and shifted his bulk onto the high seat. It was still relatively early, and the inside of the damn vehicle was already insufferable. He left the door open until Zerbe started the engine.

"Turn on the air conditioning, will ya?" Cummins said, taking off his cap and fanning himself with it.

Zerbe smiled.

"You know," he said, pausing to shake a cigarette out of his pack, "this time of the year's our winter back in South Africa."

"Big deal," Cummins said. "Why'd we have to leave so early?"

"Haven't you ever heard that old saying, the early bird catches the worm?"

"I don't like birds. And what the hell does that have to do with anything?"

Zerbe smirked and lit the cigarette. "Well, my re-working of that aphorism is the early bird never gets caught. And you were the one pissing and moaning about Wolf catching a glimpse of us yesterday."

"I wasn't moaning," Cummins said. "I just think we were taking too many chances he would."

The smoke was starting to make him feel nauseated.

"Exactly why we're going to renew our efforts to surreptitiously plant one of our trackers on their car."

"How we gonna do that?"

"Easy," Zerbe said. "We stake out that bail bonds-man's place until they show up."

"What if they don't?"

Zerbe started the car.

"They will. That place is their bread and butter. And I haven't ruled out a ruse to draw them in."

"What kind of ruse?"

"Mr. Sutter, the bail bondsman, saw you in Las Vegas." Zerbe shifted into gear and the backup cam-era feature activated, showing a live-action depiction on the dashboard. "But he's never seen me. I might pay his office a visit."

"What if Wolf happens to stop by while you're there?"

Zerbe braked and shifted into drive.

"That's why I took steps to make myself less recognizable," he said. "Or hadn't you noticed?"

Cummins didn't reply but thought Zerbe looked like an asshole, and he still smelled like a BO factory. The cigarette smoke would fade after he tossed the damn thing out, but the body odor was a permanent fixture.

"Once we get the tracker on him," Zerbe said, "it'll be a simple matter of shadowing him until we find the right moment."

"If you say so," Cummins said.

"I do," Zerbe replied. "I'd like to have things in place before the Lion Team arrives."

The Lion Team, Cummins thought. *At least then I'll have some protection.*

CHAPTER 9

THE MCNAMARA RANCH
PHOENIX, ARIZONA

After fixing himself a liquid breakfast of two raw eggs, a load of carrots, a banana, and some orange juice in the blender, Wolf pulled on his workout sweats and packed a ditty bag with his regular clothes and a towel. Hopefully, Reno wouldn't mind him taking a shower there after the workout. He hoped this newly formed friendship would extend to him getting a couple of MMA fights with the prospect of making some good money. Granted, he wasn't very familiar with the sport, but from what he'd seen, he felt he could hold his own. It looked brutal and grueling, but so did the prospect of Mac losing the Escalade to the bank or worse, should he not be able to recover from the financial hit he'd taken due to the Mexico fiasco. Initially, it had appeared to be a cakewalk to some big and easy money.

Best-laid plans, he thought.

It had been a risky venture from the get-go, and anytime there was risk involved, he knew from experience that you should plan for the worst.

Getting into the ring and maybe getting busted up a little seemed like an acceptable risk for the possibility of staying ahead of the bill collectors. He owed Mac that much.

He grabbed the ditty bag and the keys to the Hummer and trotted down the stairs, hoping he wouldn't have to stop by the house to get Mac. Wolf had no desire to be subjected to Kasey's withering gaze first thing in the morning. He thought about Rodney Shemp and felt a twinge of pity for the poor guy. Kasey obviously thought she was quite a catch.

Maybe one day, she'd wake up and find that there was a pea under her mattress, and that was what was making her so irritable.

To his surprise, Mac was waiting for him outside, with Chad and a child's car seat.

"We got to drop Chad off at preschool on the way," McNamara said.

Wolf wondered why Kasey couldn't do that but said nothing. He remembered she had a heavy course load this semester and probably needed the time to complete her assignments.

I'd better start trying to give her the benefit of the doubt, he thought. *After all, she doesn't have it easy being Big Jim McNamara's little girl.*

After they'd managed to secure the car seat to the rear seat, Chad insisted he would ride up front with Grandpa. Never one to disappoint his grandson, Mac cast a furtive glance at the house, then hopped into the front passenger seat with Chad on his lap.

"Let's vamoose," he said, slamming the door. "Before she sees us."

Wolf jumped in and started the Hummer, shifted into gear, and proceeded down the driveway. He was just making the turn onto the highway access road when he caught a glimpse of Kasey coming out the front door and running down the driveway after them.

"I think she saw us," he said.

"Well, remember what old Satchel Paige used to say," McNamara said. "Don't look back. Something might be gaining on you."

Chad squealed in delight, and Wolf grinned as he stepped on the gas.

As soon as they were on the highway, McNamara's cell phone rang. He took it out of his pocket, looked at the screen, and pressed the button to ignore the calls.

"This is fun, Grandpa," Chad said. "Mommy never lets me ride up front."

"Well," McNamara said, chuckling as he held the

child close to his chest, "after today, she probably ain't gonna let me ride up there either."

You got that right, Wolf thought.

***

Office of Emmanuel Sutter
Bail Bondsman
Phoenix, Arizona

Zerbe looked through the rangefinder binoculars as he peered through the front windshield. They were about a hundred yards away, and Cummins was sure that given the hour, which was just past eight, no one, least of all Wolf and his buddy McNamara, was going to show up at some degenerate bail bondsman's office. He was about to say that when Zerbe lowered the binoculars and grabbed his notebook. After paging through it, he grinned.

"That Toyota Corolla," he said.

"What about it?" Cummins asked. They'd skipped breakfast at Zerbe's insistence and rushed over here to do nothing but sit and watch the bail bondsman's office through a pair of binoculars. Cummins could feel his innards becoming unsettled.

"It's the same car they were driving yesterday," he said. "That means they're probably still using that big Hummer."

"So, it's obvious that they're not here," Cummins said. "Why don't we come back later or something?"

"Huh-uh," Zerbe said, opening the door. "You get behind the wheel."

"What for?"

His stomach was queasy.

"So I can put a tracker on that one." Zerbe opened the rear door and started digging in a black nylon bag. "Then we'll be able to track them from a distance."

"Is all this really necessary?" Cummins started to say. Then he felt it: the distinctive roiling in his gut that meant another episode of regurgitation was about to begin. He threw open the passenger door, leaned out, and puked.

Since they hadn't eaten yet, hardly anything came out, just a bunch of sour-smelling bile. It burned his throat, and just when he thought it was over, a subsequent attack occurred.

"Don't you ever get tired of doing that?" Zerbe asked.

"It's because we skipped breakfast," Cummins answered, his tone defensive.

"I'm glad you didn't do that while we were driving," Zerbe said with a laugh.

***

Even after dropping Chad off at the preschool, Mac's phone continued to ring as they drove to Manny's office. McNamara looked at the screen and smirked. "I wonder if I should just toss this damn thing out the window? Tell her I lost it."

"What if Ms. Dolly's flight gets in early?" Wolf asked. "She'll need to call you."

McNamara sighed and answered the call.

Once again, Wolf could hear Kasey's shrill tone even though he was a few feet away.

McNamara listened, replied in monosyllables, grunted, and occasionally said a word or two. Finally, the diatribe subsided, and he said, "Okay, sweetie. Love you too."

After he hung up, he turned to Wolf.

"I guess she's forgotten about the times when she was a little whippersnapper and I used to take her riding on my Harley back when we were living at Fort Bragg." McNamara heaved a sigh. "That girl's got a lot of her mother in her, all right."

Wolf had never met either of Mac's two ex-wives and was glad of it.

He made the turn into the parking lot of the strip mall where Manny's office was.

"There it is," McNamara said. "All safe and sound. If it wasn't so damn hard to get in and out of, I might consider buying one someday."

Wolf pulled up beside the Corolla. About thirty feet away, the unlighted office area of Manny's place was visible through the glass window. He shifted into park.

"Want me to drive it over to the gym?" he asked. "You can drive the War Wagon."

McNamara shook his head as he opened the door.

"Nah, I might as well get used to it. I gotta go get them flowers while you're doing your workout."

Wolf grinned. "You sure you don't just want to go for the air freshener option?"

McNamara smiled and shook his head.

"You want to sample that fine vintage," he said, "you got to make sure you bring the right bottle opener."

He got out, slammed the door, and walked to the Toyota.

***

McDonald's
Phoenix, Arizona

Cummins poured another mini-carton of syrup over the pancakes and sliced them with his plastic knife. It wasn't the best breakfast, but it was better than nothing.

Next to nothing, he thought as he stabbed one of the pieces with the plastic fork and shoved it into his mouth. It tasted flat, like Army food, and it brought back the uncomfortable feeling of being in the officers' mess when he'd deployed, albeit briefly, to Iraq. The discomfort increased exponentially when he remembered Wolf in his infantry armor, waiting to escort them to the meeting where they were supposed to get the Lion and the Lioness Attacking the Nubian. The meeting where all this started and where everything had gone wrong.

"They're moving," Zerbe said.

He sat across from Cummins at the table they'd secured in the far corner of the room. Zerbe had opened his laptop as soon as they'd arrived and tapped into the restaurant's Wi-Fi. Now his face had a big grin on it.

A big stupid-looking grin, Cummins thought.

He still wasn't used to the new look Zerbe had affected. Without the ubiquitous Panama hat and dark glasses, he looked like a deviant actor playing a washed-up nerd on a television sitcom. No, more like a cable sitcom. There was something about Zerbe that suggested unwholesomeness, an R-rated unsavoriness. Perhaps it was the man's perpetual body odor.

Cummins swallowed the bite of pancake and waited to test the state of his stomach.

So far, so good, he thought.

"Once they come to an extended stop, we'll—" Zerbe started, then his cell phone rang. He glanced at the screen and smiled. "*Hallo, Luan. Hoe gaan dit?*"

More of that damn South African stuff, Cummins thought. He shoveled a few more pieces of the pancakes into his mouth, wishing he could understand what was being said.

He suddenly realized he was going to be at a distinct disadvantage once this gang of muscle arrived. They could understand him but spoke a language that was foreign to him. What was to stop Zerbe and those freaks from taking the damn artifact and renegotiating the deal with Von Dien once they retrieved it from Wolf? And where would that leave him? Zerbe had to figure that with VD's wealth, he'd hunt them to the ends of the earth if they tried to cross him, but that still left him as the odd man out.

"*Hoe lank?*" Zerbe said, listened, then added, "*Dis oulik. Koebaai.*" He pocketed his phone. "The Lion Team's arrived in the US. They're clearing Customs in Baltimore now. Should be here this afternoon."

"Wonderful," Cummins said, hoping it sounded more sincere than he felt. The pancakes tasted like sugar-coated mush.

He had to figure out a way to remain in the game and safeguard his position once the new players arrived.

***

Mixed Martial Arts Fighting Academy
Phoenix, Arizona

Wolf had always enjoyed punching a heavy bag, and Reno's place seemed to have plenty of them. Mc-

Namara had taken the loaned Corolla back to the body shop in hopes of rattling their cage so he could get the Escalade in time to pick up Ms. Dolly and the P Patrol at the airport. It was closing on ten, so Wolf had driven to the gym to return the Hummer. Mac was supposed to stop by later to pick him up.

"You'll want to change clothes before we hit the airport, won't you?" McNamara had asked.

"You're acting like I should rent a tuxedo or something."

McNamara snorted a laugh. "That's up to you, but I'm planning on getting them three dozen roses. What color you want for Yolanda's?"

Wolf thought for a moment. "I know she likes yellow."

"Good choice," McNamara said. "I'm getting red for Ms. Dolly and pink for Brenda."

Wolf figured Mac had more in mind than a quick collaborative trackdown, but that would be a welcome task as well.

The sign on the uppermost part of the front of the building said this was a FITNESS CENTER, but underneath were the words Mixed Martial Arts, Boxing, Wrestling, Jiu-Jitsu, Karate Taught Here.

And big block letters painted in red, white, and blue on the front window proclaimed *RENO GARTH, MMA CHAMPION, TRAINS HERE.*

Wolf went to the front entrance doors and pulled

one open. The interior was cool compared to the wretched heat outside, but it wasn't frigid, which was good. The last thing he needed was to pull a muscle, and that was easy to do in an overly air-conditioned environment. The gym was pretty big, with an array of speed and heavy bags, free weights, weight machines, aerobics rooms, cardio machines, treadmills, a large space covered with padded floor mats, a full-sized boxing ring, and an octagonal cage like the ones used in mixed martial arts. As he walked through the place looking for Reno, he caught the stares of several guys who were working out. A few of them appeared to be in pretty good shape, others not so much. Wolf saw a group of offices behind a section of half-partitions. Next to them was a pair of signs indicating the male and female locker rooms. As Wolf was scanning the expansive room, he heard someone call to him. It was Reno, who ambled toward him using his cane, a grin stretched over his face.

He switched the cane to his left hand and held out his right, and Wolf shook it.

"I brought back your Hummer," Wolf said. "All washed and topped off. Thanks."

"No problem," Reno said, eying the ditty bag Wolf was holding. "You decided to take me up on that workout?"

"Actually, yeah," Wolf said. "There's something else, too." He hesitated, unsure of just how much he should divulge about his and McNamara's financial desperation.

Reno raised an eyebrow.

Wolf debated what to say for a few more seconds, then decided to lay his cards on the table. After all, even though their association had a rough beginning, they now shared the mutual bond of having been together with their backs to the wall as they faced a common foe—a foe who had given no quarter.

"I don't know about you," Wolf said, "but we came out of that Mexican thing pretty much the worse for the wear. Took a big financial hit."

"Yeah, I can imagine. That Mexican hospital charged me a pretty penny. I had to buy my way outta there, telling them the banditos must've stolen my passport."

"Well, you said something the other day about an MMA fight."

Reno's other eyebrow rose.

"Yeah, I could probably set something up." He pondered his next words. "I also manage fighters, and I got a guy with a match coming up on this Saturday. One of his regular sparring partners got hurt, so I'm looking for another one." He eyed Wolf's frame. "He's a heavyweight and probably has a few pounds on you. How much you weigh?"

"About two-fifteen right now."

Reno nodded. "Well, he's looking to go a couple

of rounds right now if you're interested. I'll pay you two hundred for today's session and round it up to five if you help work his corner on Saturday."

Wolf thought about it. He knew from experience that a sparring partner was hired to take a beating, but he'd done a lot of ring work in Leavenworth, so how hard could this be? Plus, the money was too good to pass up.

"Sounds good," Wolf said. "But I don't have a cup or a mouthpiece with me."

"Hell, I got all that stuff. I'll even give you some mostly unused equipment."

Wolf laughed.

Reno held up his index finger.

"Ah, look, Steve," he said. "I know you can handle yourself, God, do I know it, but this sport's kind of rough physically. You sure you're up to it?"

Wolf didn't know if Reno was trying to warn him or discourage him.

"I spent a couple of years on the prison boxing team, and the fights I got into out of the ring didn't have any rules."

Reno's eyes narrowed, and he gave a quick nod.

"All right. Come on over here, and we'll get you suited up."

Wolf followed him toward the office area. Reno swung around the end of the wall of cubicles and motioned for Wolf to follow. Six people, four women and two men, sat at desks, typing on keyboards. Reno hobbled over to a desk with a gorgeous woman with blonde hair pulled back in a ponytail. Wolf thought she was the same one who'd driven Reno out to see him and Mac the day before yesterday. She looked up at them and smiled.

"Barbie," Reno said. "This is Steve Wolf. We're hiring him on as a sparring partner for Greg Storm. Do a quick application and insurance disclaimers and such."

The woman had blue eyes, which looked Wolf up and down.

He noticed she had a spray of freckles over her cheeks.

"Sit down, why don't ya?" she said, indicating the chair on the other side of her desk.

As Wolf moved to the chair, Reno told him he was going to get a groin protector and a mouthpiece from the equipment room.

Barbie turned toward him and smiled as she sized him up. She had on a white tank top with a lacy décolletage that exposed her exquisitely tanned neck and shoulders. Wolf couldn't help but notice the garment was so tight-fitting that the outline of her nipples showed prominently through the thin fabric.

Headlights, he thought.

"Hey," she said. "My eyes are up here."

He flushed and quickly averted his gaze, not knowing whether to apologize or say nothing.

She giggled and made a dismissive gesture with her fingers.

"Don't worry about it," she said. "We wouldn't wear this kind of stuff if we didn't want a guy to look. The birds and the bees."

Wolf wondered if she knew the male birds were the ones with the more colorful plumage, but that was because, as he'd learned in biology, they didn't have a visible penis. Barbie inhaled and leaned back to stretch, and at this moment, he was glad his wasn't visible either.

Once she opened the forms on her computer monitor, she proved very expedient in taking down his information. By the time Reno had returned with a groin protector, headgear, a pair of gloves, and a mouthpiece in a box, Barbie had printed out the forms, and Wolf had signed them.

"You read them first?" Reno said with a grin. "Or were you too busy checking out Barbie's tits?"

Wolf flushed again.

"He did both," she said with a smile.

"Hell," Reno said. "I can't blame him for that. Grab me a cup from the coffee maker and heat up some water so we can fit this mouthpiece."

Barbie rose from her chair, and Wolf noticed that her tan slacks fit as snugly as her tank top. They both watched her move, Wolf trying to make it less obvious.

Reno shook his head and sighed.

"She's something, ain't she?" he asked.

Wolf agreed.

"And believe it or not," Reno said, "she's got brains, too."

Wolf stood and placed the groin protector around his waist, checking the fit. It seemed to do the job. Next, he slipped on the gloves. They were fingerless and had a ridge of padding over the knuckles, unlike a standard boxing glove. Wolf flexed his hand a few times.

"With MMA, you got to do a lot of grabbing," Reno said. "Chokes, arm-locks, take-downs. You familiar with any of that kind of stuff?"

Wolf was, having taken the opportunity to study it during his stint in South Korea. The Korean instructor he'd had, Mr. Yu, was very adept at both Tae Kwon Do and hapkido.

He nodded.

"Good," Reno said. "Expect Storm to take you down and try to choke you out. Or maybe get a kimura on you. You know what that is?"

"I guess I'll be finding out real soon," Wolf said.

Reno seemed to appreciate Wolf's insouciance.

Or maybe he's looking forward to seeing me get my ass handed to me, Wolf thought.

Barbie brought back the cup of steaming water, and Reno dropped the mouthpiece into it. After about a minute, he used a pen to fish it out and handed it to

Wolf, who put it into his mouth and bit down hard. It took about thirty seconds for the impression of his teeth and bite to set into the plastic. After that, he removed the insert and stared at it.

"Let's hope I still have all my teeth after this," he said.

"The match is three five-minute rounds," Reno said. "With a minute's rest between them."

He went over the basic rules: no kicking or punching to the groin, the back of the head, or the kidneys, no pokes to the eyes, no fish-hooking of the lips, no kicking the head of a downed opponent. Pretty much everything else, including punching a downed opponent, was allowed.

Wolf didn't particularly like that last one since it invited serious debilitating injuries, but he decided the best course would be to avoid being knocked down. Even with the green light to beat a downed adversary, it was still a cakewalk compared to dealing with a hostile con in a dark, vacant hallway trying to stick a shiv into you. There were no rules on the inside and no referee, either.

"I wish I could tell Greg to take it easy on you," Reno said. "But he's got that fight coming up, and he's gotta go hard. You sure you want to do this?"

Wolf mulled over his options: two hundred dollars for three five-minute rounds, roughly thirteen bucks a minute. It would be almost eight hundred if he put in a full hour, but the fifteen minutes was likely going to be more than enough.

"Let's do it."

***

Wolf emerged from the locker room feeling a bit self-conscious in his long-legged black sweatpants, with the obtrusive, cumbersome groin protector tied around his hips.

It beat the alternative.

He also elected to wear a black sweatshirt to conceal the residual bruise from the Luth shooting incident. It was now a nice purple, and Wolf figured it would make too tempting a target if he went shirtless. His bare feet, toughened and callused by his daily runs, felt naked and strange without shoes, bringing back memories of running barefoot outside on the rez when he was a child. The headgear, which he'd donned in the locker room, felt almost like his old Army helmet, and he wished he had the body armor to go with it.

A sparring partner's paid to take a beating, he reminded himself.

That didn't mean he wasn't going to try to give as good as he got.

When he got to the door of the cage, Reno was waiting for him. A big white guy with a muscular build who was wearing an outfit similar to Wolf's stood at Reno's side, along with an older, shorter guy. This one held a towel, headgear, and a jar of Vaseline.

"Steve," Reno said. "This is Greg Storm, one of my fighters. He's got a match coming up on Saturday."

Wolf extended his gloved hand, and Storm gave it a fist bump. His expression was blank, and he didn't make eye contact. It was as if he'd accidentally bumped into the guy who cleaned the toilets.

Just another guy to do the nasty stuff, Wolf thought. Like stand there and take punches.

He took the opportunity to size the other man up. The guy was big, bigger than Wolf, and both ears were cauliflowered, which pegged him as a wrestler. His neck was as thick as a gallon milk jug, and his nose had the look of having been broken several times. The sloping traps made his shoulders look rounded, and Wolf had no doubt the arms under the long sleeves of the sweatshirt were corded with muscle.

"And this is Nick Gill, his trainer," Reno said.

The older guy smiled and cocked his head but made no offer to shake hands, holding up the cluster of items he held.

"Now remember," Reno said, addressing both of them, "this is sparring, not all-out combat. You got to work techniques and combinations, not swing for the fences. And Greg, you can't afford to get hurt with that match so close."

I can't afford it either, Wolf thought.

Storm nodded and slipped in his mouthpiece. Wolf did the same.

Reno motioned for Gill to put the headgear on his fighter. The trainer slung the towel over his shoulder, stuck the Vaseline under his left arm, and lifted the headgear toward Storm.

"No headgear," he said, glancing at Wolf. "Don't think I'll need it."

"Come on, don't be stupid," Gill said. "You don't want to take a chance of getting cut."

He lifted the helmet again, and Storm shoved his hand away.

"I ain't stupid, and I said no." He glanced at Wolf and rolled his eyes. "This is gonna be like amateur hour."

Wolf felt miffed by the dismissal but let it ride. He wasn't here to prove how tough he was; he was here to make a couple of bucks.

And take a beating, although he was starting to have serious misgivings about this venture.

I'll just stay on defense, he thought. *I got nothing to prove.*

He also harbored no resentment toward Storm. From his own ring experience at Leavenworth, Wolf knew the delicate balancing act a fighter had to perform. You had to maintain that level of confidence and belief in yourself, and at the same time, deal with the natural anxiety of stepping up and putting everything—your body, your health, your prestige—on the line. This process included stoking your confidence with a combination of bravado and arrogance. You couldn't afford to have friends or be courteous in the ring or the octagon, not when the guy standing across from you was intent on taking your head off.

"Well," Reno said, "he's tougher than he looks, but just the same, Gill's right. You don't want to take chances at this juncture."

Storm pursed his lips and shook his head. "I ain't worried. Come on, let's go."

Gill grabbed his fighter's arm and smeared a gob of Vaseline over Storm's eyebrows, nose, and cheeks. When he'd finished, Storm stepped through the open gate into the octagon. Gill motioned for Wolf to step over and applied some Vaseline to his face as well.

Reno yelled someone's name, and a tall white guy in a sweatshirt trotted over.

"Murph," Reno said. "You up for doing some reffing?"

"Sure thing, boss."

Murph stepped through the gate into the octagonal ring.

Wolf began to follow him, but Reno grabbed his arm.

"You sure you want to go through with this?" he asked. "Ain't no shame in backing out if you don't think you can handle it."

Wolf watched as Storm danced about throwing punches and kicks, warming up. The display was formidable.

"I've been through worse," Wolf said and stepped through the gate.

Reno was closing and securing it when Storm smirked and said, "Better not lock it in case I kick his ass so bad that he wants to run outta here."

Bravado and arrogance, Wolf thought, feeling less like a man being paid to take a beating and more like a guy who wanted to administer one. He smacked his gloves together and walked around the perimeter of the ring, getting the feel of it with his bare feet.

Not having shoes on bothered him a bit, but it brought back memories of his Tae Kwon Do lessons in Tang Do Chon up by the DMZ.

Murph stood in the center and held up his arms.

"You guys ready?" he yelled.

Storm and Wolf nodded.

"Then let's get it on," Murph said and dropped his arm. "The clock's ticking."

The clock was a huge square time-board mounted on the wall above the highest rail of the octagonal cage. Two electronic displays, one labeled ROUNDS and the other MATCH LENGTH, commenced their illuminated digital counts. Wolf moved forward and held out his left hand for the customary tap. Storm slapped it hard, then swung a kick onto the outer edge of Wolf's left thigh.

The blow stung, and Wolf skipped back. Storm moved forward and began throwing punches, most of which Wolf blocked with his forearms.

This guy's got power, Wolf thought, but he also seems to be moving at an accelerated pace.

Wolf wondered how long his opponent could sustain it.

Storm stepped forward and threw a roundhouse kick toward Wolf's head that missed, then followed up with looping body blows, one of which connected. Wolf threw his first punch in retaliation: a straight right that smacked into Storm's face.

Storm took half a step back, then the outer edges of his lips twisted downward and he lumbered forward again, his eyes reflecting anger.

The guy was bigger and stronger than he was, so Wolf backpedaled in an arc, letting the bigger man pursue him. Usually the guys with the overdeveloped muscles, the weightlifter types, tired quicker, so it was prudent to let the big guy keep slugging away and, hopefully, lose steam. As Storm drew closer, Wolf snapped a front kick into the other man's abdomen. It felt like he'd just kicked a tree trunk, but Storm's guard came down a tad, and Wolf followed up with a left hook that smacked into Storm's right temple.

Wolf was a little too slow to pull his arm back and Storm grabbed it, the sleeve of his sweatshirt providing nice purchase. Storm maintained his grip on Wolf's forearm as he pivoted and used his right foot to strike the back of Wolf's left knee, sending him down to the mat.

The surface was padded, but it felt almost as hard as a paved street. Wolf tried to roll away, but Storm was on top of him in an instant, trying to straddle him.

Time to wrestle, Wolf thought.

He managed to get onto his left side and put his arms up to block the series of punches that were raining down on his head. The obstruction of the headgear made it impossible to see the punches coming, and several of them connected.

This is MMA, he thought. *The ref's not going to break us unless I can tie him up and neither of us can move.*

Storm began landing punches on Wolf's back, and one of them strayed a bit low.

A kidney shot.

The pain radiated upward. It was a cheap shot, a foul, but Wolf wasn't about to complain. He just hoped the blow had been unintentional.

Another pair of blows smacked into the top of his head and back.

No need to play the human punching bag, he thought.

With that, he reached up and grabbed the front of Storm's sweatshirt with his left hand. Storm grabbed

Wolf's hand, trying to bend it into a wrist lock. He outweighed Wolf by a substantial amount and was too heavy to buck off. Storm brought a hammer fist down onto the side of Wolf's head. The helmet absorbed much of the impact, but it also preventing Wolf from seeing the blow coming.

"Hey, Greg," Reno called. "Take it easy, would ya? This is a sparring session."

"Fuck that," Storm said and delivered another hammer strike.

Wolf wound his hand into Storm's sweatshirt and pulled the man's upper body closer. Storm flailed away with two more blows and then tried to pull back. Wolf twisted onto his back, which apparently Storm thought gave him the upper hand. He cocked his arm back, but Wolf had worked his left hand up into the collar of Storm's sweatshirt and then did the same with his right, crisscrossing his arms. He then applied a strangling technique, pulling both of his arms toward his chest and pressing the edges of his wrists to cut off the blood flow to Storm's carotid arteries. Storm's breathing became labored, and he emitted a series of hacking sounds.

Wolf increased the pressure.

"Break 'em, Murph," Reno yelled.

The referee stepped forward and tapped Wolf's shoulder. He immediately released his choke-hold and anticipated that Storm would get off of him.

Instead of standing, Storm, whose face was bright red, took a few seconds to recover, then delivered a hard punch to Wolf's head.

"Hey," Murph yelled. "I said break, Greg, dammit."

Storm cocked his arm again, and Murph grabbed it and pulled it back.

This was enough distraction for Wolf to push Storm's body off and shift his own out from underneath him. He rolled away and staggered to his feet, wobbling to a corner and checking the clock. A minute still remained in the round.

Four minutes, and I feel like I've run five miles, Wolf thought, then remembered he'd done close to that on his roadwork this morning.

Dumb move. He gripped the crisscrossed wire of the cage wall and noticed a small crowd had gathered on the outside and was watching the festivities.

Looked like a lot of people were looking forward to seeing an ass-kicking.

Reno hobbled into the center with his cane and looked angry.

"That was a cheap shot, Greg," he said. "You oughta know better."

Storm frowned and shook his head. "He cheated with that fucking choke. Grabbing my sweatshirt like that. Why, in a real match, I wouldn't even be wearing this piece of shit."

"You know I don't condone gym wars," Reno said.

He turned to Wolf. "You want to continue?"

Wolf felt fatigued but was getting his wind back.

"Yeah," he said. "But I think I'll get rid of this."

He pulled the headgear off and tossed it away. It was sliding on his face and blocking his vision. It might have been effective for a sparring match in a boxing gym, but for this MMA stuff, it was a liability.

"You can slip out of your sweatshirt, pal," he said. "If you want."

Storm glared at him and reached down, yanking the garment off to expose a chiseled and heavily muscled torso.

The timer clock rang, indicating the first round was over.

One down, two to go, Wolf thought.

He debated whether to slip out of his sweatshirt as well. Since he had a t-shirt on under it, he decided that would conceal his scarlet bruise well enough and slipped the sweatshirt off. He knew his arms were nowhere near as big as Storm's, but neither were they matchsticks. Plus, Wolf knew he had the edge in speed.

The timer bell rang again, and Reno walked out of the cage.

Wolf held up his glove for the sportsmanship tap, but Storm ignored the gesture this time.

Sensing his opponent was angry, Wolf decided to stick with his original game plan of letting the other guy punch himself out.

Block and counter.

The ball of Storm's foot smashed into the outside of Wolf's left knee. The blow could have done a lot of damage if it had hit him squarely, possibly causing a meniscus tear.

It was the third foul Storm had committed and the last one in Wolf's estimation.

This guy deserves an ass-whipping, Wolf thought and snapped a quick jab into Storm's face.

The bigger man brushed off the blow and moved forward with his arms semi-extended, obviously planning to dive for Wolf's legs for another shooting technique to repeat his mounting procedure.

He's more comfortable on the ground, Wolf thought. Like any wrestler would be.

Wolf danced away, snapping out a few more punches with his left hand.

The blows seemed to have little effect, but Wolf hadn't thought they would. He was timing Storm's approaches and watching how he lowered his arms in anticipation of initiating the shoot.

His left hand shot out again with trip-hammer speed, each jab a little harder than the previous one. Storm slowed for half a second, once again lowering his arms to do a front tackle, and Wolf drove a straight right into Storm's cheek. In an instant, he twisted his upper body and delivered a left hook to the right side of the other man's temple. He crumpled to the mat.

Wolf would have been allowed by the rules of MMA to mount his foe and keep right on punching until the ref stepped in, but such a move was anathema to Wolf in a sporting event. He stepped away from his fallen adversary.

Behind him, Reno was yelling and Murph was running toward them. Wolf continued to the edge of the cage and watched as Gill ran inside and knelt beside Storm, who was now trying to rise on shaky legs. He shoved Gill away and managed to get to his feet, but looked wobbly.

"Get away from me," Storm muttered. His eyes were loose and unfocused as his head swiveled from side to side, then his gaze centered on Wolf. "Come on over here and let's finish it, fucker."

Wolf stayed where he was, saying nothing.

Reno stepped between them and held up his hands.

"This session's over," he said. "Greg, hit the showers."

Storm's jaw jutted out, and he stared at Reno with a disbelieving look.

"No way, Reno," Storm said. "That guy caught me with a cheap shot, is all."

Wolf said nothing. His breathing was back under control, and he remained ready in case the other man rushed him. Wolf planned to sidestep while delivering another straight right.

But he didn't have to. Reno grabbed Storm's head

in both of his hands, moved his face close to the other man's, and whispered something to him.

"No," Storm said. "No, I wasn't. No way."

Reno whispered something else.

Storm's jaw was still sagging, and Wolf noticed that a stream of blood was cascading from the man's right ear.

With a pair like that, Wolf thought, he should've kept the headgear on.

CHAPTER 10

NEAR COY'S AUTO REBUILDERS
PHOENIX, ARIZONA

Cummins lowered the binoculars and rested them on the steering wheel. He didn't like being so close to McNamara, but at least, as far as they knew, Wolf wasn't with him.

"He still in there?" Zerbe asked, snapping a freshly charged battery into the drone.

"I haven't seen him come out yet," he said and then watched as Zerbe lit up a cigarette.

They'd followed McNamara in the Corolla, courtesy of the GPS tracker Zerbe had planted on it earlier at the bail bondsman's office. McNamara had appeared to be alone when he entered the building.

"Well, keep watching. He's probably going to pick up his own car."

Cummins picked up the binoculars and held them to the lenses of his glasses. It made for an uncomfortable and not entirely clear view, and he wondered if he should try contacts like Zerbe had.

His glasses were as thick as mine, Cummins thought. And it would change my appearance.

The large overhead door of the main building next to the office began to fold upward. After it locked in the open position, somebody drove a black Escalade through the door and parked next to the side door of the office. A guy in overalls got out, then McNamara emerged with somebody in a short-sleeved shirt from the office area. The two of them stood by the Escalade talking. The guy in the short-sleeved shirt was gesticulating and grinning. McNamara was smiling as well. Then they shook hands, and McNamara walked around to the driver's door of the Escalade and got in.

"Looks like he's getting ready to move," Cummins said. "A black Cadillac Escalade." He read off the plate number.

Zerbe grunted an approval and made a few adjustments to the drone before setting it down next to their Lexus.

"Get ready to follow him at a safe distance," Zerbe said. "We'll track him with the drone."

Cummins was hoping Zerbe would toss the cigarette away before he got back in the car, but he didn't.

No such luck.

***

Mixed Martial Arts Fighting Academy
Phoenix, Arizona

"Hot damn," McNamara said with a grin. "I guess I missed all the fun, huh?"

"Fun ain't the word for it," Wolf said. "But I got some money to put toward our bills."

McNamara was about to speak but glanced around and thought better of it. The crowd that had gathered to watch the amped-up sparring session had lingered. Reno walked over to them with a concerned expression on his face. He nodded to McNamara, then addressed Wolf.

"I got Barbie cutting you a check," he said.

"How's Greg?" Wolf said. "I didn't mean to hurt him."

Reno shook his head. "He's always had more muscle than brains. Gill's in the locker room now, convincing him to go to the ER to get checked out."

"The ER?" McNamara said. "What kind of sparring session was this?"

"It got a little bit out of control," Reno said, then looked at Wolf. "I ain't blaming you, Steve. I know he fouled you a couple of times."

Three to be exact, Wolf thought, but he didn't say anything.

"Yeah," a familiar voice said amongst the throng of people still milling about. "I'd call it a first-class ass-whipping."

Wolf turned and saw the two FBI men, Franker and Turner, approaching. They had on loose-fitting windbreakers and Dockers, which must have been standard Bureau garb for the casual look. Franker had a broad smirk on his face.

"You learn to fight like that in prison, Wolf?" he asked.

"No," he said. "In the Army."

"You're a pretty brutal guy, aren't you?" Turner said. His beard was so dark on his cheeks that he looked like he had a five o'clock shadow even though it was only noon.

"You learn a lot of things in combat," McNamara said. "Like how to survive and make the other guy hurt worse, but I don't suppose either of you two snowflakes would know anything about that."

Franker's eyes narrowed as he looked at him.

"Looks like you've been engaging in a little combat of your own," he said. "What happened to your head?"

"Your girlfriend closed her legs too fast," McNamara said.

The FBI man's face twitched.

Wolf didn't want Mac engaging in verbal sparring with the feds. Talking to them was a no-win situation.

"Glad you enjoyed it," he said. "Now if you'll excuse

us, I've got a hot date with a cold shower."

Reno was standing there in silence, eyeing the two FBI men.

"No wheelchair today, Mr. Garth?" Franker said.

"What are you guys doing here?" Reno asked.

Franker turned to him with an amused expression.

"We just came by to check out your facilities here. Nice place."

"Yeah, thanks. Now, if you don't mind, this is my place of business, and I've got work to do."

"Where'd you get the money to open up a place this size?" Franker asked, looking around. "Lots of equipment. Man, those two rings there? Must've cost a pretty penny."

"I won a couple of big MMA matches," Reno said. "Got me some money, so I invested it. Why? Is that a crime or something?"

Franker shrugged and scratched his ear. "That depends."

"Depends?" Reno's brow furrowed. "What do you mean?"

"It depends on how you got the capital," Franker said. "And if it was done by legitimate means."

Reno gaped and stared at the FBI man, not saying anything.

"Reno, don't pay any attention to these guys," Mc-Namara said. "They're just trying to rattle you. That's the way they work—intimidation and threats. They're a disgrace to the government."

"Would you like us to look into your finances too, Mr. McNamara?" Turner asked.

McNamara turned toward the man. "You're gonna do whatever the hell you want to do, but just make sure you do it legally and not try to trump up something like you did against General Mike Flynn."

The FBI men exchanged glances.

"What are you doing here anyway?" Reno said. "If you're looking to buy a membership, our club's closed."

"Actually, the Bureau's gym is a lot cleaner," Franker said, the cocky smile still gracing his lips. "We just stopped by today to see if your memory's improved at all."

"Imagine our surprise," Turner said, "when we happened to see all three of the principals in the Mexican murder investigation together, snug as three bugs in a rug."

"Bugs?" Reno said. "You calling me a bug?"

"Easy, big guy," Wolf said, stepping forward. "You don't have to talk to these guys. You've already given them your statement."

"Ah," Turner said. "The jailhouse lawyer speaks."

"I think it's time for you two to leave," Wolf said.

"Go find a legitimate case to work," McNamara added.

"We've got a legitimate case, all right," Franker said. "And we're working it right now."

"Then work it someplace else," Reno said. "I already told you I don't remember shit."

"Don't you want to get to the bottom of who killed your buddy Preen?" Turner asked.

"Maybe he already knows," Franker said. "How about that, Mr. McNamara? You know who killed him?"

McNamara started to speak, but Wolf grabbed his arm.

"None of us are talking to you without a lawyer present."

The feds exchanged glances again and smiled.

"Why's that?" Franker asked. "You three got something to hide?"

"That's on the advice of our attorneys," Wolf said. "Now, if you'll excuse us."

He grabbed Reno and McNamara and steered them toward the locker room.

"Barbie," Reno called out over his shoulder, "start recording them two guys. I asked them to leave, and they're disrupting the business. I'm gonna call my brother."

"Lieutenant Garth of the Phoenix PD?" Franker said, the Cheshire cat smile still in place. "I think we've worked a few cases with him."

Barbie ran over, holding her smartphone in front of her.

Franker raised his hands and said, "Sorry to hear

you're refusing to cooperate with the FBI, Misters Garth, McNamara, and Wolf. We'll be back if and when we get those subpoenas for that federal grand jury."

"If and when you get them," McNamara said, "you know where to find us. In the meantime, quit harassing us innocent victims and go find some real criminals to arrest."

The feds exchanged glances a final time, smiling as if they were sharing a private joke, and headed for the door.

***

Adjacent Strip Mall
Phoenix, Arizona

"Shit," Cummins said. "Are those guys feds?"

Zerbe manipulated the twin joysticks and the visual display on the monitor became clearer.

"US government license plates," he said. "I'd say that was a fair assumption."

"Shit," Cummins said again. "This complicates things."

Zerbe was silent, watching the monitor and manipulating the drone.

"Did you fucking hear me?" Cummins said.

"I did," Zerbe said. "Makes sense. There were

several Americans killed on foreign soil. That makes it a case for the FBI." He manipulated the joystick a bit more. "Looks like they're coming back out now. I'd better get this up higher, so they don't hear it."

"Do you realize what this might mean?"

Zerbe frowned, obviously irritated at having his concentration disrupted.

"It doesn't mean shit," he said. "As long as we keep our heads and get in and out quick."

"In and out quick? You think they aren't going to be suspicious if some South African goon squad busts in and kills a bunch of people? We need to keep our eye on the ball, which in this case is the statue."

"Don't tell me how to do my job," Zerbe snarled.

"I'm not." Cummins felt a momentary surge of panic. "But we should call for instructions."

"Call whoever you fucking want," Zerbe said. "Just quit bothering me while I'm flying."

Flying, Cummins thought. As if he was a real pilot. What an idiot.

"Okay," Zerbe said. "The federal boys are leaving. I'm going to bring the drone back, and then we're going to sneak up and put a GPS tracker on Mc-Namara's SUV."

"Huh?" Cummins felt the roiling in his stomach begin. "Are you crazy? What if they see you?"

"It'll allow us to keep track of and locate them. We can't keep flying the drone round the clock. The batteries won't last." Zerbe looked askance. "I thought you had a background in military intelligence? You should know the value of gathering intel."

"This is too dangerous," Cummins said. It was all he could do to keep the contents of his stomach down. "I want no part of it."

Zerbe turned and looked at him. "Listen to me, you…" He stopped talking and compressed his lips. "We've both got a lot on the line here. Like I told you before, it's do or die. Failure is not an option. But if we do this right, we'll both be rich."

Cummins swallowed as best he could, then nodded.

The drone swooped in, and Zerbe went back to the controls and completed a safe landing. "Now, as soon as we break down here, we're going to drive over to that parking lot. If the Escalade's still parked where it was, you're going to stop right behind it. I'll be in and out of the car in a flash, and we'll plant the tracker. Understand?"

Cummins nodded.

Zerbe got out and retrieved the drone, which he'd managed to land a few feet away.

Maybe this wouldn't be too bad, Cummins thought. After all, Zerbe was the one getting out of the car, and even though both Wolf and McNamara knew him, he had changed his appearance a bit.

And he can move a little faster than I can.

Zerbe placed the drone in the back of the Lexus

and dug around in the black nylon backpack that had his electronic stuff, then got back into the passenger side.

"Let's go," he said, holding up a small rectangular object the size of a half-eaten donut.

The thought of food made Cummins' stomach curdle again, and he placed a hand on his substantial belly for reassurance. The PI's body odor made that even more difficult.

"Let's go, dammit," Zerbe said with a wry grin. "And try not to puke."

Cummins was starting to sweat again. But Zerbe was right. The FBI had to be investigating that incident in Mexico, and both of them had been involved up to their necks. Moreover, Wolf knew they were involved. He'd seen them in the departing helicopter. If he sang to the feds, it wouldn't be long before they'd come knocking, and Fallotti and Von Dien weren't about to take the chance of putting themselves in the federal crosshairs.

Cummins tried to swallow, but his throat felt... extra dry.

They'll eliminate me for sure, he thought. *I'll be another loose end to them. Zerbe most likely will be, too. If this thing snowballs and the feds get involved, they're not going to want to take the chance on any of it leading back to them.*

That made formulating his escape plan even

more imperative.

But what about Zerbe? Maybe it was time for the two of them to start considering a bailout plan that would leave both of them financially set. The question was, could Zerbe be trusted as an ally?

Cummins trusted the sleazy PI about as far as he could throw him, and for all he knew, Von Dien might have told him to take care of *all* the loose ends, including Cummins, the permanent way. With the squad of his South African buddy-boys arriving, he'd be at a distinct tactical disadvantage.

He didn't even want to think about those jokers right now. He couldn't afford to.

But one thing he did know; he had to get himself a gun and be ready to use it discreetly when the time came.

***

Mixed Martial Arts Fighting Academy
Phoenix, Arizona

Wolf took a "combat shower" and was dressed inside of ten minutes. After packing all his gear into his ditty bag, he walked up to the front office to look for Mac and Reno. He found them in Reno's office. Reno looked nervous as he sat behind his desk, and McNamara sat beside him, leaning close and talking in a low voice.

"That's the way those bastards work, I'm telling ya," McNamara said. "They come in threatening you and making it seem like they're gonna haul you in on a bullshit charge."

"A federal grand jury ain't no bullshit," Reno countered.

McNamara brought his hand up and massaged his temples.

"It's just a damn smoke screen," Wolf said, entering the office and closing the door behind him. He dropped his ditty bag on the floor and pulled up a chair in front of Reno's desk. "If they had anything solid, they'd be giving us subpoenas or reading us our rights."

"Shit." Reno frowned. "*That* makes me feel a lot better."

"It's true," Wolf said. "Look, we were all down there to make an apprehension. Technically, we were acting without any lawful authority on foreign soil. We took Accondras into custody with the intention of bringing him back here to face charges. Then he was taken from us, and we were held as prisoners and about to be executed. We defended ourselves. What choice did we have?"

"Maybe we should just tell them that then," Reno said.

"No." McNamara's voice was loud and firm.

"That'd send us all to prison, Mexican-style."

"But if it was self-defense—"

"Self-defense don't mean shit down south of the border," McNamara said. "And up here, we'd be charged with lying to the FBI. Not to mention maybe having to go down to Mexico to prove our innocence. You got that kind of time and money? 'Cause I sure as hell don't."

Reno sat in silence, staring at the floor.

"Those bastards killed Herc," he said, his voice hardly more than a whisper.

"Yeah, and we killed the ones that did it," Wolf said. He made sure to include the "we" in that statement, even though he'd done the killing. "It doesn't alter the facts. And Mac's right. We've already given our statements to the FBI. If we change those now, we're dead meat."

Reno pursed his lips.

"How much of all this did you tell your lawyer?" McNamara asked.

"Just what you told me to say, Mac." His voice sounded strained. "You drilled it into me when we were driving. I was shot, remember?"

"Yeah," McNamara said. "I was too. Now, what did you tell your lawyer?"

Reno heaved a sigh. "I told him we went down to Mexico, me and Herc, to have some fun. Then I said we met up with you in Cancun," He nodded at Mc-

Namara, "and went out looking for some pussy. Our driver took us to the rough side of town, and some dudes jumped us and shot us to pieces. I told him I didn't remember nothing else."

"That's a good story," Wolf said, thinking they'd told Shemp practically the whole shebang, leaving out the part about Wolf tidying things up at the Mayan ruins. But if you couldn't trust your lawyer and attorney-client privilege, who could you trust? "Stick to it, and you'll be all right."

"We all will be," McNamara added.

Reno slowly nodded. "I guess you're right. Plus, you guys saved my life. I owe you."

Wolf and McNamara looked at each other, and Mac gave Wolf a fractional nod and a quick wink.

Wolf felt like he was trying to hold a shaky engine together with duct tape and baling wire.

He glanced at his watch.

Thirteen-fifteen. That gave them forty-five minutes to get to the airport, park, and pick up Ms. Dolly and the P Patrol. And Mac had mentioned something about wanting to pick up flowers.

McNamara must have seen him checking the time, and he checked his watch also, then stood. He laid a hand on Reno's shoulder and spoke in a low, soothing voice.

"Reno, don't let this stress you out none. When our backs were against the wall, we did what we had to do and came through it as brothers, stronger than we were before. It'll be all right."

Wolf knew he'd caught a phantom glimpse of Command Sergeant Major James McNamara, Special Forces, counseling one of his troops in the field and helping him through a rough patch. He thought back to his own military days in the Sandbox and the 'Stan.

Leadership, the art of leading and directing men to accomplish the mission. Mac was a master at it.

***

Adjacent Strip Mall
Phoenix, Arizona

Cummins took several long steps away from the side of the car, leaned over, and puked on the hot asphalt. His nervous stomach had done it to him again. It was so damn hot that the stench rose toward him from the puddle, and he wondered if it was simultaneously evaporating. God, he hated this desert climate. It reminded him too much of his brief stint in Iraq, even though he'd tried to remain inside the comfort of the air-conditioned structures when he was there, leaving it to grunts like Wolf to stand guard outside the walls.

His thoughts returned to Wolf, which made his stomach even more queasy, so he did his best to cast him out of his mind. Plus, he had to get back into the car to hear at least part of what Zerbe was saying. The phone call had proved to be both irritating and disconcerting.

After Cummins had called Fallotti and reported the sighting of the feds, the son of a bitch had gone silent for about thirty seconds, then said, "Put Zerbe on the phone."

Zerbe... Did they trust the sleazy PI more than they did him?

Christ, the guy probably wasn't even an American citizen. Cummins recalled his quarantine in upstate New York. It had been Zerbe who'd picked him up from the isolated cabin and brought him to see Fallotti and Von Dien. Had Zerbe been in isolation after their return from Mexico as well? That didn't seem likely, although he had expressed surprise when Fallotti let it slip that both of their debrief sessions had been recorded. Given what they'd said during those things, there was enough to ensure absolute loyalty.

Or absolute obedience.

Put Zerbe on the phone...

It was tantamount to a dismissal, and it had been a not-so-subtle reminder of who was in charge here. Cummins wondered why he'd been included, then it dawned on him. He was the only one who'd seen half of the artifact, so he had a good grasp of what this other half might look like. He'd been cast in the role of authenticator.

But once that was done, once they obtained possession of it, would he become as expendable as the plaster bandito shell that housed the damn thing? Was Fallotti now telling Zerbe to eliminate another expendable loose end?

He wiped his mouth with the back of his hand, stepped around the puddle of vomit, and got back into the car, struggling to fit himself behind the wheel.

Zerbe was still in the passenger seat and on the phone, nodding and emitting a series of monosyllabic grunts.

"Yeah... Yeah... I know... Okay..." He cradled the phone between his shoulder and jaw and fished out a cigarette.

"Lemme talk to him," Cummins said. The sour taste of the regurgitation was still in his mouth, and he imagined his breath was just as foul, but he didn't care at this point. He reached for the phone.

Zerbe leaned away from him, still muttering one-word replies. He was obviously getting instructions about something.

I wonder if they're talking about me? Cummins thought.

Zerbe lit the cigarette, and a cloud of smoke filled the interior of the vehicle.

Cummins wanted to rip the damn phone away or at least tell him to put it on speaker.

Before he could utter another word, Zerbe mumbled a quick, "Yeah, will do," then, "Goodbye." He terminated the call, looked at Cummins, and canted his head, blowing twins plumes of smoke out of his nostrils.

"They're none too pleased," Zerbe said. "But I guess you already knew that."

"Why didn't you let me talk to them?"

Zerbe shrugged. "They didn't want to stay on the line too long."

What the hell did *that* mean?

"I hope they're not trying to blame us," Cummins said, making sure he used the plural personal pronoun to designate both him and Zerbe. "It isn't our fault."

"I explained that."

"What else did he say?"

Zerbe's profile was framed with a halo of smoke. "That he wants us to proceed with the utmost caution."

"That means we can't have your South African Musketeers acting like stormtroopers," Cummins said.

"Admittedly. He also wants us to use burner phones from here on out."

"Burner phones?" Cummins tried to figure out Fallotti's reasoning for that.

"Yeah. A sensible precaution for all of us."

And a way for Fallotti and Von Dien to distance themselves should this operation go badly. Or in anticipation of tying up all the loose ends. Perhaps it was time to talk to Zerbe about an alliance.

The smoke was irritating Cummins, and he coughed.

Or perhaps not. There was no way of telling what Fallotti's orders to the PI had actually been.

"Okay," Cummins said.

"He wants me to hold on to your phone, too," Zerbe said, slipping Cummins' phone into his pocket.

"What? No way."

Zerbe laughed. "Relax. I'm not going to deprive you of it. Just lock it in my room safe at the hotel."

Cummins didn't like that one bit. He felt like they were laying the groundwork to erase him. He could refuse, but this South African prick was tough, and they still had to work together—for the time being.

"Okay," Cummins said. "But I want the combination."

"Sure thing." Zerbe blew out more smoke and looked at the drone. It had returned to their vicinity, courtesy of the auto-return feature. "Let me replace that battery, and we'll see if our friends have left the gym." He popped open the door and started to get out.

"Just remember," Cummins said. "I'm the only one who knows what this damn artifact looks like."

Zerbe paused and smiled. When he spoke, each word was accompanied by a wisp of smoke. "We're not about to forget how important you are."

We? Cummins thought. This South African prick's

grouped himself with that damn Fallotti and that bastard Von Dien and is leaving me on the outside.

A rush of bile snaked its way up his esophagus and flooded the back of his throat.

***

Phoenix International Airport
Phoenix, Arizona

Wolf watched with a mild case of amusement as Mac wheeled the big Escalade into the hourly parking lane of the airport garage and lowered the window to grab the parking ticket. As soon as the gate in front of them lifted, he zoomed through and drove up the ramp and into the structure, pausing to glance through the moon roof.

"At least around here, we lost that damn drone that was hovering around Reno's," McNamara said. "You think that was those damn feds keeping an eye on us?"

"Hard to say. Those things are pretty popular."

"Yeah, well, if it comes over my property, it'll be the last place it ever flies."

Wolf smirked.

They passed into the penumbra of the parking structure.

"Wouldn't it be simpler to go to the cell phone lot and wait for them to call us after they got their bags?" Wolf asked.

"Huh-uh. This way, we can park and meet them just outside the arrivals gate." McNamara smiled. "I don't want to miss watching the three of them sashay down the corridor." He frowned and tapped his shirt. "Wish I would've had a chance to dress up a little better."

"You look fine," Wolf said. "They'll probably be pretty casual, too. After all, they're wearing traveling clothes."

"With Ms. Dolly, there ain't no such thing as casual. She's first-class all the way."

Wolf remembered the first time he'd seen the three of them walking through the casino of the Shamrock Hotel in Las Vegas a month or so ago, looking so stunning that they could have been fashion models on a Victoria's Secret runway. Well, maybe not quite that revealing, but first-class all the way was something of an understatement.

"Didn't have time to get those flowers, either," McNamara said. "All because of them damn feds."

McNamara pulled onto the third level and began negotiating the wide circular aisles, which appeared pretty full. They passed the entrance to the terminal and began another rotation.

"What time is it?" he asked.

Wolf glanced at his watch. "Thirteen-fifty-six. You want me to start counting down the seconds?"

"Don't be a smart ass," McNamara said, continuing to scan the lot. Finally, he smiled as he saw a man and a woman moving toward a parked car near the entrance. He pulled to a stop in the center of the aisle and waited.

"Let's hope they're in a hurry to get out of here," he said, drumming his thumbs on the wheel. "Otherwise, I might have to pull out my Glock."

Wolf chuckled, imagining Mac making good on his threat.

The man unlocked the car and opened the door for his female companion. He then waited for her to enter the car and closed the door. His head swiveled toward the Escalade, and McNamara nodded, smiled, and waved. The wait stretched into the better part of a minute as the man loaded the luggage into the trunk, closed it, and entered the car.

"What the hell's taking him so damn long?" Mc-Namara asked.

Another car had pulled into the aisle behind them and honked.

McNamara ignored it and continued to wait.

The driver behind them laid on his horn.

McNamara exhaled slowly. "That guy's pissin' me off to a high degree of pisstastity."

Finally, the car in the parking spot backed out, and McNamara pulled in. The car that had been behind then gave another derisive toot as it passed.

McNamara waved.

"Maybe I'll have you drive on the way back," he said, handing the keys to Wolf.

McNamara was walking with a spring in his step again.

Wolf pocketed the keys and grinned. "Is that so I'll be the one paying the parking fee?"

They went to a section of elevators and down to the second level, then headed over an elevated walkway to the terminal building. Inside, they followed the arrow prompts to the arrivals area.

"Time?" McNamara asked, studied the list of flights arriving and landing.

"Fourteen-oh-eight," Wolf said.

"Damn," McNamara said. "Looks like their flight already landed. Hope we didn't miss them."

"You want me to go down and check baggage claim?"

McNamara was considering that when his lips curled into a smile. He shook his head as he looked past the TSA checkpoint and down the long corridor that led to the gates.

Wolf looked too, then he saw them. The three women, one white, one Hispanic, and one black, were walking abreast, each tugging a carry-on-sized suitcase.

All Louie Vuitton luggage, Wolf thought, remembering being in their suite in Las Vegas. First-class babes.

Ms. Dolly was in the center of the trio, flanked by Yolanda on the right and Brenda on the left. They were dressed in jeans and t-shirts. Ms. Dolly's was white and had a flowery design and the letter T on the front of it, stretched tight by her substantial bosom. Brenda's was a purplish mix with *¿Ahora?* in white letters across the front.

Wolf centered his gaze on Yolanda and relished the memory of their night together. Her hair was back in the familiar ponytail, and she had on dangling gold earrings that looked like Indian arrowheads. Her t-shirt was yellow and had Double Trouble written in red script across the front. She smiled when she saw them.

Or maybe she's smiling at me, Wolf thought.

After they passed TSA, Ms. Dolly and Brenda leaned forward and kissed Mac, while Yolanda embraced Wolf and planted a kiss on his lips.

"I was hoping you hadn't forgotten me," she whispered in his ear.

"No way that's gonna happen," he whispered back.

"*Siempre buenos amantes*," Brenda said, rolling her eyes.

Always good lovers, Wolf translated in his mind and hoped it wasn't far from the truth.

"Y'all been waiting long?" Ms. Dolly asked in her East Texas drawl.

"Just since the last time we saw you," McNamara said.

Ms. Dolly laughed. "Sugar, you can always make me laugh when I need it, and after dealing with those damn TSA idiots in Vegas, believe me, I need it."

"Don't tell me they wanted to do a strip search," McNamara said. "But if they did, I couldn't blame 'em."

"You wouldn't believe all the hoops they make you jump through just because you have some guns in your checked luggage." Ms. Dolly glanced at Wolf. "So, now that you and Yolanda are through swappin' spit, how you doing, Steve?"

Wolf emitted a self-conscious chuckle. The kiss had been more perfunctory than romantic.

The trio of women laughed, and they all proceeded toward the escalators.

"Why'd you need to bring your guns along?" McNamara said as they descended. "I coulda loaned you some of mine."

"We're here on business, sugar," Ms. Dolly said, then added with a crafty smile, "But I'm sure we can put that off till tomorrow, like Scarlett O'Hara used to say."

"Great," McNamara said. "I'll make reservations at a nice restaurant. Where would you like to eat?"

"How about that same place you took us to the last time? That steakhouse place."

"Ah, Mac?" Wolf started, remembering the scene in the emergency room the night before.

"Charlie's?" McNamara said, taking out his phone.

"Consider it done. I'll reserve my usual table and tell the piano player to brush up on *As Time Goes By*."

Wolf recalled the scene in *Casablanca* and remembered the result when Ingrid Bergman asked Dooley Wilson to "Play the song, Sam." He hoped it wouldn't lead to a similar result if Kasey had indeed switched her reservations to this evening.

Of all the gin joints in all the world, he thought, *I hope she doesn't walk into ours.*

***

The Elegant Suites Hotel
Phoenix, Arizona

Cummins chewed three more antacid tablets and washed them down with a substantial gulp of Mylanta. One thing was for sure; he was going to have to see a specialist about his stomach once this was over. Of course, once the stress of this whole thing ended, the perennial queasiness might just disappear. At least, that was what he told himself. It would be a relief to get away from Zerbe, who was stretched out on his bed, drinking one of the miniature bottles of booze from the mini-bar and talking on his cell phone. Cummins thought about getting up and going back to his room, but his cell phone was still in Zerbe's pocket, and the prick hadn't given him the combination to the room safe yet. He began to rethink the whole burner phone situation, but he didn't know if he could get his phone back from the sleazy PI.

Whatever I'm going to do, he thought, *I'd better get it done before the goon squad gets here.*

It still bothered him that Fallotti had told him to give the phone to Zerbe before.

After all, I've got a safe in my room too.

He listened to Zerbe's end of the conversation and watched as he shook a cigarette out of his pack.

"No, I don't know shit about this place." Zerbe placed the cigarette between his lips and lit it. "And I need to wait for my team leader to get here anyway."

Team leader… That had to mean that South African guy who headed up the Lion Team. What had Zerbe called him? Lionus or something?

"Okay, Dill," Zerbe said. "Call me when you get here, and I'll talk you in." He listened, then added, "That won't be a problem. After all, these guys are here teaching a desert warfare class." Zerbe listened some more, then laughed. "Yeah, right. Me too."

He hung up, removed the cigarette from his mouth, and took another swig from the tiny bottle.

"That was my associate Dill." Zerbe grinned so widely that Cummins could see the gold in the man's back teeth. "Our equipment manager."

Cummins figured that meant the guy driving here from LA with the weapons. He wondered if he could get a gun too.

"When's he arriving?" Cummins asked.

"A couple more hours."

"How about those Lion Team guys?"

Zerbe smiled again. "Any time now. I figure once they get here and settle in, Luan and I can go meet Dill and pick up what we need."

"Where's that gonna be?"

Zerbe drank the last of the amber fluid in the tiny bottle before he answered.

"I'll let him pick the spot. He'll call and give me the coordinates." He snorted. "The guy's a bit paranoid, but who can blame him?" He took one more drag on the cigarette and dropped it into the bottle. The ash hissed, and a trail of smoke wafted up through the tiny neck.

"Give me back my phone," Cummins said. "I need to make a call."

Zerbe shook his head. "Huh-uh. Not a good idea. Boss' orders, remember?"

"Yeah, I remember, all right. But how come you get to use your phone, and I can't use mine?"

Zerbe sighed and rocked his head to the side like he was trying to explain the concept of jurisprudence to a third-grader.

"Because," he said, "as I told you, Dill is on his way here with our equipment. He has my number, and I need to be in contact with him until we meet. Once that happens and the transaction has been completed, my phone will go in the safe along with yours." He paused and raised both eyebrows. "*Capisce?*"

"I told you, I don't speak that South African shit."

Zerbe rolled his eyes. "That's Italian, and just a word of warning—Luan and the boys are very nationalistic. Don't say anything disparaging about South Africa in front of them."

"Hey, I'm still an important part of this operation," Cummins said. "So don't tell me what I should and shouldn't do."

"Believe me, Luan's not the man you want to make angry."

"Fuck him," Cummins said. "And I want to use my phone. Give it back to me. Now."

Zerbe got up and walked to the wall safe. He pressed the keyboard and the safe beeped, then he jerked it open. He removed the cell phone from his pocket and slipped it inside. Cummins watched as Zerbe shut the door and input the locking code once more, but this time Cummins was watching more closely and saw it: P880.

"Sorry," Zerbe said. "Boss' orders."

Cummins thought, That asshole's a real prick.

They stood facing each other, saying nothing, and Cummins wondered if he could just bulldoze over the sleazebag and open the safe himself. He was bigger than Zerbe, but he'd never been good at fighting or intimidation. In the Army, he knew the enlisted men called him disparaging names behind his back despite him being an officer. If Fallotti hadn't pulled those strings to get him sent to Iraq and assigned to MI four years ago, he wouldn't be in this fucking mess now. Back then, all he had to do was pay Eagan and his Viper team under the table to get the artifact and smuggle it back to the US in hold baggage. They'd fucked that up royally, killing those ragheads and framing Wolf. This South African prick was from the same mold as the enlisted vermin.

This guy makes his living walking on the shady side, he thought, *while I'm an attorney. Better to wait.*

He looked away first and walked over to the mini-bar.

"Hey," Zerbe said. "Don't drink up all my whiskey, now."

His tone sounded almost cordial, but Cummins wasn't fooled. Before he could answer, the room phone rang.

Zerbe strolled over to the desk and answered it.

"Hello?" His mouth worked into a lips-only smile. "Yes, they're the ones I mentioned. I'll be right there."

He set the phone back in its cradle.

"They're here," he said. "I'll be right back."

Cummins continued to peruse the contents of the mini-bar and grabbed a candy bar. He began to unwrap it as Zerbe continued to the door, casting a quick glance back at the wall safe as if to confirm that he'd locked it before slipping out the door.

As soon as the door had closed, Cummins went to the safe and punched P880.

The stupid prick, he thought as the door of the safe popped open. *Did he think I wouldn't see?*

Cummins reached inside and grabbed his phone. The LCD screen was blank, so he pressed the button to turn it on. It illuminated, so Cummins brought it to his mouth and said, "Call Fallotti."

He waited for the voice activation program to begin dialing the selected number, but when he glanced at the screen again, he saw a flashing message.

NO SERVICE

How could that be? He'd just charged it this morning.

He pressed the button to activate the phone lexicon and pressed the button.

NO SERVICE flashed again.

Then it dawned on him. Fallotti had somehow canceled his phone service.

Was this the first step in erasing him as well?

He felt an almost uncontrollable urge to throw up, coupled this time with an overwhelming need to void his bowels. He shoved the phone back into the safe, closed the door, and input the locking code.

Got to go bad, he thought, digging for the key to his room.

He rushed over to the door and pulled it open, only to see Zerbe standing there grinning, along with a bunch of the biggest, meanest, roughest looking guys he'd ever seen.

CHAPTER 11

CHARLIE'S STEAKHOUSE
PHOENIX, ARIZONA

They hadn't even ordered their food yet. Wolf figured there was going to be trouble when the maître d' seated Kasey and Shemp a table away from their booth. Wolf and McNamara sat on either side with Yolanda, Brenda, and Ms. Dolly on the circular seat. Kasey's eyes widened, then narrowed as she glared at them. Shemp's eyebrows rose, and a nervous smile stretched his lips. Kasey grabbed the maître d's arm and asked to be seated at another table.

"Of course, madam," the man said, looking strained. "I'll see what's available."

Kasey and Shemp started to follow him, but McNamara was already out of his seat and calling to her. He turned to address the booth.

"Hey, it's my daughter," he said. "I'll introduce you."

In two long steps, he cut in front of them.

Ms. Dolly leaned over the table and addressed Wolf in a low whisper. "Ain't she the one that was at the airport when we dropped y'all off from getting' back from Mexico?"

Wolf nodded, not wanting to comment on how poorly that introduction had gone.

"Shucks," Ms. Dolly said, turning to Brenda. "If this goes like the last time, remind me not to say anything later about Daddy's little girl."

Brenda murmured something in Spanish that Wolf couldn't discern and wondered if Ms. Dolly was fluent as well.

Both of them switched on their most radiant smiles, as did Yolanda, when Mac came walking back, holding his daughter and Shemp by their left and right upper arms, respectively. Shemp was dressed in a gray suit and a red tie, and Kasey wore the low-cut evening style dress she'd had on the night before. Wolf and Mac, as well as the P Patrol, were all casually dressed in blue jeans and running shoes.

"Ladies, this is my daughter Kasey and her fella." He turned to face Kasey. "This is Ms. Dolly Kline, Ms. Brenda Carrera, and Ms. Yolanda Moore. They work in bail enforcement just like me and Steve, and they call themselves the P—"

"Hell's Belles," Ms. Dolly interrupted. "We're

thinkin' of changing our name to that. My, y'all look so elegant. So, how are ya?"

Brenda and Yolanda muttered the standard greetings. Wolf just sat there, regretting that he hadn't dissuaded Mac from booking reservations at this place.

Kasey raised one eyebrow and glanced away, making no effort to disguise that she wasn't liking what she saw.

"Pleased to meet you," Shemp said, the nervous smile still plastered in place.

"Actually," Kasey said, "we met before. At the airport. The last time you were here."

"That's right," Ms. Dolly said. "We did, didn't we? Nice seein' you again."

"Yeah," Kasey said. "Excuse us, we're going to another table."

With that, she extricated her arm from her father's grip and started to move away, then stopped. "And Dad, Rod's my fiancé, not my 'fella.'"

Shemp emitted a half-hearted laugh that was followed by another quick smile as he trailed her toward the front of the restaurant.

McNamara stood in the aisle in silence, looking after them with a wistful expression. He shook his head and then resumed his seat next to Ms. Dolly.

"She's a very pretty gal," Ms. Dolly said.

McNamara nodded but said nothing.

The five of them in the booth sat in silence for several seconds, then McNamara muttered, "I'm sorry."

Ms. Dolly slapped him on the shoulder and smiled. "Hey, don't be. Ain't nothin' a drink or two won't cure. Besides, this is supposed to be a working dinner. We got business to discuss." She was wearing a black sleeveless blouse, and when she lifted her arm to summon one of the waiters, Wolf was surprised to see how muscular her arm was.

"We need some libations," she told the waiter. "Make mine a whiskey sour."

McNamara, still looking forlorn, ordered a B and B, and the rest of them ordered wine. When the waiter had left, Ms. Dolly leaned forward and said with a grin, "Well, whaddaya think? Should we change our name to Hell's Belles, or what?"

"You'll always be the P Patrol to me," McNamara told her.

Ms. Dolly slapped his arm affectionately. "You got that right, sugar. So tell me, how are we gonna grab this turkey, Krenshaw?"

McNamara snapped out of his depression. "We're already working on it."

That surprised Wolf, who knew next to nothing about any efforts.

"I got Kasey looking into both the sister and the girlfriend's credit card usage," McNamara said. "Girlfriend rented a car before our boy Willard bailed out. One of the conditions of his release was that he surrender his passport and appear in person at his next court date, which he didn't. When he didn't show up for his arraignment, his lawyer filed some kind of bullshit brief to get a two-week extension date, which is up this coming Monday. If our boy don't show, the Pope's on the line for the bond."

"Lawyer on the lam," Ms. Dolly said. "But we already know all that, sugar. The trail led here, right?"

McNamara nodded. "His sister lives here, and as far as we can tell, she and the girlfriend are running interference for him. Willard and his lady have been staying in a couple different hotels and motels in the area. Most likely, they're trying to get fake passports and some funds to fly the coop."

"So, it becomes a matter of following the paper trail to see where he's holed up?" Ms. Dolly asked.

McNamara nodded. "I've got Kasey working on that. She's a whiz at tracing that kind of stuff down."

Ms. Dolly's eyes caught Wolf's for a brief moment, then she said, "Well, that's good. I've got my hacker guy doin' pretty much the same thing, so, hopefully, between the two of them, they'll come up with some good locations."

"Not to rain on this parade," Wolf said, "but isn't organized crime looking for this guy too?"

"That's the rumor," Ms. Dolly said. "Which is why I told the Pope we were gonna need you two as muscle. Plus an increase in our bonus."

"You can be our bodyguards," Brenda added.

"We'll make sure to do that," McNamara said with a wink.

Wolf felt Yolanda's hand squeeze his thigh under the table.

The waiter returned with a tray holding the drinks. The conversation paused while he set a glass in front of each of them, then left.

Ms. Dolly lifted hers and held it high. "Sounds like this is gonna boil down to a good old-fashioned stakeout. Here's to our success."

Everybody drank to the toast, but Wolf only sipped his wine. He had the feeling he wanted to stay stone-cold sober until this lawyer on the lam case was done.

***

Luan Preetorius gazed out the tinted front passenger window of the vehicle as Zerbe drove through the darkened streets. It was still early, comparatively speaking, but he was fatigued from the constant traveling. Flying from Johannesburg to Baltimore and then on to Phoenix had been taxing, and he didn't sleep well on planes. Still, the adrenaline boost of a new mission always revived him.

Zerbe had explained it as a simple mission of staking out a couple of Americans and locating an item, a plaster statue. The surveillance equipment had looked first-rate, including a fairly sophisticated surveillance drone, and now they were going to procure some weaponry. There would be, Zerbe had told him, some tidying up of loose ends to do, but the money was substantial, and it would be paid in cash. Good old American greenbacks. Perhaps he and the rest of the team would take some much-needed R and R in Las Vegas while they were still in the States.

Or perhaps not. Canada or Mexico offered as much appeal, or maybe Costa Rica. The monetary exchange rate, the liquor, and the women would be great in any of them, and if this mission involved tactical neutralizations, it might be better to make a quick exit.

Vinnige inskywing, vinnige uitgang. Quick entry, quick exit.

That was his rule, and it had served him well up to this point. No need to change what worked.

And this one had all the earmarks of simplicity. Observe and wait. Zerbe had said that the two adversaries they'd be facing both had American military experience and were to be considered formidable. Preetorius relished the thought of facing a pair of worthy foes. It had been a while. He was less impressed by the corpulent associate named Cummins, who now sat in the rear section of the vehicle next to Rensburg. Not only did this man have thick glasses and was morbidly obese, but they'd had to stop en route to this meeting to allow him to vomit on the side of the road. He was a weakling, and Preetorius had little tolerance for weakness. But they'd worked for soft, fat men before, and as long as the money was good, it didn't matter. This one apparently had connections to the power behind the operation.

The vehicle slowed and pulled into a strip mall. Zerbe stopped in the middle of the aisle and waited. Perhaps a hundred feet in the opposite direction, another vehicle was backed in on an angle, its headlights facing them. Zerbe switched his off, then on again. The other vehicle didn't move, but Zerbe's cell phone rang.

He answered and muttered a few things that seemed to indicate they'd made the weapons connection.

Zerbe lit a cigarette, and smoke billowed around him in a translucent haze. He terminated the call, and the vehicle rolled forward slowly.

Before he could say anything, Preetorius reached over and plucked the smoldering cigarette from between Zerbe's lips. He cranked the window down and tossed it out.

"I don't like those things," he said, rolling the window back up.

Zerbe stared at him for several seconds. "That's them. They're going to lead us to a more secluded spot."

That activated a caution light in Preetorius' mind.

"How well do you know this guy?" he asked Zerbe in Afrikaans.

"Pretty well," Zerbe replied. "I've used him a time or two before, but…"

Preetorius turned to look at him.

"That's not to say," Zerbe continued, "that we shouldn't exercise due caution. If he tries anything stupid, let's consider him an expendable commodity."

"The first of many, I assume," Preetorius said.

"Correct," Zerbe said, still speaking Afrikaans. "As I told you, our employer has an aversion to loose ends."

Preetorius smiled as his fingers caressed the textured handle of his KA-BAR, anticipating the pleasure of getting a chance to use it again so soon.

***

Charlie's Steakhouse
Phoenix, Arizona

Wolf and McNamara stood side by side at the urinals in the men's washroom.

"The gals are all staying in one room at the hotel," McNamara said.

"Yeah?"

"So Ms. Dolly and Brenda sort of suggested I accompany them back there to discuss some more business."

The way he said "business" told Wolf all he needed to know. He recalled that had also been the arrangement in Las Vegas.

"Well," Wolf said, finishing up, "you are Special Forces. I'm just a Ranger."

McNamara laughed. "Besides, if I remember correctly, you and Yolanda probably have some similar things you'd like to discuss in private, right?"

Wolf had been hoping to spend some romantic time with her, but he wasn't sure how this scenario was going to play out. He didn't answer.

"So, I was thinking that maybe you could maybe take a taxi or one of them Uber things back to the ranch, and I'll meet you there in the morning," McNamara said. "I'll keep the Escalade here with me."

They both went to the array of sinks and began washing their hands.

"You sure you're up to this?" Wolf asked.

"Oh, yeah." McNamara chuckled and grinned. "Like you said, I *am* Special Forces."

Wolf laughed too. "I should ask Yolanda how she feels about this arrangement, don't you think?"

McNamara shook his wet hands and reached for one of the paper towels.

"Would be a good idea, I guess. But I think Ms. Dolly already brokered the deal."

As they walked out, they saw the women were apparently still in the ladies' room. McNamara told Wolf to wait for them and went up front to pay the bill. Presently, the doors opened, and the three of them pranced out. Yolanda walked up to him and smiled.

"Where's Mac?" Ms. Dolly asked.

"He's paying the bill," Wolf said, trying to think of a way to unobtrusively invite Yolanda back to his place.

Then he thought about it. His place wasn't exactly a plush bachelor pad. It was a two-room flat above a garage. What would a high-class lady like this think about the way he lived? Maybe it would be best to tell Mac to back off on his romantic plans.

Ms. Dolly and Brenda started walking toward the front entrance, which left Wolf and Yolanda alone in the hallway.

Wolf cleared his throat.

"I, umm…" He started to clear his throat again, giving himself time to search for the right words, still trying to predict her reaction.

Before he could speak, she reached into her purse and took out her smartphone.

"What's your address?" she asked. "I'll order us up a ride, but we'll have to stop by the hotel first so I can get my go-bag."

Wolf was both delighted and surprised. He wasn't used to the woman making command decisions, but in this case, he wasn't complaining, either.

I guess that settles that, he thought and smiled.

***

Downtown Phoenix

The two vehicles sat back to back in the semi-darkness of the deserted underpass. Cummins watched as the two big South Africans inspected the array of weaponry, two long guns and an assortment of handguns. He wanted to grab one of them for himself but didn't want to approach the group while they were involved in their selection.

Zerbe stood next to Cummins and was smoking a cigarette. Dill, the black guy Zerbe knew from LA, stood by the open rear door of the dark, windowless van, along with another black guy who was armed with some sort of big handgun on his hip.

Zerbe blew out a plume of smoke, and the warm night breeze sent it across to Cummins. He coughed.

At least the prick hadn't been smoking that long in the car before that guy Preetorius guy took it away from him. That was a good thing.

My stomach was already on the ropes, Cummins thought.

The leader, the one called Luan, picked up a blue steel semi-auto, racked back the slide, checked the chamber, then eased the slide forward. He shifted to a firing position and swiveled his body. The hammer made a dull snap, and he relaxed and hefted the weapon in his hand.

"How many magazines do you have for this one?"

he asked Dill.

"I got two, and one of them's extended," the black guy said.

"Let me see them."

A South African who was even bigger than Luan picked up an AR-15, broke it open, and began field-stripping it. He said something to Luan in what Cummins figured was their native language. He tried to remember that one's name.

"You like it, Johannes?" Zerbe asked.

The big guy grinned. "It's not my Denel, but it'll do." He turned to Dill. "Do you have an extended magazine for this one too?"

"We should only need handguns for this one," Zerbe said. "We need to keep it low-key."

"Too bad," Johannes said. He slid the bolt back into place, snapped the upper and lower receivers together, pressed in the pin, and passed the AR-15 back to Dill.

These guys spoke really good English, so Cummins wondered why they'd been speaking in that other language in the car. It not only made him feel left out, but he also wondered just what Zerbe had been saying about him.

Were they plotting against him?

First Fallotti and Von Dien had kept him isolated in that damn cabin for three weeks, then they'd sent him on this excursion, where Zerbe was calling all the shots.

Then they told Zerbe to snatch my phone, he thought. And he'd canceled his service, which Zerbe hadn't mentioned to him.

They needed him on the scene to identify the artifact and probably as insurance that Zerbe wouldn't try to abscond with the damn thing and renegotiate the deal. Cummins was also the logical choice to take the artifact back to New York.

Or was he?

He watched as the perusal continued.

Zerbe took one last drag on the cigarette, dropped it, and ground it out beneath his shoe. He walked over to the van.

"You got that snub-nose I told you to bring?" he asked.

Dill, who was chewing on a toothpick, nodded and reached into the van. He withdrew a small, shiny revolver, flipped open the cylinder, and handed it to Zerbe.

This is my chance, Cummins thought and stepped over as well.

"I need one of those too."

Zerbe glanced at him. "I thought you didn't like to get your hands dirty?"

"I don't. But I also like insurance, just in case."

"In case of what?" Zerbe said. He snapped the cylinder closed, cocked the hammer, and pointed it at Cummins. "Something like this?"

Cummins felt a rush of panic and outrage, even though he was pretty sure the damn thing wasn't loaded.

"Quit fucking around," Cummins said. It took him several seconds to think of moving out of the line of fire. "You're not supposed to point a gun at anybody you're not intending to shoot."

Zerbe dropped his hand. "You're absolutely correct." He flashed a quick grin. "So the next time I do it, you'll know the jig's up, won't you?"

His laugh was staccato and phlegmy-sounding.

The two South African goons laughed and the two gunrunners did as well, which irritated Cummins to no end.

"I want a gun, too," he insisted.

"Dill," Zerbe said, "what do you have for my corpulent friend who doesn't like to get his hands dirty?"

Dill grinned, and Cummins could see the half-chewed toothpick in the corner of his mouth. The black man looked to be sizing Cummins up.

"What you got in mind?" he asked.

Appropriate question, Cummins thought. *One I should be asking Zerbe.*

***

McNamara Ranch

Phoenix, Arizona

The lights were on in the house when Wolf and Yolanda got out of the ride-share.com car, and the motion sensor light on the garage was activated. He reached for his wallet, but she shook her head.

"I'll just put the tip on here," she said. "Don't want to mess up my rating."

"Your rating?"

"You can rate the driver's service, and he can give you a passenger rating, too. It stays on your record."

Wolf was amazed. This had been his first time using such a service, and he didn't particularly care for it. The vehicle was a Honda Civic and had the feel of being somebody's private ride, which it was. The setting seemed somehow less intimate and private than a cab, and he'd found himself overcome with reticence.

Maybe it was the trust factor, he thought. It was not like this guy was a professional taxi driver or anything.

Wolf made sure to wait until the guy had backed up and left the driveway before he made any moves. They watched the red taillights disappear down the road, heading for the highway. The lights were on in the ranch house, and he thought about going to the house and checking on Chad and the babysitter but decided against it. There was too big a chance that Kasey might arrive unexpectedly. Having to constantly be worried about a confrontation or her giving him the evil eye was taking its toll on him. He needed to get his own place sooner rather than later, but to do that, he'd need to get back on his feet, pay Mac back, and start making some real money.

There I go, he thought, b*ack in the same old rut.*

"This your place?" Yolanda asked, looking at the ranch house.

He wondered what she would think of his quarters.

"Actually," he said, "that's Mac's. Mine is over there."

He pointed to the big garage.

Yolanda's eyebrows rose.

"I thought that was the garage."

"It is, but it's a big one."

She giggled, and they walked hand-in-hand toward his humble dwelling.

"I was worried you forgot about me," she said.

Amazingly, he'd worried about the same thing and told her so.

Her smile looked radiant in the moonlight, and he detected the same whiff of her perfume that he'd noticed in the car. Then he remembered Mac's suggestion at the restaurant about giving her the flowers, the yellow ones only, when he and Yolanda got to the ranch. Mac had picked up three bouquets of roses, one red, one pink, and one yellow, after dropping the women off at their hotel but had forgotten to bring them to the dinner engagement. He'd placed them in the refrigerator for preservation, and now the three floral bundles resided within the ranch house in re-frigerated tranquility.

Which is where they'll stay, he thought, worrying again that any trip into the ranch house might invite a confrontation with Kasey.

They approached the door, and the motion sensor light above it flipped on, illuminating them.

"Damn," she said. "That's bright."

"Don't worry, you look great under the spotlight. Just like a movie star."

They went inside. Wolf flipped the light switch that activated the overheads and led her around the clutter. Yolanda stopped and looked around, gazing at the shower and then the equipment in the mini-gym: the weight bar, the bench, the stacks of free weights, the speedbag, the over-under, and the heavy bag made out of the ancient duffel bag.

"Looks like you work out a lot," she said.

"Keeps me out of the bars."

"So, where do you sleep?"

"On the floor over there," he said, grinning. "I've got a mat rolled up in the corner."

Her eyes widened as if to say, "What have I gotten myself into?"

He laughed and pointed at the stairway.

"Actually, my room's upstairs. And it's got a regular bed."

She canted her head.

"And a couch for you to sleep on tonight?"

Wolf didn't respond, feeling anxious about her seeing the state of his living facility. He hadn't thought about it much when Mac had brought him here since it had been a step up from Leavenworth. He hadn't ever pictured bringing a beautiful high-class woman there.

High-class and high maintenance, he thought. Guess we'll see how high.

They went up the stairs, and he noticed that Yolando scaled them without so much as a hint of exertion. Then again, he knew from experience just how good of shape she was in.

He paused at the top of the stairs and put his hand on her arm, stopping their progress, then reached to the wall switch and shut off the lower-level lights. They were plunged into darkness.

Wolf closed his eyes for a few seconds to speed up his adjustment to the absence of light, then opened them. Moonlight filtered in through the windows in his room. He moved to the step just below hers and put his arms around her, placing them around her waist and pressing his chest to her back.

Their heads were about level now, and he put his mouth next to her ear. Her luscious hair brushed against his face, and her perfume was intoxicating.

"Did we stop for a reason?" she asked.

"Yeah." He searched for the right words. "I'm really flattered and happy you want to spend more time with me…"

"Okay…"

"And." He paused again, swallowed, then continued. "This place, it's really just temporary. Mac's been letting me stay here until I get back on my feet and—"

"Didn't you tell me all that before in Vegas?"

"Well, yeah, I guess I did." Wolf flushed in the dark.

"Then I only have one question," she said.

Uh-oh. Here it comes.

"What's that?" he asked.

She slowly turned around, pressed her body against his, and kissed him.

After their lips parted, she whispered, "Is there a bathroom in there someplace, or do I have to go back downstairs?"

CHAPTER 12

THE MCNAMARA RANCH
PHOENIX, ARIZONA

The next morning, Wolf woke up at first light as usual. Even though there were curtains on the window, he never pulled them, and he could see the nascent dawn turning from dark gray to subtle orange through the glass. He got up on his elbow and looked at Yolanda next to him. The night before, she'd twisted her hair into braids after a long session of love-making and before they'd finally decided to go to sleep. Their conversation had been all over the place but had ended when he'd asked her why she was braiding her hair if she was going to sleep.

"Don't you be asking me questions about my hair." Her tone was defensive.

"Okay," Wolf said, fluffing the pillow. "Far be it

from me to mess with perfection."

He wanted to say how delicious she looked sitting there naked and winding her tresses, but he was genuinely exhausted. "You can explain it to me in the morning."

He watched her slumber and marveled at how beautiful she was. He managed to edge out of bed and went to the bathroom. It appeared she was still sleeping when he came out, and he decided not to wake her. The sky was brightening with its unceasing regularity as he gazed out the window again, and the urge to do a quick run struck him. Wolf began searching for a pen and some paper to write her a note saying he'd gone when her voice startled him.

"Didn't you do this last time we slept together in Vegas?" she asked.

He glanced at the bed and saw her sitting up to watch him.

"Sorry I woke you," he said. "I was just getting ready to go on a run."

She smiled. "Didn't you get enough physical activity last night?"

He smiled too. "I got plenty, but I'm not sure I'd say it was enough."

She tossed the sheet off and slipped her brown legs over the edge of the bed.

"Well, let me go to the bathroom and freshen up a little, and we can do some more."

The suggestion sent an immediate jolt through him, centering in his groin. As she padded past him to the bathroom in her bare feet, her fingers traced over his abdomen and then lower.

"You never did tell me how you got that bruise," she said.

"I got shot."

Her eyes widened. "You did?"

"No big deal. Mac loaned me one of his vests."

"Did it hurt?"

"Only when I laugh."

He slapped her butt, and she scurried to the bathroom. Wolf went to the sink and rinsed his face and mouth. When she came out, he was standing by the bathroom door. He scooped her up into his arms and carried her over to the bed, their lips just touching. As he laid her dark body on the smooth white sheet, his hands went to her breasts. He leaned down to kiss her, but she put her index finger between their mouths.

"Hold on, sweetie. I still got to brush my teeth, and so do you."

***

After another hour or so of intimacy, Wolf noticed that the sky was now blue and glanced at his alarm clock. It was seven-thirty, but he figured he still had time to get that run in, albeit a limited one, before the heat of the day began. As he swung his legs over the side of the bed for the second time that morning, her hand caressed his back.

"You still want to do that run, baby?" she asked.

"If I don't, I'll find it twice as hard tomorrow."

"How far you gonna go?"

"Just to the mountain and back. A couple of miles."

"Mind if I run with you?"

He looked at her quizzically.

"I do three miles on my treadmill about every day," she said. "I've got my running shoes in my bag and a sports bra."

Wolf grinned. "Is that all you're gonna wear?"

She laughed and slid out from under the covers. "No, but I bet if I go through your clothes, I can find something I can jury-rig with a few deft folds and some good knots."

Fifteen minutes later, they were going out the side door. Wolf was in his customary shorts and t-shirt, and Yolanda clad in a similar outfit made snug by knots, twists, and safety pins.

Wolf was anticipating a more enjoyable run than usual until he stepped away from locking the door and caught sight of Kasey about thirty feet from the house, staring at them. He nodded a greeting, but she didn't acknowledge it. She had the three wrapped bouquets of flowers in her arms along with the Mexican bandito statue and was standing by the blue plastic container that held the trash for pick up and disposal.

"Good morning," Yolanda said.

Kasey didn't acknowledge her either, just lifted the lid of the trash can and dumped the flowers and the bandito into it. She let the lid fall with a thump and turned back to the house without a word.

"Why's she giving us the stink-eye?" Yolanda said. "Ain't she ever seen an interracial couple before?"

Wolf was going to offer an excuse for Kasey but decided against it. He was getting tired of her petulance.

But she *was* Mac's daughter, and he still owed Mac big-time.

"It's me she doesn't like," he said. "Resents my presence here."

"That's no excuse for being ignorant."

Wolf left the keys hanging in the lock and went to the trash can. There was no way Mac would want to leave the flowers in the trash, and he certainly wouldn't want to lose the bandito. Wolf had grown kind of fond of it too, and it was also a symbol, a remembrance of things past.

As he lifted the lid, the smiling plaster face gazed up at him from its place between the scattered bouquets at the bottom of the can. The trashcan was about four feet deep, but luckily it had two wheels built into its frame. Wolf laid it on its side and ran back to the garage to get his broom.

"What are you doing?" Yolanda asked.

"Effecting a rescue," he said.

He ran back to the garbage can and used the long broom handle to drag the flowers and the bandito within reach. The majority of the flowers had crushed or broken stems, but Wolf managed to salvage an even dozen.

Twelve out of thirty-six wasn't bad, he thought. And most of them were yellow. After righting the garbage can, he walked over to Yolanda, carrying the assorted roses, the bandito, and the broom.

She was leaning against the doorframe and looking at him with an amused expression.

"We got these for you girls yesterday," he said. "But we forgot them last night."

"Looks like *she* didn't forget." She cocked her head toward the house. "And what's that thing?"

"A trophy from Mexico. I got to put these in some water." He paused and looked at her. "You like yellow ones, right?"

"I don't want those things after they've been in the trash."

Wolf grinned. "Well, they'll brighten up my place a little bit."

He went through the door and told her to bring his keys. After trudging up the stairs and searching fruitlessly for a suitable container for the roses, he finally pulled out a razor knife and cut the top portion off an empty bottle of water.

Yolanda stood in the doorway, arms crossed, staring at him.

"Just until I get a vase," he said, placing it on the small table next to the window. He put the bandito next to it.

His cell phone rang, and he glanced at the screen. It was Mac.

Wolf wondered if he should tell him about the flowers.

No, he thought. *I'll let Kasey explain that.*

"You two up?" McNamara asked.

"We are."

"Well, quit your lovey-dovey business and get yourselves ready to roll. We're on the way, and we got to hit the ground running."

"What's the rush?"

"I told Kasey to work on finding out something about that lawyer's sister, and Ms. Dolly's hacker guy called this morning to tell her there's some credit card activity on the girlfriend's card here in town." Mac's voice sounded agitated. "Car rental and gas station. Looks like the lawyer on the lam's getting ready to book."

"Okay," Wolf said. "Something else bothering you?"

"Damn straight. I got a call from Otto at the body shop. Guess what he found on that car he loaned us?"

Wolf tried to think if it had been damaged in any way, but McNamara answered for him.

"A damn GPS tracking device."

"What?"

"It's gotta be them good-for-nothing feds," Mc-Namara said. "And remember that damn drone yesterday? It started right after they came to see us at Reno's."

"It did seem highly coincidental that they knew we'd be there," Wolf said. "You check the Escalade?"

"I did. Just as soon as Otto called. Used my cell phone app and found one."

"What did you do with it?"

"Smashed it good."

Wolf didn't tell him it would have been better to save it. It might be useful to confront Franker and Turner about their surveillance of American citizens. Of course, this might mean they had a warrant, which was even more troubling.

"Hell," McNamara said, "they're probably using the drone to track us now."

"Well, that's good news," Wolf said. "If the mob comes after us once we grab Krenshaw, they'll be able to send the cavalry."

McNamara snorted. "That'll be the day. And if they send that damn thing over my property, they're gonna find out it's a no-fly zone real quick."

Wolf laughed. "How soon before you get here?"

"Maybe fifteen minutes," McNamara said. "Well, make that twenty. Ms. Dolly and Brenda are almost ready."

"Roger that. We'll be here."

Yolanda was standing next to him, her hands crossed on top of his left shoulder.

"What's up?" she asked after he'd terminated the call.

"Mac's on his way, along with your partners. We'd better skip the run and take a shower now."

"How long do we have?"

Wolf figured the twenty minutes Mac had estimated really meant thirty or more, but he said, "Fifteen minutes tops. Guess we better shower together."

She smiled up at him.

"Sounds good to me."

***

The Empire Hotel Parking Structure
Phoenix, Arizona

Cummins sat in the back of the rented Lexus while Zerbe and the one called Luan sat up front. Zerbe was behind the wheel, and the big South African was in the passenger seat with the open laptop on his thighs. The black guy, Amiri, who'd just finished secreting another GPS tracker on McNamara's Escalade, was next to Cummins in the back. The black guy was sweating, and he stank too. All these damn South Africans did, and Cummins wondered if it was his imagination or if they had some kind of genetic predisposition for pungent body odor.

Maybe it was something in their diet, he thought. Or maybe they just didn't use deodorant.

Whatever it was, he felt a bit more secure now that he had the .38 snub-nose Smith & Wesson in his pocket. It was only a five-shot, but it was his insurance policy in case Zerbe or his friends tried a double-cross.

"You sure he's not going to find this one?" Cummins asked.

"There's no way," Amiri said. "I stuck it way up underneath on the frame."

"Plus," Luan said, "it's the kind we use on our ops. It can be remotely turned on and off, so it won't show up on the scanner if he uses his phone again."

"Plus," Zerbe said, "since he already found one, he'll probably not look for a second one."

"These bastards aren't that sophisticated."

"They're slicker than you might think," Zerbe said. "That guy Wolf took out a whole squad of highly trained professionals by himself in Mexico."

The recollection of that nightmare confrontation made Cummins feel nauseated. His fingers sought the comfort of the hard planes of the revolver. But these South African assholes looked as tough, if not even more so, than Eagan's Viper group had.

"Those were Americans," Luan said. "Not Afrikaans."

"Highly trained Americans," Zerbe corrected.

"Whatever," Luan answered. "I still think it'd be a lot quicker if we just grabbed the two of them and made them talk."

"Negative. We still don't know where Wolf stashed the statue," Zerbe said.

"We'll make him talk in short order," Luan said. "We've had a lot of experience doing that, haven't we, Amiri?"

The black South African goon grinned.

"Not that I doubt your veracity," Zerbe said, shaking his head. "Or your interrogation abilities. But we're operating by an intricate set of rules here. Our employer is something of a fanatic about keeping a low profile and tying up any loose ends."

"So we don't leave any," Luan said.

"Right. And that includes not making our move until we figure out where he's got it hidden."

Cummins wanted to make it clear to these two mercs that he was not just wallpaper, but rather, he was as in charge of things as Zerbe was. "He might have stashed it in a safety deposit box for all we know."

Luan snorted derisively. "So we grab him and make him take us there."

Cummins shook his head. "Not the way things work in the US."

Zerbe said. "Right. If he's got it in a bank somewhere, we can't go waltzing in there with guns and make him go to his box. Besides, all this is speculation at this point."

"As long as you're paying us," Luan said, "we don't mind playing the big cats waiting for that herd of gazelles to get closer."

Zerbe hissed and scrunched down in the seat. "Look out. They're getting into the Escalade now. We'll track them with the GPS and then use the drone."

***

McNamara Ranch
Phoenix. Arizona

Wolf stood by the window, watching for Mac and drinking bottled water as Yolanda worked on her makeup at the mirror by his bathroom sink. His window air conditioner was working overtime, but the thin stream of cool air felt nice.

"So, what do you do at night?" she asked. "You don't even have a TV."

"Usually, I read or study," he said. "I'm taking some classes."

"Neat. What subjects?"

"Right now, I'm taking Intro to Law Enforcement— Mac's idea—and I've got an English lit class too."

"So, you're studying to be a cop?" she asked.

He turned and watched her use what looked like a

huge artist's paintbrush on her cheeks and jaw.

"No chance of that," he said. "I told you I was in prison for four years, didn't I?"

"Yeah, that's right. You did. But I thought you—"

She stopped in mid-sentence.

"You thought what?" he asked.

She finished her dusting and slipped the brush into her makeup case.

"I thought you told me you didn't do it, and you had somebody looking into it."

Wolf chuckled and turned back to the window.

"One thing you learn in prison is that everybody says they didn't do it." He drank more water as all the bad memories came floating back to him. "And the person who's looking into it is Kasey's fiancé."

"That dude we saw at Charlie's?"

"One and the same."

Yolanda laughed. "I think you better get yourself another lawyer."

Wolf was about to reply when he saw Mac's Escalade heading down the road toward the ranch.

"They're here. You ready?"

"I'm always ready," she said and smiled at him.

He thought she was fishing for a compliment about her appearance, and she deserved one.

"Wow, you look great," he said. "You ever think about being a model?"

"Models are usually flat-chested white girls with

no booties."

"Not for *Playboy*," Wolf said as they moved to the stairs. "Maybe we can do a photo layout after we catch this lawyer on the lam, and I'll become a professional photographer."

She snorted. "In your dreams."

He wondered if she was talking about the photo session or his possible new vocation.

The Escalade pulled in as Wolf locked the garage. Mac jumped out and opened the rear door for Brenda, who was in the back seat on the driver's side. He then rushed around to open the front passenger side for Ms. Dolly, who got out and stretched, looking around.

"You're moving pretty good," Wolf said. "Considering."

"Considering what?" McNamara said, leaning close. "That I was using a cane earlier in the week, or that I spent the night in heavenly bliss?"

"Both, actually," Wolf said. "But after all, you *are* Special Forces."

McNamara laughed and slapped him on the back. The blow felt hard and sure, and Wolf had to think that this liaison with the P Patrol had been just what Mac had needed to get him back on track.

"My, my," Ms. Dolly said. "So this is the famous McNamara Ranch, huh?"

"This is it," Mac said, smiling broadly. "But it's also our informal office. My daughter does all the computer stuff and keeps the books, and me and Steve do the heavy lifting. And wait till you see the special surprise that's waiting for you when we get inside."

"Can't wait." Ms. Dolly smiled.

Wolf knew Mac was talking about the flowers.

I guess I'll have to tell him after all, Wolf thought.

"You should see the gym first," he called and tossed his keys to Yolanda. "Hey, sweetie, will you show them?"

Yolanda caught the keys and gave Wolf a sideways glance.

"Come on over here," she said and walked to the garage door.

McNamara started to follow, but Wolf grabbed his arm. Mac regarded him strangely.

"You said you smashed that tracker you found on the Escalade?" Wolf asked.

"Sure did. I was gonna put it on one of the cars in the hotel parking lot to confuse those fuckers, but I was so mad, I smashed it under my heel."

"I hope you got a lot of pleasure out of doing that," Wolf said. "Because there's a slight problem with the flowers."

McNamara's brow furrowed. "What?"

Wolf debated what to tell him. He hated being a snitch, but the last thing he wanted to see was another argument flare up between Mac and Kasey, especially in front of the P Patrol. He took a deep breath.

"There's no easy way to say this, but this morning when I came out of my place with Yolanda, Kasey was tossing them."

McNamara's face reddened, and he started for the house. Wolf tightened his grip on Mac's arm, which felt like a bundle of iron.

"Hold on," he said. "You don't want to get into an argument with her right now, and I managed to save a dozen or so, which I've got in my room."

McNamara said nothing, but Wolf could tell he was furious.

They stood there for a good ten seconds, then Mac took a deep breath.

"What color are they?" he asked.

"The flowers?" Wolf shrugged. "Some red, a few pink. Mostly yellow."

McNamara considered that, then nodded. "Best leave then in your place till we get ready to go. They in water?"

Wolf nodded, thinking he still had to tell him the rest of it.

"I've got the bandito in my place, too," he said, trying to sound matter-of-fact.

"The bandito?" McNamara's eyes narrowed. "She throw that out too?"

Wolf felt Mac's biceps swell with his growing rage.

"Well, uh," he muttered, trying to figure out how to handle this part. He realized he'd put himself right in the middle of another family dispute.

But I was there anyway, he thought. Still, if he could mollify the situation...

"Yolanda wanted to see it," he said. "So I..."

"You can't lie for shit," McNamara said, pulling his arm away. "Wait till I see her."

"Like I told you," Wolf said, "keep your cool in front of the ladies. Okay?"

McNamara closed his eyes and inhaled, then nodded.

"Hey, sugar," Ms. Dolly called, exiting the garage. "I sure hope your house has better air conditioning than your garage."

Brenda followed her with Yolanda, who locked the door and gave Wolf his keys back.

All three of them were dressed in running shoes, blue jeans, and tank tops. Working uniforms, Yolanda had told him.

McNamara made a sweeping gesture toward the house. "You'll think you were in the Arctic."

"Good," Ms. Dolly said. "This heat here's as bad as in Vegas, and it ain't even afternoon yet."

Once inside, McNamara made a lot of noise, showing them around.

"Look at all them medals in that shadow box," Ms. Dolly said.

"And I love that hat," Brenda said.

"It's a beret," McNamara said. "A green beret."

Wolf separated himself from the group and went to the office. Kasey sat behind the computer, her fingers dancing over the keyboard.

"Hi," Wolf said, taking pains not to address her by name.

She replied with a quick glance and nothing more.

"Your dad's hoping you had a chance to run down some info on that lawyer case we've been working on," Wolf said.

"I have to go to class soon," she said. "And I have to drop Chad off at daycare."

Wolf nodded, hoping she'd continue voluntarily. She didn't.

"Okay," he said. "But did you find anything out yet? We're gonna be working the case today."

From the other room, he heard some commotion and Ms. Dolly saying, "Don't tell me this adorable little cowboy's your grandson?"

Kasey rolled her eyes and started to get up.

Wolf stepped closer. "Look, I know how you feel, but don't embarrass your dad in front of his friends by arguing. Please," he added as an afterthought.

Her eyes flashed. "Don't you dare tell me what to do."

"I'm not, but—"

"But nothing. You haven't earned that right. You haven't earned—"

McNamara walked in carrying Chad. "This little

guy's getting so big! We're gonna have to buy him a horse pretty soon."

The P Patrol entered beside him.

Kasey compressed her lips. "That's the last thing he needs, Dad."

"Can I, Mommy?" Chad said. "Please."

"We'll talk about that another time," she said, stepping forward to lift Chad out of her father's arms. "We have to go to daycare now, honey."

"Say," McNamara said, "did you get a chance to run that—"

"It's over there," she said, pointing to the out basket on the side of her desk. She started to walk out of the room.

Wolf walked over to the basket and picked up a sheaf of papers. It was a list of names and addresses under the heading Willard Krenshaw. It looked like she'd come through on that stuff. Wolf wanted to ask about the info he'd requested regarding the names on his list but kept his mouth shut.

"Well," McNamara said in a loud voice, obviously trying to ameliorate the situation, "we might as well get started then. You gals ready?"

"We were born ready," Ms. Dolly said.

Kasey was standing next to the door, and she plucked her car keys from the pegboard on the wall.

"Let's get in the Escalade," McNamara said. "I'll fire up the air and spring for the drive-through at your choice of Dunkin' Donuts or Mickey D's."

"I'm a Dunkin' gal myself," Ms. Dolly told him.

Kasey opened the door and grabbed Chad's hand, then turned and said, "Make sure you take the Escalade through the full-service car wash afterwards."

She slammed the door, and McNamara looked both livid and embarrassed. He glanced at Wolf. "Steve, will you show the gals here where the washroom is while I take care of something?"

"Sure," Wolf said.

McNamara strode out the door, slamming it behind him.

The four of them stood in awkward silence for a few seconds, then Ms. Dolly said, "Ain't she the sweetheart."

It wasn't a question.

Wolf said, "Ah, the washroom's over here."

He started walking through the house. Ms. Dolly caught up to him.

"If you ever want to get away from the Wicked Witch of the East, honey," she said, "just let me know. You got a job waitin' for you in Vegas."

Wolf chuckled. "I don't know if I'd fit in with an outfit called the P Patrol."

Ms. Dolly laughed, grabbed his arm, and leaned her red tresses against his shoulder. "From what I hear, you'd fit in real good."

Wolf glanced at Yolanda, who put her hand in

front of her mouth and made a motion as if she were twisting a key in a lock.

"I might take you up on that once I pay Mac back what I owe him."

"You just let me know, sugar," Ms. Dolly said.

"*Tal vez si su novio se hizo el amor con ella, que la calmaría un poco*," Brenda said.

Ms. Dolly laughed.

Obviously, she was fluent in Spanish, as Wolf had figured. He smiled too and said, "That's probably what she needs, all right."

Brenda and Ms. Dolly looked at each other and laughed.

After the women had used the facilities, they waited inside for McNamara to return. Wolf was standing near the door perusing the stuff Kasey had printed out when he heard the shot. He dropped the papers on the floor and went to the grandfather clock. After pressing the sequence of buttons on the side, the tray slid out, and he grabbed the Glock 43 Mac stored in there. Ms. Dolly, Brenda, and Yolanda were suddenly next to him, holding handguns at the ready. Ms. Dolly's was a chrome Colt Python with a six-inch barrel.

Wolf glanced at it. She said, "I like my guns the same as how I like my men. Big and bad."

Brenda's pistol was a much smaller stainless steel Taurus Spectrum trimmed in purple, and Yolanda's was a Beretta Px4 Storm with a nickel satin slide over a black frame.

"Fashion statement," she said when Wolf glanced at her.

"I guess it won't do any good to tell you girls to stay inside, huh?" Wolf asked as he cracked the door and peered out through the opening.

McNamara was walking in the driveway, fully exposed, his smoking Glock 19 in his right hand.

What the hell kind of use of cover was that?

Wolf moved through the door and the P Patrol followed, spreading out along the front of the house.

McNamara stopped near a long, flat object lying on the driveway, replaced his Glock in his holster, and bent over. When he straightened, he had an elongated piece of plastic in his left hand. He turned back and waved at them.

Wolf relaxed slightly and saw that the elongated object had four propellers, a triangular body, and three landing wheels.

The drone.

He rose from his crouch and told the P Patrol everything was clear. They assumed non-combat stances as well. McNamara walked toward them, grinning.

He held up the damaged drone.

"This son of a bitch didn't know he was coming into a hot LZ," he said as he turned it over.

"One shot, and with a pistol at that," Wolf said. "Pretty fair shooting."

"I wanted to try it after seeing Hondo do it on TV." Mac rotated the drone. "Make a nice trophy to set next to the bandito, won't it?"

"Might be best to dispose of the evidence," Wolf said. "If it belongs to the feds."

McNamara shook his head. "No registration number and the serial number's been burned off. If it is theirs, they went to some pains to hide it, but that doesn't surprise me."

He started to stick the drone in the trash.

"Let me hold onto it," Wolf said. "Maybe Kasey can do some searching as to who in the area sells that model and we can get a lead. When she's feeling better, that is."

McNamara hesitated, then pulled the drone out of the container and let the lid of the garbage can fall.

"I need to apologize to the girls about the way she acted." McNamara handed him the drone. "Maybe you could go get the remainder of them flowers for me? I'll get the bandito later, after I have a talk with her."

Wolf took the shattered remnants and headed for the door to his dwelling, fishing in his pocket for his keys.

***

Strip Mall Parking Lot
Phoenix, Arizona

Cummins was getting more comfortable in his current position of being relegated to the back seat of the Lexus. Zerbe was in the front passenger seat, and that Luan character, the leader of the Lion Team, was in the driver's seat. They both peered through binoculars at the bail bondsman's office. It seemed to Cummins that they were wasting a lot of time, but he knew better than to say that. The more time and resources they spent on watching Wolf and his buddy, the less time they watched him.

And he was already gathering information. Last night when Zerbe was in the bathroom, Cummins had snuck a look at his phones, both his personal one and the burner, and written down the numbers he'd called. The one with a New York area code had to be Fallotti's. That might come in handy if the shit hit the fan again the way it had in Mexico.

"*Drie mooi vrou,*" Luan said.

"*Ja,*" Zerbe said. He looked at Cummins. "They're just coming out. You should see the three babes they got with them."

Cummins thought about asking for the binoculars so he could look, but he didn't. He figured he'd have plenty of time to think about women later.

"We going to follow them again?" he asked.

Zerbe lowered his binoculars and sat pensively for a few seconds.

"No," he finally said. "I think not. Hand me my bag, would you?"

Cummins blew out a heavy breath and shifted in the seat, straining to lift his bulk high enough to reach the black nylon bag in the rear that held Zerbe's surveillance equipment. When he shifted back into a comfortable position, he saw Zerbe duck and realized the Escalade was driving past them. It was still a good sixty feet away, and Cummins felt secure behind the dark tint. When Zerbe straightened, he reached back and grabbed the bag.

"Pull up to the front of the place," he said. "I want to plant a listening device in there so we can find out what they're working on."

"Is that smart?" Cummins said. "I mean, after that guy McNamara shooting down your drone."

Zerbe gave him a disparaging look as Luan shifted into gear, and the vehicle lurched forward. "Let me worry about what's smart and what's not."

"*Die fokken vark,*" Luan said.

Zerbe grunted something.

"What did he say?" Cummins asked. He was tired of these two conversing in a language he didn't understand. "The least you two could do is keep in it English."

"You don't want to know," Zerbe said. "Believe me."

Cummins was about to say something when Luan spoke.

"I called you a fucking pig. Do you have a problem

with that?"

Cummins pursed his lips. Who did this South African prick think he was?

"It's actually a term of endearment in our native country," Zerbe said with a wry smile.

Cummins believed that about as much as he believed in the tooth fairy.

"Oh, yeah?" he said. "Well, just remember I'm still the only one who can identify the artifact."

"How can we forget?" Luan said. "You keep reminding us all the time."

The van jerked to a stop a few parking spaces away from the front of the bail bondsman's office, if you could call it that. Zerbe set a frequency on a receiver and placed it on the dashboard.

"Here," he said. "You can both listen to a master at work."

He got out of the car, slammed the door, and walked a few feet away.

After pinning something small and metallic to the underside of his collar, his voice came through the speaker: "How do you read me?"

Luan held up his thumb. Zerbe grinned and began walking toward the bail bondsman's office. "You two play nice."

Cummins leaned forward to listen but not too far forward. He didn't want to get too close to the head lion.

"Good afternoon, mate," Zerbe said in a faux accent. "Carter's the name. Earl Carter from down under. You Manny?"

"No," another voice said. "I'm Fred Sutter. Manny's my uncle."

"Ah, outstanding. Maybe you can help me then. But first, who were those three fine-looking ladies I just saw walk out of here?"

They heard an obnoxious-sounding laugh. "They call themselves the P Patrol, and you can guess what that stands for. They're bounty hunters out of Vegas. Fine bitches, ain't they?"

"To say the least. You say they're from Vegas?"

"Yeah, they're here working a skip—" Fred's voice paused. "You said you needed something?"

"Yeah. When's your uncle expected back?"

"He's here. He's taking a… He's in the bathroom."

"Mind if I sit down a moment?"

Cummins heard something creak. This was like listening to one of those old radio plays.

"Those two mates with the pretty ladies," Zerbe said. "They looked familiar, too. They from Vegas as well?"

"Huh-uh. They're from around here. Why?"

"I think I met them at the Bounty Hunter Convention a couple of weeks ago. McNab or something?"

"McNamara."

"Right," Zerbe said. "And the other one's named Wolf."

"Yeah."

There was the sound of a toilet flushing, then somebody swearing, along with what could have been a door slamming into a wall.

"Hey, Sherman," another voice said. "What did you do with the fucking plunger?"

"My name's—"

"Oh, hello. I'm Manny Sutter. What can I do for you?"

They heard what was probably a large man drop into a padded chair that groaned in protest.

"Sherm, go find the plunger, will ya? And take care of the toilet. What'd you say I could do for you?"

"I'm from out of town," Zerbe said. "Out of the country, actually. Australia. I was here to attend the Bounty Hunter Convention and met a guy who told me to look him up if I ever got to Phoenix. A Reno Garth. I take it you know him?"

"Yeah, I know him."

"Would you happen to have his number so I could call him? I owe him a beer."

"Try his gym. It's called the MMA Fitness Center."

"Yeah, he did mention that. You mind if I grab a fag?"

"Huh?"

"Oh." Zerbe laughed. "Sorry, that's Aussie for cigarette. Want one?"

"No thanks and I don't allow smoking in here."

A peculiar sound resonated, along with more swearing.

"Jesus, Manny! What'd you do to this toilet?"

"Will you knock it off?" Manny said in a loud voice. "We got a guest here."

"Say, what was the P Patrol doing here?" Zerbe asked in a matter-of-fact way. "They working on something for you?"

"Not for me. For the Pope. Now, if you'll excuse me..."

"The Pope? The Roman Catholic one?"

"No, the Vegas one."

After a few more innocuous exchanges, Zerbe excused himself. They saw him exit the office and head back toward them. Luan adjusted the frequency on the speaker, and the voices of Manny and Fred became audible, along with a toilet flushing.

"Man," Fred's voice said. "You're lucky we didn't have to call a fucking plumber."

"Who was that asshole, anyway?" Manny asked.

"I don't know. Said he knew you. You talked to him."

"Whew," Manny said. "Good thing I didn't let him light up that cigarette. The son of a bitch stunk. You smell him?"

The door opened, and Zerbe slipped in.

"How's the transmission?" he asked. "Coming in okay?"

"Lima Charlie," Cummins said with a grin. "Loud

and clear."

Zerbe glanced at him, then took out his burner phone and looked up to dial the number listed in pink neon in the window. He then reached over and adjusted the volume on the speaker.

"Hello, Mr. Sutter?" Zerbe said in another faux accent, this one distinctly tough and distinctly American. "This is Tommy Martin out of Vegas. I'm working for the Pope." He paused, then said. "The P Patrol touch base with you yet?"

After another pause, he said, "We're talking about the same skip, right? What's his name?" He let the sentence drop off, then said, "Yeah, Krenshaw, right. Any progress?"

After a couple more exchanges, Zerbe thanked him and terminated the call. He then pulled out his own smartphone and texted something with his thumbs, repeating, "Krenshaw, Krenshaw, Krenshaw..." He finally said, "Willard Krenshaw, here it is. Hmmm..."

"Willard Krenshaw?" Cummins said, recognizing the name. "Isn't that the lawyer who was mixed up organized crime?"

"One and the same," Zerbe said, smiling. "And he's facing charges himself. A mobster's lawyer on the run. This gives us a perfect way to start to tie up some of our loose ends."

***

Car Rental Center
Phoenix International Airport

Yolanda's cell phone rang, and Wolf watched as she answered it, put it on speaker, and set it on the dashboard of the rented Jeep Cherokee. The call was from Ms. Dolly.

"Okay, look alive, you two," Ms. Dolly said, her Texas twang clearly evident in her excited tone. "Girlfriend's gonna be on the move in a white Toyota Corolla."

"We're by the exit now," Yolanda said. She turned to Wolf. "You ready?"

He nodded and shifted into drive, watching the access road from the garage of the car rental structure. Two cars pulled up to the checkpoint, one of them a white Corolla.

"Brenda, I'm coming back to you," Ms. Dolly's voice said over their portable radio. Ms. Dolly had brought her team's walkie-talkies, and although they had a limited transmission range, they worked flawlessly.

"Roger that," Brenda said.

The white Toyota pulled up to the checkpoint, and Wolf saw the driver's side window lower with electronic efficiency. A bare feminine arm extended and handed some papers to the guard, who took them and walked around the car. Wolf edged closer to the exit ramp that led to the street. He didn't want to stay too close, and the assumption was that Krenshaw's girlfriend, Lola Crest, would either head back to the hotel she'd been staying at to pick up Willard or to his sister's house. By the time Ms. Dolly's hacker buddy had gotten the latest charges on Lola's credit card and relayed them to the P Patrol, they had been a lap or two behind. Willard Krenshaw and Lola had been skipping from hotel to hotel almost every night under her name, and now they were apparently changing cars. Unfortunately for them, Lola had used her real name for the car rentals.

"Sounds like the son of a bitch is getting ready to make a run for the border," McNamara had said.

"If they get down to Mexico, we'll never be able to track them," Ms. Dolly replied.

"You got that right," McNamara said. "Me and Steve don't even eat Mexican food no more."

The plan was to follow Lola, figuring she'd lead them to Willard eventually.

"There she goes," Yolanda said.

Wolf pulled out slowly and eased into traffic a couple of cars behind her.

"Don't stay too close," Yolanda cautioned.

"Not planning on it."

They knew she had one of two destinations in mind. Their quarry was either at the hotel or his sister's place, and from the looks of it, Lola was taking a circuitous route to wherever she was going. Additionally, she'd slowed down considerably, and the other two cars that had been behind her had vanished.

Probably wants to make sure no one's following her, he thought.

He grabbed the walkie-talkie but held it out of sight on his lap.

"Mac, where you at?"

"Coming up behind you, partner."

"All right," Wolf said. "It looks like she's taking the long way, probably trying to look for a tail. I'm going to turn off and let you take over."

"Roger that," McNamara said.

As soon as he caught a glimpse of the Escalade with Mac driving and Ms. Dolly riding shotgun, Wolf hit his right turn signal and turned off. When he got to the first intersection, he turned left and zoomed down a side street.

"We're running parallel," he said.

"Good," McNamara said. "Just leave the following to us pros. Besides, you two stand out too much."

Yolanda huffed and grabbed the walkie-talkie from Wolf.

"What's that supposed to mean?" she said, feigning anger.

"Salt and pepper, honey," Ms. Dolly said. "They're either cops or crooks."

"Or bounty hunters," Yolanda said and smiled at

Wolf. She lowered the radio. "Sounds like we got a chance to stop somewhere for a latte."

Wolf chuckled. He knew she was kidding. They came to a stop sign, and he turned left and proceeded toward the main road to get behind the Escalade.

The cat and mouse continued, with Wolf and McNamara switching positions a few more times. Yolanda flopped down in the seat to conceal herself when it was their turn.

Finally Lola slowed, and Wolf saw her turn into the parking lot of the Coral Reef Motel. It was a cheap place; the individual rooms opened out into the lot. Wolf radioed the information and drove past the motel. In the rearview mirror, he saw the Escalade hang a left and pull into the lot.

"We don't want to overplay our hand," Ms. Dolly said over the radio. "We ain't sure if Willie boy's in there."

"What's the plan?" Yolanda asked.

"Looks like the maid's doing the rooms. Me and Mac will play lovey-dovey and act like we're inquiring about a room. You swing around the back and come up acting like housekeeping. Try to get a gander inside to see if the pigeon's in the coop."

"Roger that," Yolanda said, then smiled at Wolf and added, "You two make a good-looking couple."

"Get to work," Ms. Dolly said.

Wolf swung a U-turn and pulled into the fast-food

joint adjacent to the motel. Yolanda got out as she was pulling her long tresses into a ponytail. She'd pulled a black t-shirt out of her purse and slipped it on. Wolf thought she was the best-looking motel maid he'd ever seen. She was also the best armed since Wolf knew she was wearing the Beretta in a Sport Tuck Belly Band under the loose-fitting shirt.

"See you on the flip-side," she said as she clipped the radio to her belt.

"Stay in touch," Wolf said, picking up his radio and turning it on.

"You know it," she said and ran through the dirt lot area separating the fast-food parking lot from the motel. Wolf pulled into a vacant parking space and watched. The Toyota was parked in front of room eight, and Mac and Ms. Dolly were ambling toward the front entrance of the office. Yolanda came up behind the maid's cart, which was sitting on the sidewalk in front of room eleven. She said something to the maid, showed her what Wolf figured was her Bail Bond Enforcement Officer badge, and took something from her before wheeling the cart down to room eight.

The curtains in the window were drawn, and the door was closed. Yolanda paused to place her ear against the door. After a few moments, she went to the window and appeared to be trying to peer through a divide in the curtains. She stepped back and shrugged, then took the card she'd gotten from the maid, knocked, and opened the door. Wolf watched carefully as she conversed with someone.

Yolanda's voice came over the radio. "Single female in room eight's checking out at this time. I'll be cleaning it shortly."

So he wasn't in the room, Wolf thought.

Wolf saw Lola pulling two suitcases out of the room. She went to the rear of the Toyota and opened the trunk. After loading the suitcases inside, she went back to the room. Yolanda exited and pushed the cart back to its original position. After dumping the master key card on top of the stack of towels, she kept walking, draping one of the towels from the cart over her head like a burka. When she got to the end of the walkway, she darted across the dirt to Wolf and the Cherokee. Mac and Ms. Dolly were already back in the Escalade and pulling out of the lot.

"She's either going to pick him up at a restaurant somewhere or he's sayin' his goodbyes to his sister," Ms. Dolly said over the radio.

Lola put two more bags in the trunk and slammed the lid, then got into the car and backed out. Wolf did the same.

"You know," he said. "I've always wanted a souvenir towel from the Coral Reef Motel."

"Then this is your lucky day," Yolanda said. "I'll let this one go cheap."

They followed the Toyota for several blocks, with Wolf staying primarily in the first position. Yolanda leaned forward, looking through her binoculars. "Looks like she's talking on her phone." Wolf relayed the information over his radio.

It soon became obvious that the destination was the sister's house. Wolf backed off, and Ms. Dolly went over their ops plan on the radio.

"Steve, you and Yolanda stay behind on her tail. We're gonna pass her and set up on the house. Let her park and go in, and we'll grab him as soon as he comes out. We want to get him before he gets in the car, so if she just honks, we'll move up and block her in."

"Roger that," Wolf agreed.

From the file pictures and the times Willard had been on television, he looked slim and trim and carried himself with an affected toughness. Wolf wasn't worried about mixing it up with a lawyer, but this guy was in desperate straits.

"Tempt not a desperate man," he said.

"What?"

Wolf smiled. "Just a quote I remembered from my lit class. I'm wondering if this guy's going to fight or run."

"Let's hope he just surrenders," Yolanda said.

The Toyota turned right into a subdivision, went through a series of winding streets, and appeared to be heading to the sister's place.

"We're watching the house from down the street," Ms. Dolly said. "Waitin' on y'all."

"Girlfriend's coming your way," Yolanda told her.

Wolf continued to follow at a discreet distance. They were almost there.

As she pulled up in front of the house, Wolf hung back and stopped down the block. The target house was approximately thirty yards away. Lola stayed at the curb rather than pulling into the driveway. Another vehicle, a Lexus, sat in the drive next to the house.

"Looks like they're plannin' on a quick getaway," Ms. Dolly said. "She just honked."

Yolanda brought the binoculars up to her eyes and held the radio next to her mouth.

"Wait for it," Ms. Dolly said. A few more seconds passed without anything happening. "Waaaiiit for it," Ms. Dolly repeated, drawing out the sentence like she was narrating a striptease.

Wolf was still at the curb about ninety feet away, with the vehicle in gear.

"Jackpot," Ms. Dolly said. "There he is."

Wolf tore down the street and saw the Escalade trundling toward the Toyota. Willard was halfway between the car and his sister's house, frozen in place. He shook his surprise off and started running, his longish black hair streaming in an arrow shape behind his head. The Escalade swooped in front of the Toyota. Wolf pulled up in back of it and started to get out. The Toyota slammed into the front bumper of the Cherokee, then lurched forward and slammed into the Escalade just as Mac and Ms. Dolly and Brenda were exiting. Wolf saw McNamara tumble out of the Caddie and hit the pavement hard. Ms. Dolly ran to the driver's window of the Toyota and pointed her big Colt Python at Lola. Wolf and Yolanda were already running after Willard. Yolanda closed in fast and the fleeing lawyer cut to his left, only to come within grabbing distance of Wolf.

His right hand grabbed Willard's collar, and Wolf used his momentum to force him to the ground, steering him into the grass. The two men landed in a tangle, and the lawyer yelled, "Don't kill me. Don't kill me. I won't talk."

Wolf straddled the guy like the MMA opponent had done to him, but instead of delivering punches, Wolf twisted Willard's arms behind his back and ratcheted on a set of handcuffs.

"You're under arrest," Wolf said.

"What!" Willard exclaimed. "You're fucking cops?"

"Bail Enforcement Officers," Yolanda said. "We're better because we don't have to advise you of your rights."

Wolf stood and pulled the lawyer to his feet, glancing back to check on Mac.

He lay on the ground, with Ms. Dolly kneeling beside him. Brenda had Lola out of the Toyota and bent over the hood, her small Taurus Spectrum pressed into the other woman's ear.

Wolf power walked Willard over to them, the lawyer spouting a bunch of legal threats.

"You'd best shut your mouth before I tear off your toupee and stuff it down your throat," Wolf said. "And you better pray that my partner isn't hurt."

This ended the lawyer's protestations.

"You okay, Mac?" Wolf asked.

McNamara's face was creased with pain, but he nodded. "Just had the wind knocked outta me, is all." He slowly rolled to his feet, but when he stood, he emitted a gasp and lurched to the right.

"Sugar, what's wrong?" Ms. Dolly asked, moving her body against his to steady him.

"Nothing," McNamara said, smiling weakly. "I was just hoping you'd do that."

Ms. Dolly laughed, but it was plain to see that McNamara was in pain.

"Let's vamoose with our prisoner before the authorities get here and we have more explaining to do," McNamara said. He looked at Wolf. "Stick old Willard in the back with me, and you drive." He limped to the Escalade, opened the rear door, and slid inside. Once he was on the rear seat, he slid over and held his arms outward. "Come to papa, Willie boy. We ain't gonna hurt you."

Wolf shoved the lawyer into the vehicle and opened

the driver's door. He looked at Ms. Dolly, who was going through Lola's purse.

"What are we going to do with her?" he asked.

"Oh, we're gonna take her on a little ride and do some girl talk. Maybe get Yolanda one of those latte things she likes so much." She grabbed a handful of Lola's blonde hair and pulled. Her voice coarsened as she put her mouth next to the other woman's ear. "Now listen, sweetie pie. Right now, you're facing a charge of harboring a fugitive and causin' bodily injury to an officer unless you can convince me otherwise."

"You hurt my boo daddy," Yolanda said, her face contorting in a mean expression.

"*Pendeja*," Brenda said. "I should break your fingers one at a time."

Lola looked terrified as Ms. Dolly and Brenda walked her to the Cherokee and shoved her inside. Yolanda gazed after them with a smile, then walked over to the still-open driver's door of the Escalade.

"Looks like for now, I'm the designated driver," she said.

"Enjoy your latte," Wolf said.

CHAPTER 13

NEAR WILLIAMS, ARIZONA

They'd been on the road for several hours, and it was close to midnight.

"For Christ's sake, I gotta piss, I tell ya," Willard Krenshaw said from the back seat of the Escalade. Not only was he seat belted in, but he was wearing a leather security belt that had a metal loop in front to accommodate the securing handcuffs and leg irons. Wolf had also slammed a loop of the shoulder restraint belt inside the rear door to prevent any further movement. "You want me to go all over the floor back here?"

Yolanda was now sitting in the front passenger seat next to Wolf. "You'd better not. It runs under the seat and messes up my new shoes, I'll make sure any water that's poured into you is going to be coming out red for a month."

Wolf glanced back at the lawyer and smirked. He'd always looked so smug and self-assured on TV, but up close, he saw that the guy wore makeup and a toupee. And as garrulous as he'd been on the talk shows, spouting off about defending the innocent against injustice, he'd offered them substantial bribes ranging from money to sexual favors if they'd let him go.

This guy's going to fit right in on the cellblock, Wolf thought. If the Mob lets him live that long.

Wolf figured the lawyer would most likely spill his guts to the feds and agree to testify so he could live a life of comfort and ease in Witness Protection.

"Come on, man," Krenshaw said again. His once-sonorous professional voice had degenerated to a whine.

The long day's activities and the endless drive through the desert-like terrain had worn Wolf down as well. In some ways, the scenery reminded him a bit of Iraq except this desert wasn't really empty and endless. And here there were no hostiles out to kill him or blow him up with an IED should he venture down the wrong avenue. The freeway here was just that; free and clear. He knew they'd have to stop for gas pretty soon. The needle was dropping dangerously close to the bottom. Yet escorting a guy in handcuffs and leg irons into a gas station men's room invited problems. The last thing they needed on this trek was to be stopped on the highway by some state troopers due to a call from a nervous or bored gas station clerk of a possible abduction. And there was also no guarantee that Krenshaw wouldn't call out just to cause a problem in the hopes he could escape. It was standard prisoner transport precautions to be reasonable with a prisoner, but not to take unnecessary chances.

A blue sign with white lettering appeared that said REST STOP 25 MILES.

That might be a solution to everyone's problems, Wolf thought. This time of night, it would be most likely be sparsely populated or hopefully, deserted. It would offer everyone a chance to stretch a bit and maybe grab a snack from the vending machines, gas up, and finish the last leg to Vegas.

Wolf wondered how Mac was doing back at the ranch. His ankle had ballooned up, and although he'd insisted he was all right, Ms. Dolly had instructed him to stay home and keep it elevated.

"Don't worry, sweetie pie," she'd said. "I won't steal Stevie here away from you. Yet."

Wolf evaluated her job offer again. Moving to Vegas had its appeal, and from the looks of things, Ms. Dolly would be a dynamite boss. And he'd also be close to Yolanda. Plus, it would be a godsend to get away from Kasey and her constant bitching. He was a man caught in the middle, torn by his loyalty to his best friend and mentor and his urge to get a fresh start. But getting a fresh start was off the table until he helped Mac get solvent again and paid him back for giving a second chance to an ex-con he treated like the son he always wanted. And still, in the back of his mind, was the slim hope that he could one day somehow clear himself, but this seemed quixotic at best.

"Come on, man," Krenshaw repeated. "I can't hold it anymore."

"Just stop and let him piss along the road," Yolanda said. "I won't look."

"Then he couldn't wash his hands," Wolf said with a grin. He picked up the radio and keyed the mic. "Ms. Dolly, you there?"

"Sure enough, honey," she said. "What's up?"

"Our pigeon's got a PR problem," he said.

"Public relations?"

"No, personal relief."

"Well, la-dee-da. You tell him to take a number?"

"There's a rest stop coming up in a bit. Let's stop."

"All right," she said. "I could kinda go for that myself."

"Hold on for a few more minutes, Willard," Wolf said.

"About fucking time. I'm going to sue you all for the way you've treated me."

"Good luck with that," Wolf said. "As the saying goes, I haven't even got a pot to piss in."

He saw Krenshaw's frown in the rearview mirror.

"Actually, Yolanda said, "that last latte I had is weighing heavily on me, too."

"Then we're all in agreement," Wolf said. "This next stop will make everybody happy."

***

Near the McNamara Ranch
Phoenix, Arizona

They were in a dark van rented earlier by Zerbe and Luan, who were in front as usual. The other three South African mercs sat in the very back near the rear doors. Once again relegated to the back seat, Cummins sat and listened to the ongoing conversation in front of him.

"Almost there," Amiri's whispering voice said over the comm. "No lights inside."

Preetorius had set the volume so high that it came through with the clarity of a speaker. He'd also told the black guy to speak in English, not Afrikaans, in case the transmission of their comm was somehow intercepted.

Smart move, Cummins thought. *And it also allows me to stay in the loop.*

They were a hundred yards away on the access road. With Wolf and McNamara gone to Vegas to drop off that arrest, they should have a good chance to find and recover the statue of the bandito in Mc-Namara's house. Then his two men following the Escalade could eliminate the troublesome pair and their companions by making it look like a mob hit on the lawyer in their custody. Cummins had to admit Zerbe's plan did seem pretty ingenious, but it was also precipitous. Everything was dependent on Amiri finding the bandito and getting out. Then the three South Africans following the pair on the freeway would have to take them out. Preetorius assured them it would not be a problem.

"I'm sending Bash and Gerhardus and Ryband," he said. "They're more than capable of taking out a couple of American *moffie.*"

Cummins didn't know what that word meant, nor did he care to ask. He was just grateful that the two of them had been conversing in English for the most part since he'd requested it. He also felt that if they both started talking in Afrikaans again, it might be time to worry. It could mean he was going to be edged out.

"Don't forget they want that lawyer here in Phoenix taken care of, too," Cummins said. "Shemp."

"That should be easy enough," Zerbe said. "He didn't look too formidable."

Luan's cell phone rang and he answered it, once again speaking in his native language. Cummins assumed it was the three on the road.

"*Waar?*" he said, then turned to speak to Zerbe. The other man cocked his thumb toward Cummins, and Preetorius switched to English.

"They have pulled off into a rest stop," he said. "It's just south of a city called Kingman. It looks deserted. A good place to make the kill."

"We need to make sure we have the bandito statue before we do that," Cummins said. "Maybe they can just take them hostage until we're sure."

"Where are your men exactly?"

Preetorius spoke again and then said, "They're sitting on the entrance ramp to the rest stop, blacked out. No one else is there at the moment except for a truck on the other side of the place."

"Tell them to make their move," Zerbe said. "But to do it discreetly. And hold off on killing anyone until we give the order."

Preetorius spoke in Afrikaans again and placed the phone against his chest.

"And where's your other man at?" Cummins asked. "The one doing the burglary?"

Preetorius keyed the mic on his comm and asked, "Status?"

"I'm inside," Amiri's voice said over the comm's speaker. "And I think I see it on the mantel."

"Confirm and advise," Preetorius said, then put the phone to his mouth and said something else in Afrikaans.

"What did he say?" Cummins asked.

Zerbe turned to him and smiled. "He said, prepare to terminate the subjects on my command."

Cummins nodded, suddenly feeling his stomach roil again.

It was almost over, at least this part. He hoped it wouldn't turn out to be a whole new set of problems for him.

***

Rest Stop
Near Kingman, Arizona

Wolf watched the three women rush ahead of him into the rest stop bathroom as he walked Krenshaw up the cement path. The building was brick and shaped like a long hallway with entrances at both ends. The far one opened into the truck section, whereas the one they were going through was on the car side. Rows of vending machines lined the walls, along with a section of maps and tour books. What they could be advertising in this bleak desert terrain area made Wolf wonder. There was also a big sign at the entrance advising that this building was under video surveillance, which made Wolf doubly glad he'd removed the leg irons from Krenshaw and covered his handcuffed arms with the towel from the Coral Reef Motel.

Wolf pulled open the entrance door and motioned for Krenshaw to go in. He saw another vehicle, a dark-colored Ford van, pull up next to Ms. Dolly's Cherokee, and three guys got out.

Big guys, Wolf thought, feeling the hairs on the back of his neck stand up.

It wasn't that uncommon for three men to be in a vehicle together, but added to the equation were the factors that this was a very remote location in the middle of nowhere, and it was closing in on midnight. Not only that, but they seemed to be fiddling with something on their heads.

Stocking caps?

Who the hell would wear a stocking cap in the middle of the Mojave desert?

He took out his radio and pressed the button to key the mic as unobtrusively as he could.

"Ms. Dolly," he said, "we have three males coming in here, and they might not have good intentions."

Krenshaw's head swiveled. "What? Where?"

"Armed?" Ms. Dolly asked.

"Unknown," Wolf said and backed Krenshaw into the corner by the display of maps and tour magazines.

Outside, the three men were barely visible through the glass, but Wolf saw one of the trio angle off toward the side of the building.

He's going to flank us, he thought.

***

Near the McNamara Ranch
Phoenix, Arizona

"I'm inside," Amiri's voice said over the comm. It was *sotto voce* but came through with crystal clarity.

"In and out," Preetorius said. "You know what you're looking for."

"Roger."

Cummins could feel the pressure building in his stomach again. He didn't want to have to scramble out of the car to puke, but neither did he want the vomit to explode all over the inside of the car.

I've got to keep control, he thought. *He's inside the house. Now it's just a matter of him finding that damn statue.*

Another whispered transmission. "I think I see it."

"See?" Preetorius said, smiling. "Did I not tell you this would go down easily?"

"We're not out of the woods yet, Luan," Zerbe said. "Ask him if he's sure."

Preetorius held up his hand. "He will advise."

"Ask him, dammit," Zerbe said.

Preetorius glared at him. Even in the dim moon-lit interior of the van, Cummins could see that the leader of the Lion Team did not like to be rushed or questioned. He still held the cell phone that had an open connection to the three mercs tailing Wolf and McNamara and the women.

Then another transmission came, this one in a regular conversational tone.

"Yes, I've got it," Amiri said.

"Good," Preetorius said. "Now, set fire to the place to cover your tracks."

"No," Zerbe said. "Not until we verify that it's the right statue."

"How many could there be?" Preetorius said. He was obviously irritated.

"We can't afford to take the chance," Zerbe told him.

Preetorius heaved a sigh and pressed the key on his mic.

"Belay that last command," he said. "Bring us the statue immediately."

"Roger."

Preetorius turned to Cummins. "May I at least tell Ryband, Bash, and Gerhardus to proceed with their strike?"

Zerbe nodded. "Tell them to abduct, but not to kill until we've verified the authenticity."

Preetorius snorted in disgust and spoke into his phone: "Take them."

***

Rest Stop
Near Kingman, Arizona

"Oh, shit, shit, shit," Krenshaw said. "It's gotta be the Bellottis. Those dago fuckers musta put a hit out on me. We gotta run."

"We'll never outrun them," Wolf said, picking up a magazine. "Besides, one of them just went to cover the other end of the building."

"Fuck, what are we gonna do?"

"Stay calm for the moment," Wolf said. "And do exactly what I tell you."

Urine streamed from Krenshaw's pantleg and puddled on the floor.

Two figures were silhouetted just outside the entrance doors. The door at the other end burst open, and a man wearing a ski mask pushed through. He had a wicked-looking semi-automatic in his right hand, holding it in a Weaver stance.

A gunshot exploded in the building, and Wolf pushed Krenshaw toward the open entrance to the men's room as the mounted camera exploded over their heads.

Shock and awe, Wolf thought and regretted that he hadn't taken Mac up on his offer to loan him a weapon. He was dependent on the P Patrol, and he hoped they were as good as their reputation. He also wondered how many firefights they'd been in.

He rammed Krenshaw into the wall, then twisted and threw him under the line of wall sinks. Whirling, he searched for anything he might use as a weapon. A three-foot-tall metal trash receptacle stood by a paper towel dispenser. Wolf grabbed it and lifted the white outside covering off the metal base, then kicked that on its side. The circular receptacle rolled toward the opening as one of the masked men rushed through the door, a big Glock extended out in front of him. He kicked the can out of his way but slipped in the trail of urine Krenshaw had left.

Wolf wasted no time in swinging the hollow metal tube like a baseball bat into the intruder's outstretched hands.

The man's Glock went off with an explosive roar, and the outside edge of the metal receptacle displayed a ragged circular hole.

Wolf jumped forward and grabbed for the gun.

The sound of several shots being fired outside might mean Ms. Dolly and the girls got the drop on the other two. At least, Wolf hoped so. His survival was dubious at the moment, but he hated to think that any of them would be hurt.

With his hands on those of the masked man, Wolf and his foe slammed into the brick wall like two football players scrambling for possession of the game ball, neither wanting to relinquish his hold.

More shots came from outside, then someone

screamed, "*Wat's fout?*"

Oh, God, Wolf thought. *Please don't let one of us be hurt.*

He brought his foot up in a quick kick to his opponent's groin.

The other man shifted his body slightly, and Wolf's foot struck only the inner portion of a meaty thigh. The guy was strong and bigger than Wolf. They slammed into another wall, still struggling for possession of the gun. It went off again, and Wolf felt the sting of the gunpowder blast as the bullet whizzed by the left side of his face. The slide had become blocked upon its return, and he saw that the weapon had stove-piped. For some reason, he was able to identify the snagged shell casing in the ejection port as a .45.

He adjusted his grip, wedged his right hand under the partially extended slide, and twisted the weapon. The other man grunted and tried to kick Wolf, but he managed to shift and deflect the blow.

Outside, it sounded like a war zone. He hoped the P Patrol had brought extra magazines.

Wolf ripped the Glock away, but they both tumbled forward, and the weapon hit the floor with a metallic snap. It skittered a few feet, and they both scrambled for it. Wolf got there first, still prone. The fingers of his right hand curled around the polymer handle, and he racked back the slide with his left. The stove-piped round popped free, and the slide carried the next round forward. Twisting, he pointed the weapon at the figure looming over him and pulled the trigger.

A black hole appeared in the man's gray shirt, and he reeled back with a heavy gasp. Wolf squeezed the trigger again, but the projectile only chipped flakes off the brick wall by the other man's head. The masked man turned and ran out of the washroom. Wolf scrambled to his feet and followed, holding the Glock at combat-ready. He glanced at Krenshaw momentarily.

"Dros!" a masculine voice yelled.

Wolf stopped at the entry and did a quick peek.

There was no way of knowing what waited for him on the other side.

His ears were ringing, and the voices he heard sounded like they were coming down a long tunnel.

But they were female voices.

Screams were more like it.

He stepped to the second wall of the cove-like entrance and did another check. Splashes of crimson dotted the floor, along with a plethora of expended shell casings. Ms. Dolly was wedged against the far wall in a cover position behind a vending machine. Several holes decorated the shiny metal. Yolanda was at the entrance to the ladies' room holding her Beretta in a combat stance, using the outer edge of the wall as an effective buffer. Brenda was flat on the floor by Yolanda's feet, her Taurus Spectrum in her hands.

Wolf shifted and saw that the glass doors leading into the place were riddled with bullet holes. Three men were heading for the van with ragged steps. A flash of light appeared from the group, and a bullet crunched through the perforated glass window. Wolf moved to the entry, hugging the wall for part of the way and then kneeling.

The three men scrambled into the van, and it started up. Another muzzle flash came from the big SUV, but the round didn't impact anywhere close. The vehicle backed out, cut hard to the left, and zoomed behind the parked Cherokee and the Escalade. It then shot forward, going the wrong way down the entrance ramp with no lights. Wolf ran out and leveled the Glock at the fleeing vehicle but hesitated. They were accelerating at such a fast clip that the accuracy of any shot he might make was questionable, and he didn't want to waste the ammo.

Seconds later, he realized he didn't need to fire. The van continued its rapid wrong-way unlighted flight as the headlights of a semi-truck abruptly swung into view. The truck's horn blared, then there was a squeal of brakes, followed by a thunderous clap as the van slammed head-on into the big semi. Despite his gunshot-induced hearing impairment, Wolf could discern the distinctive metallic crunch and saw the headlights of the semi on either side of the crumpled van. A few seconds passed, and the crushed vehicle ignited in a mushroom of orange, yellow, and red.

He took a deep breath and went back inside, holding the Glock down by his leg.

Ms. Dolly and her compatriots met him in the hallway. They were breathing hard.

"Whooeee," Ms. Dolly said. A wisp of smoke lingered around the muzzle of her Python. "They gone?"

"They went the wrong way," Wolf said, cognizant that his hearing was mostly back now, although still distorted by a constant ringing. "Smashed into a truck."

"Couldn't have happened to nicer guys," she said. "Where's Willard?"

Wolf ran into the men's room, almost slipping on the trail of blood and urine. He looked under the sinks where he'd left Krenshaw and saw he was gone.

Ms. Dolly and the others were right behind him.

"You see him leave this place?" Wolf asked.

"Huh-uh," Ms. Dolly said. "Nobody came out."

There wasn't a back door, either.

Wolf went past the urinals to the stalls that housed the toilets. One of them had a trail of urine leading to it. He kicked open the door and saw Krenshaw crouching on the black half-moon toilet set with an expression of sheer terror on his face.

"If you're all finished in there," Wolf said with a smile, "it's time to go."

CHAPTER 14

MCCARRAN INTERNATIONAL AIRPORT
LAS VEGAS, NEVADA

Wolf leaned back in the seat and closed his eyes. He knew he should try to sleep, but he was still feeling the adrenaline boost from the shooting and the conversation with Mac. After hightailing it out of the rest stop, they'd driven as quickly as they could to the Clark County Detention Center, where Ms. Dolly and the girls introduced him to Alexander Pope, who was waiting for them in a limo in the parking lot. Krenshaw, soiled and smelly, was more than subservient and ready to kiss the ring, but the Pope was having none of it. He admonished the lawyer that their association was finished and that court proceedings to take his worthless house in Palm Springs and his piece-of-shit Mercedes were already in the works.

"You can sell your soul to the feds if you want to live," the Pope said, as solemn as if he were administering penance in a confessional. "But do not ever call me again for bond money. *Capisce?*"

Krenshaw was in tears when Ms. Dolly, Brenda, and Yolanda walked him into the jail to collect their booking slip. That was when Wolf got the call from McNamara.

"Where you at?" Mac asked.

"Fabulous Las Vegas, Nevada," Wolf said, trying to sound light-hearted. Something was wrong. Why was Mac calling him at two-thirty in the morning? His voice sounded tense. "Everything okay?"

Wolf heard Mac blow out a long breath on the other end.

"Not really," he said. "Some asshole broke in here."

"Broke in? To the ranch?"

"Yeah," McNamara said. "Everybody's okay, Kase, Chad, and me."

"What happened?"

"Well, I was sleeping on the couch with my damn leg elevated," McNamara said. "And I got up to take a piss. I was in the downstairs bathroom when I thought I heard something. I peeked out the door and saw somebody sneaking around inside the den, shining a flashlight. I'm in my fucking underwear and no shoes, and I'm about forty feet away from my damn gun clock, not to mention my ankle being like a ball and chain."

Wolf tried to picture the scene. The fact that Mac was taking his time and relishing the account let him relax a little.

"So, I was trying to figure out if there was more than one and what the chances were of me making a dash for the clock when I hear the son of a bitch talking. But he wasn't talking to anybody close. He was on a comm."

That set off a red flag for Wolf. It didn't sound like a run-of-the-mill burglar.

McNamara continued, "I slipped out the bathroom and started sneaking toward the clock, being so quiet and smooth that a whole company of NVA wouldn't have heard me. Then I hear the son of a bitch saying he's 'got it,' and a voice telling him to set the house on fire and scoot. I figured, sore ankle or no sore ankle, I had to make my move before he did." McNamara paused and took a deep breath. "I made a beeline for the clock and got it open just in time to see this black guy coming at me. I turned and shot. Point-shooting, not even aiming. No time. He went down. When my hearing came back, I could hear the son of a bitch on the other end of the comm asking him what the hell was going on."

He paused and Wolf waited, saying nothing.

"Well, Kasey had heard the commotion and called nine-one-one. I checked the motherfucker, and he was unconscious. My round hit him a little off center mass. Missed his heart, but sure enough, it caught his right lung. I cleared the rest of the house and got back on the phone with the cops, telling them there were more of them in the area. Pretty soon, the whole place was lit up like Christmas in Times Square."

"You know the guy?" Wolf asked.

"Nah, never seen him before. A black guy. But I do know what he was after." McNamara paused. "You'll never guess what."

"What?" Wolf asked.

"The damn bandito," McNamara said.

"What?"

McNamara chuckled. "Yeah, I thought that would get you. I can fill you in on the rest of it when you get here."

Numerous questions circulated in Wolf's mind. Why would a burglar be after that thing? Was Mac right about that? Could this somehow be connected to Mexico?

"Where's the bandito at now?" Wolf asked, still wondering about its significance.

"He's standing guard in my super-secret gun safe," McNamara said.

The safe was hidden behind a false wall in the master bedroom and housed Mac's rifles, pistols, and a whole lot more. The metal door was secured by a biometric lock.

The unanswered questions kept swirling, then

Mac made the mistake of asking him how his trip had gone.

"It was eventful," Wolf said and related the details of the shootout.

"Holy shit," McNamara said. "My three darlings all right?"

"All right and combat-tested. I was thinking it must have been some Mafia guys, given who we were transporting, but after what you just told me, I'm not so sure anymore. Plus, one of them said something that sounded like German."

"Damn! I'm glad you guys didn't sustain any casualties."

"Well," Wolf said, unable to resist giving it back to him a little, "there was one."

"Huh? Who?"

"Not who, a what. The Escalade caught a bullet in the radiator. I tried to drive it away, but it conked out, and I had to leave it on the side of the road on I-93. We didn't have time to wait around, not knowing if a second wave was coming."

"Smart move," McNamara said. "It was probably gonna get repossessed pretty soon anyway."

"Not with the paycheck we'll be getting for this one. Ms. Dolly said she'd split it with us fifty-fifty."

The flight attendant came by and told him to turn off his cell phone and buckle his seatbelt. He told Mac he'd call him when he arrived and hung up. The flight attendant's eyes widened as she looked down at his pants, which were spotted with blood and smelled slightly of urine. He wished he'd had time to buy a new pair, but Yolanda had driven him directly to the airport so he could catch the redeye out. It had turned out to be a three-hour wait, and he'd regretted not just renting a car and driving back. But he knew he was in no shape to try it alone. Fatigue was eating into the adrenaline rush that had sustained him, and now all he wanted to do was sleep.

He buckled the seat belt and asked, "How soon will we get to Phoenix?"

"It's a short flight once we take off," the flight attendant said and moved on.

The way he smelled, he couldn't blame her.

***

The Elegant Suites Hotel
Phoenix, Arizona

Luan Preetorius tossed the phone on the bed and felt like slamming his fist into the wall. Make that through the wall. Still no acknowledgment from the three of them. Was it possible that this Wolf fellow had bested them all? Gerhardus, Bash, and Ryband... Three of his best men, albeit not as good as him or Henrico, and maybe not even Gidea and Francois.

But if that was the case, he was now down to him and three others. Well, four, counting Zerbe, who couldn't be trusted for much more than observation and intel. The fat American was useless, and according to Zerbe, a weak link that was eventually to be dealt with after they had verified this artifact they were seeking. It was some rich man's holy grail but essentially worthless outside of certain select circles. Like being paid in Bitcoin, intangible and essentially worthless unless you held a certain key.

"Any word?" Cummins, the American, asked.

Luan despised the man so much he didn't bother to answer.

Cummins tried again. "Any word from your three men we sent after Wolf?"

Luan shook his head.

"Damn," Cummins said. "I told you it was risky sending just three of them, didn't I? Wolf was an Army Ranger and his partner a Green Beret. It was a mistake to underestimate him."

Preetorius grabbed him by the throat, slammed him against the wall, and lifted him up. "You keep your fat mouth shut. I have apparently lost part of my team."

Cummins gurgled as Preetorius held him there.

"Luan, we still need him," Zerbe said in Afrikaans.

Preetorius dropped Cummins and stepped away.

Cummins rubbed his throat with both hands and

peered up at him.

Preetorius met the other man's gaze and held it until he looked away. It only took about ten seconds, then Cummins bolted for the bathroom and slammed the door. The sound of retching quickly followed.

"It's too bad they all aren't soft pussies like him," Preetorius said. "It would make things a lot easier."

Zerbe scrolled through some numbers on his burner phone and saved one.

"I've located the hospital where they took Amiri," he said. "He's been admitted and is under police guard."

"How did you find that information?"

"Easily enough," Zerbe said. "I pretended to be a reporter seeking information on a news story about a home invasion."

Preetorius was impressed. Despite Zerbe's short-comings as far as fighting skills, he was a good intelligence-gatherer.

Inside the bathroom, a toilet flushed.

Preetorius smirked.

"The question is," Zerbe continued, "how do you want to handle it?"

"Amiri knows better than to talk."

"That's good, but how long will that last? How long will it be before they identify him?"

"All the more reason we have to get back to South Africa," Preetorius said.

"It's only a matter of time before he's identified and

traced back to the Lion Team and when you entered the country. We can't afford for that to happen."

"Of course not. Amiri's a liability to me and the rest of us. An expendable liability."

Zerbe was silent for a moment as if he were contemplating what had just been said.

Yes, Preetorius thought, *I have agreed to eliminate one of my team.*

"And you're all right with that?" Zerbe asked.

"Why do you think I sent *die neger*?" Luan said. "It's a soldier's duty, and it will be painless and quick."

"How will you do it?"

"Leave the details to me. Merely give me the hospital specifications and drive me there. It shouldn't take long. We'll need some hospital nurse's uniforms and an empty syringe. Knowing American hospitals, he's probably on a morphine drip, which will make it even easier."

Cummins came back into the room. He looked at Preetorius and then at Zerbe.

"I'm going to my room," he said. "My throat hurts."

With that, he stormed out of the room.

"I should have kicked his ass instead," Preetorius said.

"He'll get his soon enough. Now remember, we need to take care of a few more loose ends, like that lawyer, Shemp."

"Let me see the file you prepared."

Zerbe sorted through a group of manila folders and handed him one.

Preetorius flipped it open and studied the 8x10 headshot of the lawyer. It was a boyish-looking face, devoid of toughness. This one, at least, should be easy.

"And we still have to get that statue," Zerbe said.

"Yes," Preetorius said, still perusing the file. "We will do that tonight."

***

The McNamara Ranch
Phoenix, Arizona

Wolf's plan to take a combat nap of one hour had stretched into eight. The short airplane flight had been unexpectedly delayed by a computer problem in the cockpit, which had required a technician to be summoned to replace the entire unit. The whole time, the antsy passengers moved and spoke, preventing even the least bit of slumber on the plane. The woman next to Wolf was constantly getting up; he imagined she wanted to get away from the smell of him. He wanted to get away from it too, which was why he'd taken a taxi from the airport to the ranch without bothering to call Mac. When he arrived, he saw no signs that anyone was stirring inside the house at the still-relatively-early hour, so he went to the garage, showered, and then hit the sack.

His cell phone woke him, and he stared at the screen in disbelief.

Was it really fifteen-thirty?

He punched the icon and heard Mac's chuckle coming from the phone.

"They let you sleep like that in the Rangers?" he asked.

Wolf yawned. "I can't believe I've been out this long. Why didn't you wake me?"

"Aw, hell, after what you told me and then talking to Ms. Dolly, I figured you earned the rest. She sends her regards, by the way, and says you saved the day."

"Hardly," Wolf said. "More like the other way around."

"She also gave me fair warning she's gonna steal you away from me."

Wolf hadn't been expecting that. Maybe she'd been sincere about the job offer, and he was tempted. It would be a good way to get away from the Wicked Witch of the East, but he could hardly tell Mac that.

"Ain't gonna happen until I pay you back," Wolf said. "In fact, I probably should be paying you rent now."

"Hey, like I said before, we'll worry about that once we get you back on your feet. And me, too." He laughed again. "Did I tell you that my ankle's good to go? Well, almost. But that little after-midnight exercise seemed to pop everything back into place. I got an elastic bandage on it now, and it's feeling great."

Wolf's head was starting to clear, and he had a bunch of questions he wanted to ask.

"Come on up, and I'll make some coffee," he said. "We can figure out our next move."

"I already got our first move," McNamara said. "We're gonna see if Manny can get us any info on this burglar guy, but first, look out the window."

Wolf got out of bed and padded over. He looked down in the driveway and saw McNamara standing next to a rather shop worn silver BMW X-6.

"Where'd you get that thing?" he asked.

"Lonnie Coats," McNamara said. "I put in a good word with Manny when we dropped him off, and Manny reposted his bond. After you told me about the Escalade, I called him and asked if he had a loaner. He give me this baby. It's got some miles on it, but the air-conditioning works."

"Sweet."

"See? It's like I always say it pays to be nice to people because you never know when you'll need a favor down the road."

"Let's hope we don't have to call for a tow truck, then," Wolf said.

***

Office of Emmanuel Sutter
Phoenix, Arizona

Manny stirred the plastic fork through the leafy assortment of vegetables in the bowl on his desk. He picked up a packet of dressing and looked at it, then clamped his teeth on one end and pulled. Some of the orange liquid squirted onto the papers on his desk.

"Goddammit," he said, then squeezed the rest of the contents over the lettuce. "Fucking Paul Newman. What the hell did he know about fucking salad dressing?"

"Since when did you start eating salads?" McNamara asked.

He and Wolf sat in the two chairs in front of Manny's big desk, and Wolf was glad he wasn't within squeezing range.

"Doctor's orders," Manny said. "I gotta lose some weight and cut down on my sugar. Otherwise, there's a chance I could get diabetes."

"That's nothing to fool with," McNamara said.

"Tell me about it." Manny glanced over his shoulder at his nephew. "Hey, Sherman, go get me one of them paper towels, will ya? You forgot the napkins again."

Freddie pursed his lips as he got up, glaring at his uncle. "It's Fred, not Sherman."

"Yeah, whatever."

As soon as Freddie had gone to the closet and

stuck his head in the open door, Manny pushed back from his desk, pulled open the top drawer, and removed a long, flat candy bar. He winked at Wolf and McNamara as he swiftly unwrapped it, broke off several chunks, and dropped them into the salad.

"If I cheat on my diet," he said with a wink as he concealed the half-gone candy bar under his desk, "Sherman here will rat me out to his mother, and she in turn will tell my old lady."

You can't cheat the Grim Reaper, Wolf thought and figured Manny's diet plans weren't headed for a happy ending. Neither was his health.

"So, like I was saying," Manny continued, still stirring the vegetables around with his fork. "Ms. Dolly called me. I heard about your little shootout."

"It wasn't so little," Wolf said.

"So I heard." Manny finally shoved some of the salad into his mouth, which remained partially open while he chewed and spoke. "Ms. Dolly said you thought the guys mighta been Mafia?"

"It's anybody's guess," Wolf said. "But what I couldn't figure out was how they knew we'd be transporting Willard on that route."

"Willard," Manny said and stuffed some chocolate-laden lettuce into his wide-open mouth. "Ain't that a funny name?"

"Funny guy, too," Wolf said. "Pissed his pants."

Manny laughed, expelling a few chunks onto his

paper-strewn desktop. "Ain't that the luck?"

"Actually, it was," Wolf said. "One of the gunmen ended up slipping in it, and I was able to get his gun away from him."

Manny leaned back and laughed so hard Wolf was worried he was going to topple over. When he shifted back to his regular posture, he slammed his massive forearms on the desk. "So, what brings you two gents here now?"

"I shot a burglar in my house last night," McNamara said.

"No shit?" Manny plucked a few pieces of chocolate from the salad and tossed them into his mouth.

"And at the same time," Wolf said, "three guys attacked me on the road to Vegas."

McNamara leaned forward. "Like we said, those bastards knew exactly where to find Steve and the crew last night, and the only place we went after nabbing him was here."

Manny's eyebrows rose. "You don't think I ratted you out, do ya?"

"I don't know," McNamara said. "Did ya?"

"Hell, no."

Wolf could see the color rising on Manny's cheeks and neck.

"Did you call anybody and tell them?" Wolf asked. "Maybe drop a hint that we'd be driving?"

"Huh?" Manny's face scrunched, then relaxed.

"Well, I did call the Pope to tell him you was on your way, but Ms. Dolly told me to do that."

"And you gave him the route?" Wolf asked.

"Well, yeah. He asked, so I told him."

McNamara slammed his open palm on the desk so hard it caused the plastic salad tray to jump. Something fell to the floor from under the desk.

Wolf reached down and picked it up. It was two small circular devices stuck together. They were about the size of a quarter, and the one on top had a small netted circle off to one side.

"What the hell?" Manny said. "Lemme see that."

Wolf handed it to him, and Manny rolled it around his palm.

"This is a fucking bug," he said. "A listening device."

He whirled his chair around. "Sherman, you put this in here?"

"What? No."

"Then how in the fuck?" He dropped the bug onto the floor and stomped on it.

"I found a tracker on my car, too," McNamara said. "It's gotta be tied together."

"You know," Freddie said. "Come to think of it, that one Aussie guy was monkeying around over there while you was in the john."

Wolf was confused. Aussie guy?

"And you didn't fucking tell me?" Manny rose from the desk like a behemoth and strode across the small space separating the two of them, cocking his right arm back. "Why, I oughta kick your—"

"Manny, it's not his fault," Wolf said. "These guys are pretty slick. Pros."

Manny kept glaring down at Freddie, who had an expression like a fearful puppy.

"If you wasn't my sister's kid..." Manny said finally, then traipsed back to his chair. He settled into it with a tremendous plop, causing the chair's metal framework to give what almost sounded like a scream for mercy.

"You think it was the Outfit?" Manny asked. "The Mafia?"

Wolf shrugged. It was like they were trying to put together a jigsaw puzzle without an overall picture of what it was supposed to be, but he was leery of divulging too much to Manny.

"Somebody's stalking us," McNamara said. "And we don't even know who the hell it is."

"But now we know how," Wolf said. "All we gotta find out is why."

"How you gonna do that?" Manny asked.

"You got contacts in the PD," McNamara said. "Do me a favor and call one of them. Find out where they're keeping that guy I shot and anything else they'll tell you."

"I'll get on it," Manny said, stirring the salad some more.

"Now," McNamara said in a voice that meant business.

"Okay," Manny said, setting the salad aside and reaching for his phone. "Now it is."

***

Office of Rodney F. Shemp
Attorney at Law
Phoenix, Arizona

"We gotta interrogate that prisoner," McNamara said in a stentorian voice. "And according to the cops, he's already lawyered up."

Wolf felt sorry for poor Shemp as Mac leaned over the guy's desk and continued to address him.

"Listen, Rodney," McNamara said. "I told you this ain't gonna take that long. We just need you to get us past the police guard."

"But I'm not even the arrested man's attorney," Shemp said, leaning back in his chair. He was wearing a crisp white shirt, which was rapidly flagging in places, and a red necktie. "Besides, Mr. McNamara, I'm supposed to pick up Kasey at six-thirty. It's important."

McNamara raised an eyebrow.

"Important?" he repeated. "How so?"

Shemp's eyes darted to Wolf, then back to McNamara, then downward.

"We're... I'm... You see—"

"Spit it out, dammit," McNamara interrupted. "We're talking about my little girl here."

"I'm going to ask her to marry me tonight," Shemp blurted.

McNamara was silent, eying the man for several seconds, then his head began a slow rocking.

"Well," he said. "From a father's perspective, it's good to know you have honorable intentions regarding my daughter."

A weak smile formed on Shemp's lips, then vanished.

"I didn't mean to be so vociferous," he said. "But you see, I have to get home and shower and change and—"

"And nothing," McNamara said. "I'm giving you my blessing. She needs a good strong man she can depend on."

Shemp's smile returned, but it was still tentative.

"So," McNamara said, extending his big open palm, "welcome to the family."

Shemp took McNamara's hand and immediately grimaced.

Wolf knew from experience that Mac had one of the strongest grips he'd ever had the misfortune of feeling.

Shemp was still wincing as McNamara raised his arm upward, bringing Shemp out of the chair.

"So, here's the way this evening's gonna play out,

Rodney," he said. "You, me, and Steve are gonna take a little ride over to St. Francis Hospital, which is only a few blocks out of your way, right?"

"Well, it's actually not—" Shemp stopped talking and went up on his toes. McNamara was still pumping the man's arm.

"Not what, Rodney?" Mac asked, a big smile stretched across his face.

"It's not," Shemp said, "that far out of my way, I suppose."

"Now we're talking," McNamara said and winked at Wolf.

***

Outside the Office of Rodney F. Shemp
Attorney at Law
Phoenix, Arizona

"Isn't that Wolf and McNamara with the lawyer?" Preetorius asked from the front seat of the van. They were parked about fifty feet from the lawyer's office.

Cummins felt a surge of panic even though he was in the back seat and mostly concealed by Zerbe and Preetorius. The last thing he needed was for that one-man killing machine to see him or Zerbe. Even though both of them in the front seat were armed, and Preetorius was huge, he wasn't sure they could stop

Wolf. Eagan had been big, too, and look how easily Wolf had taken him out.

"Duck down or something," Cummins said. "What if he sees you?"

"Relax," Zerbe said. "I've got my contacts in and combed my hair differently. No way they'll recognize me, and they've never seen Luan."

Cummins noticed that Zerbe did slip on a baseball cap and pull it down over his forehead.

"Looks like they're getting into two different vehicles," Preetorius said. He was dressed in hospital scrubs in anticipation of his visit to his wounded comrade. "McNamara and the lawyer in one and Wolf in the other. An old used BMW."

"Let's see if they're splitting up," Zerbe said. "If they do, we follow Wolf and try to put a tracker on his Beamer."

Cummins scrunched down as best he could. This van had dark windows, and he felt fairly invisible behind the tint. Two cars passed, one of them the Beamer.

Wolf was driving the BMW, Cummins thought as a shiver ran through him.

What if Wolf discovered the artifact and was now anticipating making a deal of his own? But he didn't know about Von Dien...or did he? There was no telling how much information Eagan had given him in Mexico before Wolf killed him. Cummins debated whether to bring this up to Zerbe and decided against it, but he had to start planning an exit strategy for himself.

They followed the BMW through the city streets for several blocks until Shemp's car and Wolf's both turned right into the parking lot of St. Francis Hospital.

"This is working out better than we expected," Preetorius said, activating his own turn signal and entering the parking lot.

"All roads lead to Rome," Zerbe said.

Rome...

Cummins wasn't comfortable with that metaphor. Right now, he felt a bit like Nero.

***

The woman at the front desk was hesitant at first to give them the room number of the patient in police custody. Manny had found out that the police were holding him as John Doe because thus far, he'd either been unable or unwilling to give his real name. Shemp showed her his Bar Association card, but she eyed Wolf and McNamara with suspicion.

"These are my associates," Shemp said.

The woman's fingers tapped the keyboard, and she reluctantly told them it was Room 628.

As they headed for the elevators, McNamara reached into his pocket and pulled out a small black velvet box. He slapped Wolf's arm as they entered the elevator car.

"Look at this," he said, popping the box open to display a beautifully cut diamond set in a ring of white gold. "Ain't that a nice-looking rock he's got for my little girl?"

"It is," Wolf said. "But why are you holding it?"

"So I could show it to you, of course," McNamara said. He closed the box and slipped it back into the pocket of his BDU blouse.

Shemp's brow furrowed, and he bit his lip.

"Uh, Mr. McNamara—" Shemp started to say.

"Hell, son," McNamara said. "Since we're gonna be family, you'd better start calling me Mac."

Shemp nodded and swallowed.

"The ring, Mac," he said. "I'd like to keep it."

"Keep it?" McNamara grinned at Wolf. "I thought you were gonna give it to Kasey?"

"Well, I am, but—"

"Mac," Wolf said. "Give him back the ring. The guy's doing us a favor here, and you're being a bully."

McNamara looked wounded. "Me? A bully? I thought I was just being a father."

He reached into his pocket, withdrew the ring, and handed it to Shemp. Then he leaned close. "You better be good to her. She's my little girl."

Shemp flashed another weak smile and slipped the ring into his pants pocket. He was still wearing his gray suit, white shirt, and red necktie, although the collar of the shirt was sweat-stained and starting to wilt. Wolf hoped he wasn't getting cold feet about the whole thing. Having Kasey happily married and out of the picture would make things a whole lot easier in his world. He'd have to have a talk with Mac and tell him to quit being the prospective father-in-law from hell.

"Rod," Wolf said, glancing from Shemp to McNamara to Shemp again, "we appreciate you doing this."

Shemp nodded, and the elevator doors opened.

The uniformed police officer in front of Room 628 looked young and bored. He was a good-looking guy, and he was holding his hat in his hand while conversing with a young and very pretty nurse. He straightened when Wolf, Mac, and Shemp walked up and slipped the hat back on his head.

"May I help you?" he asked.

Shemp held up his Bar Association card and identified himself as a lawyer needing to speak to Mr. John Doe, who had requested legal counsel.

The young officer stared at the card intently, then scribbled down the name in a small notebook.

"Who are these guys?" he asked, cocking his head toward Wolf and McNamara.

"They're my associates," Shemp said.

He shot a nervous glance at McNamara, who said, "If you need to pat us down, feel free, Officer. I left my gun in the car."

The cop's eyes widened, but he smiled when Mc-Namara let out a friendly laugh. It bridged the gap with the implied brotherhood of two men who knew what it was like standing guard on the line.

The unspoken camaraderie of mutual respect, Wolf thought. Mac's experience as a leader of men seemed to automatically place him above question to most who'd been there.

McNamara lifted his arms and the cop did a quick pat-down of him, then Wolf, and finally Shemp.

The cop opened the door, and Shemp started to walk through but stopped as McNamara placed his hand on the lawyer's shoulder. They both turned to the police officer. Mac said, "It goes without saying that this interview falls under attorney-client privilege and is confidential, right?"

"Of course," the cop said. "I won't be listening. Call me if you need me."

Shemp nodded, but from the expression on his face, Wolf sensed that the lawyer was having serious misgivings.

We'll have to make this short and sweet, Wolf thought.

But if they could just get one clue about who this guy was working for and why he was after the bandito, it would be worth it.

It was a private room and the burglar lay on his back, tubes and IV lines connected to various parts of his body. There was a bag of clear liquid suspended on a metal hook on the left side of the bed; the line connected to it went to the inner aspect of the supine man's elbow, where an IV was connected. A set of telemetry machines overhead flashed numbers, and one showed a static line of heartbeats. His right arm was handcuffed to the metal handle of the portable gurney. His eyes were closed, and he had an oxygen tube in his nose.

Wolf assessed the man. He was very dark-complected, and his hair was cut military short. He looked to be fairly young, late twenties or not much beyond that. It was hard to tell much else due to the medical equipment and attachments.

McNamara strode over to the bed and smiled. "Don't he look peaceful?"

With that, the man's eyes fluttered open.

"How you doing?" Mac asked.

The man's head turned slightly. "I'm...who the hell are you?"

His words had a foreign sound to them.

"Well," McNamara said. "That depends. I could be your savior, or I could be your worst nightmare." He placed his hand on top of the man's chest and pressed down.

The man grunted.

"I'm surprised you don't remember me," McNamara said.

He exerted more pressure and elicited another grunt.

"I already told you," the man said. "I've got nothing to say until I talk to my counsel."

"We ain't cops," McNamara said, leaning close to the man. "And I ain't above finishing what I started last night."

The man's eyes widened. "You... You're the one who shot me."

"And you're the one that was gonna burn my house down, motherfucker."

Shemp cleared his throat. "Mac, please. I can't be a party to this. I'll be disbarred."

"Then go get a drink of water or something," McNamara said.

"They have my name," Shemp said.

"Well, we'll have to keep that in mind. Now take a quick walk and leave us be for a couple. This ain't gonna take long."

Shemp's mouth twitched, then he headed for the door.

***

Preetorius watched as the lawyer, Shemp, came out of Amiri's room. The cop was still in front, but he was busy chatting with the pretty nurse again. Shemp walked quickly toward the elevators and Preetorius followed, moving easily in the comfortable blue scrubs. As he passed the nurse's station, he scooped an empty clipboard off the counter and quickened his pace to catch up with the lawyer, who was now standing by the elevators, jamming his finger against the summoning button. He looked to be in a hurry to leave and separate himself from the other two.

"Excuse me," Preetorius said as he stepped up to the other man. He was fairly tall but soft around the middle and not at all rugged. "Is your name Mr. Shemp?"

The lawyer's jaw sagged slightly. "Yes."

"I believe you were in Mr. Doe's room just now?" Preetorius kept his expression neutral.

Be professional and non-threatening, he thought.

"I was," the lawyer said.

"Would you step this way, please? Doctor Sterfgeval would like a word with you."

He couldn't resist using the Afrikaans word for death.

Shemp's face twitched. "What's this concerning?"

"Doctor will explain," Preetorius said, affecting a benign smile and stepping to the side. "Please."

Shemp went along, glancing toward the room as they got into the main hallway. Instead of turning to the left to revisit Room 628, Preetorius turned right and walked briskly down the hallway, cognizant that Shemp was only a few steps behind him. They got almost to the end of the corridor, and Preetorius stopped by the stairwell door and pushed it open. Shemp balked.

"The stairwell?" he asked.

Once again, Preetorius flashed the benign smile.

"Oh," he said, holding the door open and lightly placing the fingertips of his gloved hand on the lawyer's right shoulder. "His office is only one floor down. I hope you don't mind."

Shemp nodded and stepped forward.

Preetorius went in after him and let the door swing closed. Shemp had barely taken two steps toward the stairwell before Preetorius dropped the clipboard on the floor. The lawyer stopped abruptly and was glancing downward as Preetorius shot forward and delivered a knife-hand chop to the back of the other man's neck. He collapsed without a sound, and Preetorius stooped and scissored his beefy forearms around the lawyer's rather thin neck. With the deft twist he'd practiced and used many times, the dull crack told him it was over.

Quick and easy, he told himself.

Now it was time to tie up that other matter.

***

Wolf was increasingly less comfortable the longer this went on. While he knew Mac's threats were meant more to intimidate than anything else, the repercussions of what they were doing could work against them.

Maybe it's time for a little good cop, bad cop, he thought.

"Let me talk to him," Wolf said, placing his hand on McNamara's arm and gently steering him away from the bed. "What's your name, brother?"

The man said nothing, his dark eyes defiant.

"Look, you're in some real trouble here," Wolf said. "And all we want to know are a few minor things. Who are you working for, and why were you after the bandito?"

"The what?" The man's face reflected confusion.

Wolf and McNamara exchanged glances.

"All right," Wolf said. "Let's go back to the original question. We know you weren't working this thing by yourself, and it's obvious that you're just the middleman. Tell us who put you up to it, and we can put in a good word with the DA for you."

The man just kept staring at him.

McNamara lurched forward, his face full of bluster.

"You goddamn well better talk, buster, and talk now. Otherwise—"

He smacked his right fist into his left palm with a loud cracking sound.

The man's eyes widened again. He seemed on the verge of saying something when the door opened, and a big guy in hospital scrubs stepped into the room. He had a clipboard and a pen, and he looked at Wolf, then McNamara.

"What is going on here?" he said. His speech had a foreign sound to it as well, but Wolf couldn't place it.

Neither Wolf nor McNamara spoke.

The man on the bed did, however: "Boss, help me. Please. These men are threatening me."

The big guy's eyebrows rose, and he studied both of them.

"Is this true?" he asked.

"Nah," McNamara said. "We were just having a little conversation, that's all."

"No, it is not true," the man said.

The big guy regarded both of them. "Perhaps it is best if you two left. Immediately."

McNamara started to argue, but Wolf grabbed his arm and walked him out of the door. They'd overstayed their welcome. It was time to boogie. As they left the room, Wolf glanced around for Shemp but didn't see him.

"Where's Rod?" he asked.

"Who gives a shit?" McNamara said. "That little weasel ran out as soon as things started to get hot. If one of my men had done that under my command, I'd have him brought up on charges after I beat the holy hell out of him. And that's only if I didn't shoot him for cowardice first."

Wolf smirked. "This ain't the Mekong Delta, and

we better beat feet before that cop decides to follow up and get our names."

McNamara nodded as they turned into the corridor leading to the elevators.

"Yeah, you're right," he said. "But that damn Shemp's gonna be lucky if I don't put a boot up his ass."

"I think poor Rod's probably got other things on his mind," Wolf said. "But at least you gave him back the ring."

***

Preetorius walked briskly to the cop and the flirtatious nurse in front of Amiri's room.

"Officer," he said. "There seems to be an emergency in the stairwell down the hall. I heard someone say a man fell down the stairs."

The cop's head shot up, the smile disappearing from his face. He immediately began a quick jog down the hallway, the nurse on his heels.

Protect and serve, Preetorius thought as he watched them. You do that so well.

He opened the door of room 628 and let it close behind him as he walked over to the bed.

"Are you all right?" he asked in Afrikaans.

Amiri opened his eyes. "Yes. I told them nothing. One of them was the old man who shot me last night."

"I know," Preetorius said.

"You've come to get me out of here?" Amiri asked.

"Yes." Preetorius studied the equipment and the IV lines, paying particular attention to the morphine drip gauge.

"How are you going to do it?"

"Easily," Preetorius said, adjusting the flow meter on the morphine bag's line to its fully open position and then picking up the pump. This would be better than inducing air into the flow line. With his other hand, he reached up and switched off the telemetry recording Amiri's heartbeat and vitals. The displays went silent, and the images disappeared from the screen. Amiri stiffened, and his eyes closed.

"And silently," Preetorius said as he continued to work the morphine pump.

CHAPTER 15

PHOENIX, ARIZONA

"That was a damn waste of time," McNamara said as he steered the BMW off the hospital exit ramp and onto the street. "That guy sound foreign to you?"

"He did," Wolf said. "But I couldn't place the accent."

"And how about King Kong in the nurse's outfit?"

"Who?"

"The guy that interrupted us."

Wolf thought about it. "Yeah, come to think of it, his words did sound a little foreign as well. But again, I'd be hard-pressed to say from where?"

McNamara went silent, but Wolf could see he was still frustrated and angry.

"You want me to call and check on Rod?" Wolf asked. "I have his cell."

"Check on him?"

"Yeah, you know. Tell him Elvis has left the building."

"That little weasel ran out on us as soon as the going got a little bit tough," McNamara said. "Like I said before, if he would've been on my squad—"

"Mac, give the guy some slack," Wolf said. "He's obviously not cut from the same cloth as you and me, but he's not that bad a guy. And it looks like he's going to be your new son-in-law."

"That's why I'm so goddamn upset. You don't treat family like that."

"Think about Kasey. What's best for her? She obviously loves the guy."

McNamara chewed on that; he was silent for the rest of the drive. After they'd arrived at the ranch, he pulled the BMW in front of the house, shifted it into park, and shut the engine off. It shuddered to a stop. Mac's phone chirped with a text, and he glanced at it. Wolf started to get out, and McNamara placed a hand on his arm.

"You're right," he said. "I do need to quit acting like an asshole and start thinking of Kasey and what's best for her."

Wolf was relieved to hear that and nodded.

"Actually," McNamara said. "Her and me had a little talk earlier while you were sleeping."

Wolf waited for him to continue.

"We got a lot of things out in the open," McNamara

said. "Including how she's been unfair to you."

Wolf felt awkward. That wasn't a road he wanted to go down. He started to say something, but Mc-Namara cut him off.

"She made that comment about you being the son I always wanted and how I was never there for her when she was growing up." He paused, and Wolf thought he saw tears glint in Mac's eyes. "I told her that was one of my biggest regrets. I also told her how you saved us down in Mexico and that I was the one that dragged you down there."

They sat in silence for a few moments, then Mc-Namara added, "She wants to apologize to you."

Wolf was stunned. Not only couldn't he believe it, it wasn't something he wanted to deal with at the moment.

McNamara held up his phone. "She just texted me to remind me to bring you into the house."

Wolf blew out a slow breath.

Was the Wicked Witch of the East about to turn into Glenda the Good?

They got out and walked to the front door. Wolf felt conflicted and wondered if this apology was something Mac had demanded or if it had been Kasey's idea.

When they went inside, Chad ran to greet them, punching McNamara's legs and then Wolf's.

"Where's your cane, Grandpa?" he said. "If you're

not going to use it no more, then I want it."

Wolf glanced over, saw the cane was still hanging on the grandfather clock by the door and surmised that Chad was almost tall enough to retrieve it. The kid had good manners, though.

A fresh-faced teenage girl with her hair pulled back in a ponytail approached and steered Chad away from them. Wolf knew she was Bonnie, Kasey's regular babysitter.

Kasey came in from the other room, once again dressed in an evening dress. This one was navy blue and had fine netting along the neckline. Her short hair looked to have recently been styled, and she'd obviously taken her time doing her makeup. The angry glower that had so often marred her looks, like the other night at Charlie's, had been replaced by a tentative yet seemingly genuine smile. Wolf thought she looked pretty.

In a sisterly way, of course.

After dispatching her son and Bonnie to his room for a few minutes, she approached Wolf and McNamara.

Wolf knew the presence of Bonnie the babysitter portended the imminent arrival of Shemp for the all-important dinner date. He hoped to get out of here before the lawyer's arrival.

"Steve," Kasey said, walking toward him with a sheaf of papers, "this is for you."

He accepted them and saw they contained a lot of printed documents and pictures.

"I finally got a chance to run those names you wanted and did some more digging on things. I did checks on Jack Cummins, that guy named Eagan, Jason Zerbe, the Viper PMC, and the Fallotti and Abraham Law firm. I even found some stuff out about that Von Dien person; that is, if his first name is Dexter."

She was talking faster than normal, and Wolf took that to mean she was nervous. He tried to make her feel at ease.

"Wow, this is great," he said, not wanting to use her name for fear of breaching some yet to be established etiquette rule.

"You'd better wait before you say that," she said. "At least until you've read it. The law firm's been dissolved, and a couple of the names have been virtually erased from the Internet."

"I appreciate all your work. Thanks."

"Actually," she said slowly, "I'm the one who should be thanking you. For saving my father's life. He told me what you did in Mexico."

"Well, I didn't do that much…"

"That's not what he told me," she said. "And I believe him. You're a special kind of person. A special kind of man. A special kind of soldier."

Wolf was embarrassed by the praise she was heaping upon him.

"There's something else I need to say," she said. "I apologize for the way I've been treating you."

"That's not necessary."

"Yes, it is." Her eyes locked with his. "I've been a...a real bitch lately, and I want you to know I really am sorry."

Wolf felt like clicking his shoes together and saying, "There's no place like home."

Instead, all he could think to say was, "Apology accepted."

In his peripheral vision, he saw that Mac was standing off to the side, grinning.

Kasey's cell phone, which was on the desk by the computer, rang, and she turned toward it.

"That's probably Rod," she said. "He was supposed to be here by now."

Wolf and McNamara exchanged glances, and Mac smirked and shrugged.

"I think I'll retire to my humble abode and peruse these," Wolf said, holding up the papers.

"Aw, hell, why not stay here instead? We can order a pizza, grab a couple of beers, and go over this stuff together."

Pizza did sound good, and Wolf was getting pretty hungry. He was just about to agree when they heard Kasey's semi-scream. They looked at each other, then ran into the other room. Kasey stood with one hand touching her face and the other holding the phone down by her leg.

"Honey, what's wrong?" McNamara asked.

Her hand dropped and she looked up, tears streaming down her face and causing black streaks of mascara.

"It's Rod," she said between sobs. "He's dead."

***

Preetorius watched as he listened to what Zerbe was saying, formulating the plan of attack in his mind. The ranch house lay before them, no more than seventy meters away. Even though it was still light out and less than ideal for a hard assault, the area was remote enough that they shouldn't be noticed or disturbed. Although he was unsure of how long this interrogation would last, in many ways, he was very much looking forward to it. This fellow Wolf was responsible for the deaths of three members of the Lion Team, even though the Internet newspaper account said three unidentified men had been killed in an automobile crash outside Kingman.

Accident, my ass, he thought. Wolf killed them.

Not only had he lost three comrades, but their defeat had impinged upon his reputation as a leader.

A good leader takes responsibility, he thought. And holds people accountable.

Not to mention that he was now curious about the

prowess of this Wolf. The fat American had extolled their adversary's strength and cunning and said not to underestimate him. He'd proven his mettle a bit by besting three of the Lion Team.

Preetorius smiled. He was looking forward to testing himself against this American Airborne Ranger warrior.

But first, they had to secure the damn artifact, then Wolf would be dealt with appropriately. Preetorius hoped he would not give up the artifact easily. He and Henrico and Gidea and Francois were running just ahead of the clock now. There was little time. They had to finish this mission and then make a hasty exit, perhaps to Canada or Mexico.

The fingers of his left hand caressed the KA-BAR he'd affixed to the belt around his waist. He looked forward to using it on Wolf.

"Let's do it," he said. "Gidea and Henrico, take the back door. Francois and I will hit the front."

He shifted the van into drive and floored the accelerator.

∗∗∗

Wolf thought he heard a vehicle accelerating, but it didn't sound real close, and it was hard to discern much detail over Kasey's sobs. Mac had taken her in his arms, and she was crying against his shoulder.

Wolf was glad the two of them had made amends before this tragedy. He was also wondering what had happened. Kasey had not been forthcoming, other than saying Shemp was dead. Questions began to formulate in Wolf's mind, and some of them caused some alarm bells to go off. He didn't feel like intruding on Mac and Kasey at this moment, but this wasn't the time to drop their guard, either.

In fact, he thought, it would be the perfect time for an attack.

But an attack by who?

He noticed that Chad and Bonnie were standing off to the side with expressions of horror on their faces.

"Mommy, what's wrong?" the boy asked. He was crying as well.

Wolf was just about to tell the babysitter to take him out of the room when he heard a crunching sound coming from the kitchen. His head swiveled toward it, as did Mac's, then the front door burst open from a stunning impact that sent the door flying inward, accompanied by a flurry of broken wood from the frame. Men entered from both directions, holding semi-auto pistols in front of them in combat-ready position. They moved like pros, using that modified Groucho Marx half-crouch-shuffle, issuing commands of "Nobody move" in foreign-sounding English. They were all good-sized white guys. The one who'd come in the front was the big nurse who'd kicked them out of John Doe's room.

This was all coming together now, and Wolf wasn't liking it one bit. Just when he thought it couldn't get any worse, another man entered who looked vaguely familiar. He certainly wasn't commando material—doughy-looking with a rotund middle—and neither was the one who waddled in behind him.

A chill went through Wolf as he saw who it was: ex-Lieutenant Jack Cummins.

The other doughboy was Jason Zerbe.

A Mexican reunion, thought Wolf. With a new Viper team.

***

After searching all of them and finding Mac's gun in his holster, they made everyone kneel in the center of the living room and told them to put their hands on top of their heads—with the exception of Kasey, who they allowed to hold Chad. He buried his face against her, obviously terrified. One of the crew laughed.

"If you hurt them," McNamara growled, "you ain't gonna have enough rounds to keep me from tearing your head off."

The man stepped forward and backhanded Mac in the face.

Wolf debated making a move, but he knew that in this position, it would be akin to suicide.

Zerbe stepped forward and grinned.

"Nice to see you two again," he said, pausing to light a cigarette. "Now, we can do this the easy way or the hard way." Turning, he motioned to Cummins. "Pull down all those window shades. We don't want to take the chance of anybody seeing this little party."

Wolf saw that Zerbe had a revolver tucked into the left side of his pants.

Cummins, who looked as white as sailor's cap, waddled over to each window and pulled down the shades. It caused the room to darken, so Zerbe said, "Turn on the fucking lights."

Cummins flipped the switch, then put a hand on his immensely distended gut.

"I gotta wait outside," he said, his voice a whine. "My stomach's bothering me."

"When *isn't* your stomach bothering you?" Zerbe said, his tone dripping derision. "Go ahead, get the hell out of here, and let us men do the work. We'll come and get you when we have it."

Have *it*?

Wolf wondered what that meant. Were they talking about the bandito?

Cummins shuffled out the door and disappeared.

Déjà vu all over again, Wolf thought.

Zerbe leaned his head back and blew a smoke ring, then looked down at Wolf.

"How about it, Stevie boy?" Zerbe said. "Which

way is it gonna be? Easy or hard?"

Wolf tried to figure out a way to buy some time and also to separate some of the bad guys from the innocents. The military tactics that had been drilled into him advised that if captured, the best chance for escape was at the earliest possible time. The longer it went on, the less chance you had.

But there were four guns pointed at them, and Zerbe was armed as well.

And none of us are, Wolf thought.

The best tactical plan he could come up with was to split their forces. If he could draw a couple of them away from here by leading them to his place, perhaps he could get the jump on them. It also might give Mac a chance to strike, but he was at a supreme disadvantage with his daughter and grandson in harm's way.

Still, if I know Mac, Wolf thought, *he's probably thinking the same way I am.*

"What the hell do you want?" Wolf asked.

Zerbe blew another smoke ring. It floated toward the ceiling smoke detector. Maybe if that went off, it would provide a diversion...

"You know what I want," Zerbe said. "That fucking statue Accondras had in Mexico. The one in his backpack."

"The statue?" Wolf said, trying to sound confused. "Why?"

"That's for me to know," Zerbe said. "Now, where

is it?"

Wolf searched for something to say.

The big guy who'd played the nurse spoke up.

"Let me get it out of him," he said. "It won't take me any time at all."

Zerbe contemplated that, then shook his head. He drew on the cigarette and released a cloudy breath as he spoke. "No, I think not. Mr. Wolf prides himself on being tough, and we are pressed for time. I believe it will go a lot quicker if we start with one of the less formidable subjects. Which one do you want, the child or one of the ladies?"

"Zerbe," McNamara snarled. "You son of a bitch."

Zerbe held up his index finger and waggled it dismissively.

"I'm not an unreasonable man," he said. "I have no desire to see Luan here start chopping off fingers or other parts." He paused to let that sink in. "But I'm also ready to do whatever it takes." He grinned sardonically. "Just like in Mexico."

"What's all this about?" Wolf asked, trying desperately to buy some time. "At least tell me that."

"You have no fucking idea," Zerbe said. He blew out a plume of smoke. "Well, what's it going to be?"

Wolf tried to glance at Mac to signal him that he was going to try something, but the big nurse slapped his face.

"Don't look at each other," the man ordered.

Wolf's mind raced with various scenarios, none of which seemed to have a snowball's chance in hell of working.

"I'm waiting," Zerbe said. The tip of his cigarette glowed bright red. "Ever seen an eyeball used for an ashtray?"

"All right," Wolf said. "I'll give it to you."

Zerbe's smile widened. "Now we're talking. You do that, and I promise we'll just tie all of you up and be on our way."

Wolf didn't believe that for a moment but pretended he did. He knew Mac didn't either, and he also knew through the gut instinct of combat brotherhood that Mac knew Wolf was trying to split the enemy force.

"It's in my apartment," he said.

"Is it now?" Zerbe waggled his eyebrows. "And where exactly is that?"

"Above the garage. In the other building."

"And where is it in there exactly?" Zerbe asked.

Wolf hesitated for a moment. "I've got a gun locker over there. It's hidden. I'll have to show you."

Zerbe laughed. "Oh, come on."

"No," Wolf said. "It's in there, but you won't be able to open it without me. It's a bio-lock. Requires my handprint to open, plus a combination."

"How about I just cut your fucking hand off?" the big nurse asked.

"Luan," Zerbe said, "That would be messy and time-consuming. Why don't you escort Mr. Wolf over there and see if he's telling the truth? If he's not, then let me know, and I can't decide which of these pretty girls I will let you start with."

"You better not hurt my mommy," Chad shouted.

Kasey put her hand over his mouth and pulled him closer to her breast.

He's gonna be a Ranger someday, Wolf thought. Or maybe Special Forces like his grandpa, if we can get out of this.

"May I stand?" Wolf asked.

Zerbe stepped back and tossed the cigarette on the floor. He stepped on it, then stooped and picked it up.

He doesn't want to leave his DNA, Wolf thought. That's a sure sign they plan to kill us as soon as they have what they want.

"Rise, Sir Prince," Zerbe said.

Wolf got up slowly and started to lower his hands, but Luan, the big nurse, punched him in the back. "Keep your arms where they are."

As they walked toward the front door, he leaned closer. "Do you know that Amiri's name means 'prince' in Afrikaans?"

"Who the hell is that?" Wolf asked, debating his chances of whirling and trying to strip the big asshole of his Glock. It was a long shot.

Too long, he decided and kept heading for the door.

"You saw him in the hospital," Luan said. "He was one of my men. The Lion Team."

The Lion Team, Wolf thought. How trite, and hopefully overrated.

"Oh, yeah, he's a prince, all right," Wolf said. Maybe if he could bait the big guy, he'd stand a better chance. Or maybe that would just make him mad. "I suppose those other three weak sisters you sent after me on the freeway were lions too?"

Luan hit him hard in the back.

"Shut up and keep walking," Luan said. "It is bad enough that I have lost four of my comrades."

Four? Did that mean Amiri was no longer alive?

He must have killed his own man, Wolf thought. These guys were brutal.

The door flew open, and Cummins stuck his head in.

"Zerbe," he said. "A car's coming. I looked through the range finder. It's the feds."

"Shit," Zerbe said. He dug into his pocket, removed a set of keys, and tossed them to Cummins. "Get the van out of sight on the other side of that other house and wait for us there. Hurry your fat ass up."

***

Cummins hurried to the van and slid in behind the wheel. He jammed the keys in the ignition and started the vehicle.

No lights, he told himself as he shifted into gear and floored the gas pedal. Can't afford to let them see me pull out of here.

The van shot forward, and he twisted the wheel to loop behind the big garage to his right and kept going. The ride was a bit uneven, but he reached the other side of the structure and pulled up to the corner. A dust cloud was rising behind him.

Wait for us there, Zerbe had said.

Cummins had no doubt that he and the South Africans were going to kill everybody in that room once they had the bandito.

It was all about tying up those loose ends.

And I'm one of them, he thought. Once they have me identify the artifact, I'm toast.

Wait for us there.

Yeah, right, he thought. They'll probably get into a firefight with those feds.

The realization came over him quickly: He had one chance, and that was to run. He floored the van once more.

I owe nothing to Zerbe or any of the rest of them, he told himself. And he certainly wasn't going to stick around to get killed pursuing some rich bastard's obsession—a devil's fancy. He made it out onto the road without any problem, traveling over the uneven ground. He saw the oncoming headlights were still about fifty feet away as he got onto the access road, switched on the van's lights, and sped toward the highway.

There were two men seated in the oncoming dark sedan. It looked like a Crown Vic and had US government plates.

It was them, all right. The feds.

As the two vehicles passed each other, Cummins held his hand in front of his face. He tried to make it look like a casual gesture but realized it probably looked like anything but that.

The feds went past him, and he kept his eye on the side-view mirror, his stomach roiling until he saw them turn into McNamara's driveway. A burning flood of bile snaked up his esophagus and flooded the back of his mouth before sliding back down. His throat burned.

Then he floored the gas pedal again. It was time to get the hell out of there, Zerbe and his band of killers be damned. He was going to drive straight to the hotel and grab everything out of the safe in Zerbe's room: the cash he was going to use to pay off the mercs, both cell phones, and whatever else the son of a bitch had stuck in there. Hopefully, they'd get the damn artifact and kill Wolf and forget all about him. And with those FBI agents on the scene, who knew what was going to happen?

The chances of them coming after me are slim, he thought. *But God help me if Wolf somehow survives.*

He swallowed hard at that thought and steered the van onto the main highway and toward the hotel, feeling like he was running from the devil himself.

***

Luan kept pushing him toward the door.

The feds, Wolf thought. This could either be the break they needed or a total disaster. If it was Special Agents Franker and Turner coming back for Round Three, they were walking into what could turn into a hell of a firefight.

One for which they were totally unprepared.

"There's a dust cloud settling out there," Luan said. "I think that fat fucker took off in the van."

"Shit. Push that damn door closed," Zerbe said. "And shut off the lights. As long as the van's out of sight and nobody in here makes a fucking sound, they'll go away. We can deal with Cummins later."

One of the South Africans hit the switch, placing the room in semi-darkness.

"The door is broken," Luan said. "They'll notice it."

Zerbe swore. "Francois, go crouch by the door and lean against it. Keep it closed."

The big guy on the far side of the room moved to that position like a trained bear.

"Now, nobody make a sound," Zerbe repeated. "And nobody move. Otherwise, you're all going to be shot."

The room was as silent as a melting ice cube.

Outside, Wolf saw a pair of headlights pull up and then extinguish. Next came the sounds of a couple of car doors closing. It had to be Franker and Turner, the Penn and Teller of the Federal Bureau of Investigation. But what good were they in this situation? If this went bad, they'd just be two more bodies to add to the crime scene.

He swallowed and waited.

The doorbell rang.

No one made a sound.

The doorbell rang again.

More silence.

A sharp knock came, accompanied by Franker's voice saying, "Mr. McNamara. Mr. Wolf. This is the FBI. Open the door, please."

Still, no one spoke.

"Look," Franker said. "We know you're in there. We saw the lights go off when we rolled up. Now, if you don't open the door and talk to us, we'll be forced to call the local authorizes to assist us in a well-being check."

"Luan," Zerbe whispered. "Take him to the door. Wolf, you get rid of them. Otherwise, you're dead. Understand?"

Wolf nodded.

He walked to the door, with Luan following close behind him, the gun pressed against the small of Wolf's back. The room was a monochromic pattern of soft shadows. When they got to the door, Luan grabbed Wolf's shoulder and halted him. The big South African then stepped back at an angle and motioned for his compatriot Francois, who was on all fours, to move away from the door so Wolf could open it. The big man on the floor set his weapon down in front of him between his hands and edged over a foot or so.

Wolf debated his chances of kicking the man in the face and diving for the gun, but Francois placed his left hand over it.

A southpaw, Wolf thought.

"What's it gonna be?" Franker called.

"Just a moment," Wolf yelled and took hold of the knob to pull the door open slightly. He wondered if he could somehow alert the two feds to the circumstances without the shit hitting the fan.

"Good evening, Special Agents," he said, keeping his voice as even as he could. "What can I do for you?"

The FBI men exchanged glances.

They have to be sort of suspicious at this point, Wolf thought. *A dark house, me answering the door instead of Mac...*

"Where's Mr. McNamara?" Franker asked.

"He's...tied up," Wolf said, hoping to sound evasive.

"May we come in?" Franker asked. "We'd like to talk to you. Both of you."

"Uh, we've got company," Wolf said. "It wouldn't

be a good idea right now."

Please, he thought. *Let them detect the meaning I'm trying to convey.*

Franker's brow furrowed. "Company with the lights off?"

Wolf caught a glimpse of Mac's cane hanging on the grandfather clock to his left. There was a knife blade inside the cane, and hopefully, Mac's Glock was inside the clock. Or had the police taken it after the shooting? Even if it was in there, he'd have to reach up and hit the proper button sequence to release the lock. It would take too long.

Way too long.

"Just what are you trying to hide, Wolf?" Franker asked. "You're not making a lot of sense."

"It'd be best for you to cooperate," Turner said. "Believe me, you don't want to play hardball with the FBI."

"That's the last thing on my mind right now," Wolf said, trying desperately to remember if Mac had said the knife blade could be released with a right twist or a left twist.

Mac's right-handed, Wolf thought. So it's most likely a right twist. But what if, for safety reasons, they'd made it a left twist to guard against an inadvertent release?

"You guys are *this close*," Franker lifted his right hand and held his index finger and thumb a few millimeters apart. "This close to being charged with obstructing a federal investigation."

"That's the least of my problems at the moment," Wolf said and shifted his body to allow his left hand to grip the lower portion of the cane.

"Is that a fact?" Franker said, his head bobbing up and down. "Well, let me tell you something, mister…"

Wolf's fingers tightened around the base of the cane and he shifted again, stepping back slightly. "Shut up."

Franker's face registered surprise, then settled into a frown.

"Why, you—"

It's now or never, Wolf thought and yelled, "Gun!" He stomped on Francois' left hand as hard as he could while ducking and twisting the cane's handle.

The blade slipped free, and Wolf rolled and slashed at Luan. The Glock the man was holding exploded in a burst of flame and a puff of smoke.

Wolf felt the round sear his left side, but he didn't think it had penetrated his torso. He swung the knife blade downward; it connected with something solid, rolled off, and then embedded in a thick softness. Below him, Francois made gurgled.

The door smashed into Wolf's leg, obviously kicked by one of the feds.

Wolf pulled out the blade and dove for Luan, who was bringing up his Glock to point it at Wolf's face.

He grabbed for the weapon and slashed at Luan's hands, feeling the edge of the blade connect with a hard, flat surface. The Glock fired again, and the round zipped past Wolf's face, so close that he felt the burning sensation once more.

He and Luan fell to the floor in a tangle. Wolf gripped the other man's hands with one of his, but the Lion's were slick with blood. They began rolling over and over, struggling for dominance. Wolf caught a glimpse of movement farther back in the room and saw that Mac was engaged in a struggle too. Another gunshot reverberated in the confines of the house, and someone hit the floor.

God, I hope it's not Mac, Wolf thought.

He had his left hand wrapped around Luan's two as well as partially on the slick metal of the gun. His right hand still held the knife blade, so he began jamming it into the big South African's side, working his way up like he was climbing a ladder until he reached the neck. Luan released the Glock and grabbed Wolf's right hand, which was enough for Wolf to gain control of the Glock. Using his non-dominant left hand, he pressed the weapon against Luan's abdomen, adjusted the muzzle slightly so it was operational, and pulled the trigger.

The other man's body jerked as it absorbed the round.

Wolf rolled off and stretched out on the floor,

extending the Glock as he surveyed the scene in the living room. Late evening light streamed in behind him through the open door. Mac was straddling one of the South Africans on the floor, and they were wrestling for control of a gun. Zerbe held a small snub-nosed revolver and was pointing it at Mac.

Wolf acquired a sight picture as three tritium night sight dots appeared to frame Zerbe's center mass. He squeezed the trigger this time, and Zerbe did a quick stutter-step and then looked at Wolf, his mouth sagging open. He tried to raise the revolver to point it in Wolf's direction, but Wolf squeezed the trigger again, let it slip forward until he felt the slight click, and fired a third time.

Zerbe tumbled forward as Mac fired his weapon into the underside of the last assailant's chin.

Wolf twisted to check on what was going on behind him and saw that Luan and Francois were dead. A narrow sliver of light angled through the space between the open door and the jamb, touching the upper portion of Luan's face. His head was tilted slightly, and his dead eyes stared vacantly at Wolf.

"Drop your weapons and surrender," Franker's voice called from outside. Wolf's hearing was still distorted from the gunshots, but he understood the message. "This is the FBI."

Wolf relaxed and let the Glock slip from his fingers and thump onto the floor in front of him.

EPILOGUE

FIRST FEDERAL PLAZA BANK
PHOENIX, ARIZONA

SEVENTY-TWO HOURS LATER

Wolf reviewed the events of the past three days as he and McNamara stood in the cool, air-conditioned room while the pretty bank clerk put the finishing touches on the safe deposit box signature card. Mac had taken out his two South African foes Green Beret-style, and Zerbe, Luan, and Francois had gone to that big game preserve in the sky as well. Franker and Turner were shaken but unharmed. They were a bit perturbed by the professed ignorance of Wolf, Mac, and the rest concerning what the deadly group had been after, however.

But that wasn't far from the truth.

There were still too many missing pieces of this jigsaw puzzle, but Wolf now had the FBI on his side, at least as far as trying to trace who was behind this. He'd given them the name Von Dien and the law firm of Fallotti and Abraham and Jason Zerbe, an associate of the law firm who had approached them about doing some illegal work during their "preplanned trip" to Mexico.

"Luckily, we turned them down," Wolf said.

He knew he was getting into deep water lying to the FBI, but the bullshit was flying fast and furiously, so he felt a small lie was necessary.

Famous last words, he thought. *They'll probably come back to haunt me.*

He also knew this was way too big for him to figure out on his own. It was somehow tied to Iraq and what happened there four years ago—the missing eight to ten minutes he could not recall—and the debacle in Mexico. This time, all the buzzards had come to Phoenix to roost.

No, not buzzards, lions.

Some of them were, anyway.

And best of all, Cummins had been picked up by Phoenix PD in the van Franker and Turner had seen fleeing the scene.

Maybe that would shed some light on the situation.

"So, you're sure you two are the only ones to be on the card?" the woman asked.

"Yes, ma'am," McNamara said with a smile. "We might be putting my daughter on when she gets back from her trip. She's visiting her mama's folks back East for a week or two."

The clerk gave them a perfunctory lips-only smile. "All right, here are the two keys. Make sure you don't lose them since they must be returned when you close out the box. If they're lost, there's an additional fee since it's very expensive to replace the locks."

"I'll keep mine close to my heart," McNamara said. "Right next to my dog tags."

The woman smiled again, less perfunctorily this time. "Are you both going to go into the room?"

"We are," Wolf said.

The three of them walked together into the vault, and the woman placed Wolf's key, then the bank's key into the two slots. After she twisted each, the door opened, and she pulled out the substantial metal box.

"This is the largest one available," she said, handing it to McNamara.

"Looks fine to me, ma'am," he said.

"Okay," she said, her smile growing warmer. "The review rooms are over there, and I'll be waiting until you're done."

Once inside the confines of the review room, Wolf removed the bundle from the canvas bag he'd been carrying. He slowly unwrapped the newspapers and exposed the smiling face and body of the bandito. He and Mac looked at each other without saying a word, but Wolf knew they were both thinking the same thing.

How in the hell did this thing figure into all this?

He replaced some of the wrappings, leaving the face exposed, then carefully set the bandito inside the box and closed the lid.

"Think that asshole Cummins will spill his guts?" McNamara asked.

"After trying to get away and leading the cops on a pursuit?" Wolf said, "I'd say no. He is a lawyer, after all."

McNamara blew out a heavy breath. "I sure hope he doesn't spill his guts about what happened down in Mexico. If he does, we could be up Shit Creek without a paddle with the feds."

"I've been thinking about that," Wolf said. "At the moment, they really don't have him on anything more than state charges of fleeing and eluding and unlawful firearms possession. Franker and Turner and the cops will be trying to unravel this one till next Christmas."

"And they can't do that without our little buddy here." McNamara patted the box. "But I still got a bad feeling about that Cummins asshole."

"Me too. I asked Manny to look into posting bond for him once they charge him."

"You did?"

Wolf smiled. "Once he's out, we can grab him and

do our own interrogation."

"Minus Miranda and all that jazz," McNamara said. "I like the way you think."

"Maybe we can—"

Wolf's cell phone rang, and he answered it.

"Hey, Wolfman," Manny said. "If you're through getting in shootouts for the week, I got some skips for you guys to work."

"We'll be right over," Wolf said.

"Good. Hey, guess what." Manny paused and let out a long belch. "You know that guy Cummins you wanted me to look into bonding out?"

"Yeah," Wolf said. "What about him?"

"Well, I checked into it. Funny thing is, he's gone. Somehow, somebody already posted bond for him or something. He's in the wind, so to speak."

Wolf let the arm with the phone sink to his side. He could hear Manny saying, "Hey, you still there?"

"Yeah," Wolf said, bringing the phone back up to his mouth to say goodbye. He looked at Mac, who shrugged, then smiled.

"Well, there ain't nobody better than us at tracking people down," he said. "We might as well start with him and that other guy we got on the list. Von Dam."

"Von Dien," Wolf corrected as he opened the lid of the box and stared into the opening.

The bandito's smile was reminiscent of mockery, just like the first time he'd seen it.

You can run, Cummins, Wolf thought, *but you can't hide. And I'm coming after you no matter how far you run or how long it takes.*

The old airborne refrain echoed in his mind.

How far?

All the way.

How long?

As long as it takes.

Yeah, Wolf thought. *As long as it takes.*

A LOOK AT: DEVIL'S BRIGADE (TRACKDOWN III)

A LIFE HANGS IN THE BALANCE, AND THE STAKES ARE DEADLY.

After having been court-martialed and sent to prison for a war crime he didn't commit, former Army Ranger Steve Wolf has taken up bounty hunting with his friend, mentor, ex-Green Beret Big Jim McNamara. Having survived a brutal confrontation south of the border and a recent attack by mercenaries hired by his mysterious and incredibly wealthy foe, Wolf also finds himself being badgered by the FBI.

A lucrative bounty takes him and Mac to a lawless encampment inside a large city in the Pacific Northwest, but the same powerful, rich man who set Wolf up years ago is still shadowing him hoping to gain possession of a priceless artifact that is in Wolf's unknowing possession. To accomplish this end, the sinister rich man employs still another professional killer, a former CIA fixer who is set to come at Wolf with unrelenting efficiency. Just when it seems things couldn't get worse, Wolf and McNamara must suddenly rescue Mac's grandson who has been taken to a militia compound and held hostage. Facing CIA killers, crazed militia forces, and overwhelming odds, Wolf once again finds himself outnumbered and outgunned.

AVAILABLE NOW

ABOUT THE AUTHOR

Michael A. Black is the author of 36 books and over 100 short stories and articles. A decorated police officer in the south suburbs of Chicago, he worked for over thirty-two years in various capacities including patrol supervisor, SWAT team leader, investigations and tactical operations before retiring in April of 2011. He has a Bachelor of Arts degree in English from Northern Illinois University and a Master of Fine Arts in Fiction Writing from Columbia College, Chicago. In 2010 he was awarded the Cook County Medal of Merit by Cook County Sheriff Tom Dart. Black wrote his first short story in the sixth grade, and credits his then teacher for instilling him with determination to keep writing when she told him never to try writing again.

www.MichaelABlack.com.

Made in the USA
Monee, IL
01 November 2021

81232986R10239